Soap-Stud & Blue-Movie Girl

STORIES OF HOLLYWOOD

DAVID GODOLPHIN

Soap-Stud & Blue-Movie Girl

Published by The Conrad Press Ltd. in the United Kingdom 2022

Tel: +44(0)1227 472 874

www.theconradpress.com

info@theconradpress.com

ISBN 978-1-915494-03-0

Copyright © David Godolphin, 2022

All rights reserved.

Typesetting and Cover Design by: Charlotte Mouncey, www.bookstyle.co.uk

The Conrad Press logo was designed by Maria Priestley.

Printed and bound in Great Britain by Clays Ltd, Elcograf S.p.A.

for Katherine M. and the KBO gang

A NOTE FROM THE AUTHOR

This is a novel – so, reader, expect to meet people you don't know, as well as some that you do know who hopefully will enjoy being press-ganged into this collaboration. You will also meet people you thought were dead (a not uncommon occurrence in the City of Angels). Some of your favorite stars have disappeared from pictures you remember to provide casting opportunities for resurrected players. Oscars and other awards have been re-allocated. I have also reopened studios and restaurants that closed down long ago in the real Hollywood.

If there is – or ever was – a 'real' Hollywood.

David Godolphin
June 2022

www.davidgeebooks.com

CONTENTS

A note from the author   5

SOAP-STUD

1. Wicket, WY   11
2. San Diego, CA   19
3. Special Extras   25
4. Learning and earning   35
5. Dave Crowe: the dick of death   47
6. Two old broads   63
7. Who killed Topaz Leon?   75
8. The Man from Nowhere   91

BLUE-MOVIE GIRL

1. Baton Rouge, LA   107
2. The Seldom Motel   117
3. Le Bayou   125
4. All the way ... and then some   139
5. Kitten Kandy   167
6. Pussy-Kat Kane   175
7. Kate comes clean   203
8. Poor Nellie   213
9. Revelation   231
10. A phone call   247

Soap-Stud

1. WICKET, WY

'That boy's so god-darned cute he's gonna be a movie star,' his grandmother predicted when the boy in question was barely two weeks old.

'That boy's gonna be sheriff of this here town,' countered the boy's pa who was, as had been pa's pa and grandpa, the town sheriff.

That boy's ma, nursing the black eye which she often did after the sheriff had sustained heavy losses at his weekly poker game, failed to join in this speculation about the future of her firstborn son. After eleven months of marriage she dreamt only of getting herself and her blue-eyed black-haired baby out of this here town.

The blue eyes came from his mother, the blonde daughter of third-generation Swedish Americans. Marlene was small but busty – cheerleader cute if none too bright (especially when it came to choosing a husband).

Sheriff John Howell III, known as 'Jack', was tall and craggily handsome in a Randolph Scott sort of way. His hair was dark, but not the jet-black 'Junior' was blessed with – '*Injun*' hair, some of the townspeople would whisper (out of earshot of Jack Howell, who was capable of killing anyone who suggested that anything other than hundred percent WASP blood ran in his or his son's veins). Perhaps some ancestor of the sheriff had married him a squaw.

Cornflower eyes, jet-black hair. Jason's fortune was already made.

'This here town' is Wicket (pop. 889 in March 1974 with the addition of John Howell IV) in NE Wyoming, on the western fringe of the Black Hills and the Bad Lands. The township's name is an obvious corruption of 'wicked', its origin either dating from the era of Prohibition and Bonnie & Clyde or from the great westward march of the Early Settlers (the latter distinctly improbable since the graveyard boasts no headstone earlier than 1880).

Before it became the birthplace of Jason Howl, only one thing distinguished Wicket from a hundred other Nowheresville pit stops on the tourist trail between Yellowstone, the Devil's Tower and Mount Rushmore. The nearest mountain produces a gushing cold spring of premium purity. If you order a bourbon and branch water anywhere west of Kansas City, there's a twenty-five percent chance that the water hails from Wicket. The town makes its own bottles as well as supplying their content. In 1974, pre-computerization, the bottle-making plant and the bottling plant between them employed almost half the town's population including, prior to the birth of her son, Marlene Andersen Howell.

The beatings had started on their wedding night when Jack Howell knocked Marlene off the bed for not being a virgin, too drunk to remember that he'd deflowered her six months earlier. He then hauled her back onto the bed and resumed conjugal relations with enough vigor to make her bleed. In the morning he was too hung-over to attach any significance or guilt to the blood-stained sheets.

By the time Junior was two, his mother's bruises and black eyes had escalated to intermittently fractured cheekbones, cracked ribs and a twice-broken wrist. Jack wanted a big family and forbade the use of the Pill, but Marlene made sure he was impotent-drunk during her most fertile days. Another baby would make escape harder.

'I'm leaving him,' she told her mother who'd never received so much as a harsh word from her gentle and gentlemanly high-school teacher husband in twenty-one years of marriage. They had been 'peaceniks' during the Vietnam years.

Had Alzheimer's not struck him down in his early fifties, Marlene's father would surely not have tolerated the sheriff courting his eighteen-year-old daughter. He'd always viewed John Howell III as a near-as-makes-no-difference-fascist like John Howell II. A few months before her wedding, on what he must have thought of as one of his 'good days' and his wife the exact opposite, Marlene's father jumped to his death from the fire-station tower; he left no note. Her brother-in-law gave her away when she married Jack Howell whom she now, three years later, intended to leave.

'Are you sure about this?' her mother asked. 'Junior needs a daddy.'

'Not one who beats him, he doesn't.'

'He's beating the boy now?'

'Not yet. But it's a matter of when, not if. I'll find him a better daddy someplace else. Ingrid says I can go to her.' Her sister, two years older, had married a Californian she'd met on holiday.

'Marlene, honey, don't you leave too. I couldn't bear it here without you.'

'You can come to California with me and Junior.'

'Baby, you know I can't leave your daddy.' Mom took flowers to her husband's grave each Wednesday morning and refreshed the water after church every Sunday. 'Give me time to get used to the idea of you going. Give me a year. Promise me you'll stay one more year.'

Marlene sighed a deep sigh that pained her newly re-cracked ribs and gave a promise that she would only have to keep for seven months. Five weeks after Junior's third birthday a massive coronary sent his maternal grandma to join her beloved husband in Boot Hill, as the sheriff and his buddies called the cemetery with predictably crass Bad Lands humor.

Marlene let four weeks go by, taking flowers to the grave on each of the Wednesdays, changing the water on Sundays. Ingrid had come from San Diego for the funeral and the packing-up of the family home. She confirmed her offer of sanctuary. Marlene discussed her escape with none of her friends from high school days or the bottling plant. If one word got back to the sheriff he would hospitalize her before he let her leave Wicket with his son.

She chose Monday for her departure because the sheriff and the fire chief always had a morning meeting with the mayor and the town treasurer followed by a liquid lunch at The Wicket Lady. While Junior played in the yard she packed his clothes and toys and her own clothes, making a point of leaving behind her wedding dress and two evening gowns Jack had bought her for Town Hall dinner-dances. She had kept a few treasures from her parents' house and these she carefully encased in bubble-wrap. By ten a.m. she had loaded her car, an eight-year-old Ford station wagon, and was ready to go.

She phoned Dorinda, her closest friend, to say farewell and asked her to call the realtor on Tuesday and give him Ingrid's number for when the sale of their parents' house went through. Then she called Junior in from the yard.

'Where we going, Mommy?'

'To your Aunt Ingrid's.'

'Wow! In Californ-eye-ay?'

She nodded.

'Is Daddy coming too?'

'No, honey: just you and me.'

'Are we gonna say him goodbye?'

'He's in a meeting right now. We'll call him from Aunt Ingrid's.'

'Aunt Ingrid said she lives not far from Disneyland.'

'We can go there on the way – and Las Vegas, if you like.'

'If I like!'

She left her house and her hometown with no more backward glances than were necessary to check the mirror before turning or braking. The Black Hills had loomed over her life for twenty-two years; now they receded to a rear-view smudge. Her son went from excited to bored to fractious to asleep as they headed west on I-80 toward Rock Springs and the state line. She planned to overnight outside Salt Lake City.

It took another hard day's driving before Marlene, wearily checking herself and her fretful son into a motel at the tackier end of the Las Vegas Strip, felt safe enough to draw her first deep breath of the hot dry air of freedom.

*

All our lives have key moments, turning points. This was the first in the life of the future Jason Howl.

How would it turn out? Did Sheriff Jack drag them back after a high-speed pursuit for more – and more brutal – beatings? Did Marlene wind up in a tacky trailer park on the outskirts of San Diego en route to the *Jerry Springer Show*? Did her son become a foul-mouthed vicious thug?

Let's start with John/Jason since he is to be the hero of our story. He will not return to Wicket until the town makes him an 'Honored Son' many years hence. Nor does he become a thug, though he will play some on screen.

From his mother he inherited a plucky independence that would stand him in good stead when he ventured down the yellow-brick road to Hollywood. Growing up in an unsentimental age and an ungentlemanly society, he would get by without his grandpa's courtesy or his grandma's winsomeness. His other grandmother, killed in a car smash outside Wicket with her husband drunk at the wheel, was a church mouse who put nothing detectable into the gene pool. More importantly, John would never develop the aggressive streak that ran through at least three generations on his father's side. No wife of Jason Howl's would ever bear a bruise inflicted by him.

Sheriff Jack Howell did not send cars in pursuit of his fugitive wife. It was early evening on that Monday when he weaved his way home from The Wicket Lady. Even drunk he immediately noted the missing photographs and knick-knacks of his Boot Hill in-laws. He checked his son's stripped room and his wife's wardrobe, bare of all but her bridal gown and evening dresses.

Then he sat down and drank his way through a six-pack of Buds. During the night he tore the three gowns to shreds and trashed the furniture in Junior's room, unthinkingly conceding that they were gone for good.

'I never shoulda married that cunt,' he said. 'Schoolteacher's daughter, always thought she was too good for me.' (Actually, after the bottling-plant Marlene had imagined she was bettering herself by marrying the sheriff.)

His lawyer counseled against contesting the divorce, since there was medical as well as anecdotal evidence of maltreatment. The judge gave him limited supervised access rights which he never got round to avail himself of. A sheriff's life is a busy one, particularly when he drinks both on and off duty.

He remembered Junior's birthday for two years and sent checks care of Ingrid for three Christmases. The checks were acknowledged with notes in a childish scrawl, but the sheriff's birthday, along with Baby Jesus's, went unremembered by his son and ex-wife.

Over the next few years he proposed to two more factory women, but his reputation as a wife-beater caused the proposals to be declined. Aside from the occasional adulteress (none of whom came Sheriff Howell's way) no wicked ladies patronized The Wicket Lady; the sheriff had to make a foray to Cheyenne or Billings and get himself laid by whores.

Long before his son achieved star status, John Howell III was sacked as sheriff. It was he who ended up living in a moldy trailer on a small pension and Welfare, one of Wicket's dozen or so town drunks.

2. SAN DIEGO, CA

From this unpromising beginning Marlene's life went uphill all the way – as, give or take a few glitches, did that of her son. They stayed two weeks with Ingrid while Marlene found a job and an apartment of her own. John started school, the first of several.

Within six months of her divorce Marlene married Bill, a co-worker of Ingrid's construction-worker husband. Bill was a Polack, twenty-four, single, a tad lardy, not especially handsome but especially not a wife-beater. The brothers-in-law went into business on their own and, as they prospered, the two families moved into increasingly better neighborhoods, into houses the two men had built, always within hailing distance of each other. Marlene had three more children and gained a little weight. She loved San Diego's malls and beaches; she did not sing 'Take Me Back to the Black Hills'. The sisters sometimes went to the opera, although Grand Ole Opry was more to Marlene's taste.

Her son called his stepfather 'Dad'. Now that there was no longer another John Howell in his life he stopped being 'Junior': he was John. He and his stepbrother and stepsisters and Ingrid's four kids got used to changing school every few years: new teachers, new friends, new malls, new venues for barbecues and sleepovers.

John got only average grades. He rose in height and strength but did not excel at team sports although he was a good, if not exceptional, track athlete and swimmer. He took part in school plays and pageants, clearly sowing the seeds of his future career, but even here he showed no early promise.

By the time he turned fourteen he had, however, developed in one area that literally made him stand out from his peers in Hope Valley High School, a school built by his stepfather and his uncle.

'Why, John Howell, you naughty boy, you've been hiding your light under a bushel.' The speaker's father was an Episcopalian Minister; she tended to speak in parables.

'What d'you mean, Rebecca-Ann?'

'This thing –' (it was in her hand) – 'is the biggest in Hope Valley High.'

'How can you know that?'

'Believe me, baby, I know.' Slumber parties and the girls' locker room were gold mines of information and comparison. More to the point, Rebecca-Ann Blake, nine months older than John, had been round a few blocks.

She did not, in the strictest sense, relieve him of his virginity (a few of her father's Thou-Shalt-Not's prevailed, but Reverend Blake had not thought to admonish that 'Thou Shalt Not Jerk Boys Off under the Bleachers'). Rebecca-Ann gave John his first hand-job that was not self-administered.

It was the first of dozens – only three more of them from Rebecca-Ann. She couldn't keep her big mouth shut and Hope Valley, like every other high school, bred a competitive spirit. There was always a new girl after him, after *it*. Sometimes a girl played hard to get, though usually not for long. Ten or twelve girls later, John encountered Maybelline who opened and then closed her big mouth around that which other girls had been content just to manipulate. And on the eve of his fifteenth birthday a girl named Moniqua who had herself just turned fifteen gave him a pack of condoms and showed him what they were for.

It was the age of AIDS, of safe sex, of self-restraint and abstinence, wasn't it? Was it ever! By the time he graduated from Hope Valley High three years later John had fucked every available senior, plus a few from the younger grades. He'd been treated for crabs and was responsible for two abortions.

The school stud. The envy of his peers.

And there were girls from other schools in other suburbs, a handful of local shopgirls. There were some married women. A classmate's mother taught him to give head as well as receive it, something high school girls seemed not to expect (now they did). A neighbor's wife liked it up the ass. His stepfather's secretary liked dirty talk and handcuffs. John was a fast learner and always happy to oblige.

They came, these girls, these women – some even *came* – and they went.

'I love you,' a few of them told him – with or without a proceeding 'oh' or 'ooh baby'. It seemed only right to reply in the same vein:

'Yeah, babe/darlin'/(name),' he would say in a throaty, breathy tone cultivated from the male stars of the soaps his mother and stepsisters were always glued to (a voice coach would later perfect this tone). 'I love you too, babe/darlin'/(name).'

It wasn't love, of course. John, a teenage cynic, knew that what these girls were really saying was: 'I love *this*. It.' He loved it too.

For most of them, whether or not he was the first, he would remain unforgettable. It wasn't just his size, he was good. In years to come many of them would boast (even to their husbands), 'Jason Howl screwed me when he was just plain ordinary John Howell' (clearly neither plain nor ordinary). An improbably large number of them would say, 'I was the first girl/woman he ever screwed'. Moniqua, who had true title to this claim, would not be among the boasters; she would die when a forest fire consumed her grandparents' house in Oregon at the end of her sophomore year at college.

As for Rebecca-Ann Blake, the Minister's daughter, she emulated Marlene and married a sheriff, another of the kind who gave his wife an occasional belt.

What to do next? There had to be more to life than getting your rocks off – didn't there?

His stepfather was willing to pay for college but there was no course of study John was inclined to pursue. Playing for time, he joined the family firm, as had his uncle's two sons before him, one of whom was now a site manager and the other gone to college to study architecture. Like them, John was started at the bottom, dirtying his hands: hauling bricks, mixing mortar.

This he hated. So he quit after two months. And went to work in a sports shop owned by a classmate's father in the Hope Valley Mall. That lasted six weeks. A job in mall security lasted less than a month. New guys had to take the night shift. No shoppers; just clock-on patrols. Mind-numbing. And a real bummer for a guy's sex-life.

Next: Mission Beach. A logical stop for a six-foot-plus swimmer with a runner's body. A lifeguard. Day work.

It was pure *Baywatch*, of course. Babe-watch. More pussy than you could shake a dick at (or you could die trying!).

'Is this what he's gonna do with his life?' Bill asked Marlene. 'Hang around at the beach. Chase after girls?'

'At least he's keeping himself in clothes and gas,' she replied defensively. Bill had given John a small used Jeep as soon as he was old enough to drive.

'The kid's lazy, Marlene. D'you think he's doing drugs?'

'He doesn't look like he is.' Marlene, in her new life, was not a worrier.

'All the kids do drugs today. Maybe I should talk to him.'

'Leave him be, honey. He'll find something he's good at. Or something will find him.'

He wasn't doing drugs. Not seriously, anyway. Bill was right. Like many California kids John's age, he smoked dope pretty regularly, dropped a few tabs of this and that at parties and discos, snorted a little coke. But the thing he got most high on was pussy, and he didn't need drugs for that.

Turning nineteen, he quit Mission Beach and went to La Jolla, then to Solana, inching his way up the coast: Encenitas, Carlsbad, San Clemente. He grew his hair to shoulder-length; girls said he looked like *Renegade*'s Lorenzo Lamas. He traded in the old jeep for a Reno Raines-style chopper. To save on driving he moved into a scruffy apartment a couple of blocks from the ocean at Newport with three other guys from the beach.

On some beaches he worked as a lifeguard. On others he sold ice-cream, rented skates or taught windsurfing. He turned twenty.

It wasn't only girls who came on to him. Some of the fags might mince but they didn't mince words:

'Hi there, handsome, you look like you could use a blowjob.'

'Wanna come home and sit on my face?'

'How'd you like to get that big dick out and ram it up my ass?'

He'd heard of guys who picked fights with the Muscle Beach gays and then had the crap beaten out of them, so he shrugged off these generally unthreatening overtures with a good-natured 'Get lost, fruitcake' or 'Fuck off, Mary'.

For a while it looked as if Bill might be right about his stepson's prospects – or lack of them. Pot. Booze. Babes. The longhaired rock-n-roll/hippie scene that was now into its fifth decade.

And then Marlene was proved right. He found something.

Something found him.

3. SPECIAL EXTRAS

'How d'ya like to be on TV?' the woman asked. She was a peroxide blonde somewhere between thirty and fifty with a face that was either naturally hard or frozen from too much sun and/or surgery.

'Yeah,' he grinned. 'Like video porn!' He knew guys who'd done this, had thought about doing it himself. The money wasn't bad but – hey! – he didn't need to be paid to fuck pussy.

The woman cracked a heard-it-before smile. 'No, like *Baywatch*.'

'You're putting me on.'

'That's right,' she said. 'I'm putting you on TV.'

Used to eating lamb, he wondered if he'd be able to eat mutton. But luckily for John, Cora Quinn turned out to be a dyke.

And she was a talent scout, obviously. She and others were always on the lookout for new faces, new bodies, for *Baywatch*, *Santa Barbara*, *Solana Beach* and other soaps that made extensive use of the California coast. The good-looking young men and women who filled in as extras (swimmers, sunbathers, ice-cream vendors, volleyball players, passing skaters, washed-up bodies) soon got themselves egos and agents and moved onto something bigger: modeling, advertising, walk-ons in other shows or movies – if they were really lucky, a part with lines.

Or they got pregnant or bored or too spaced-out and drifted back to lives in the 'real world', occasionally to real deaths.

Nobody asked if he could act. Or wanted to.

Cora's agency, Special Extras, signed him up and took some photos.

And then – just like that – he was being filmed for *Solana Beach*, Series Four. One morning's work, although he'd taken the whole day off his current day job at Huntington. Half a week's pay for half a day's work.

Blink and you miss him. It's a two-second shot in which, hair flying, he roller-blades past bikinied beach-babe Darla Dawson. Of the two profiles there are no prizes for guessing which one catches the viewer's attention. Even his stepfather failed to spot him when it first aired until Marlene replayed it in slow motion.

By this time Cora had gotten him into a couple of commercials. In the first only his feet were filmed, again in skates: one of a line of people in assorted footwear crossing a giant new credit card. He was paid $400 for this, which took a whole day to film.

For the second ad he had to admire *Eldorado*'s Tawdra Thanatos in a new shade of lip-gloss. He didn't get to meet the star since they filmed on separate days. The makeup company vetoed a shot of his face because it distracted from their product.

In the version that aired he was only seen from the rear, in jeans and a white tee-shirt, watching Ms. Thanatos admire herself in a mirror. '*And her boyfriend likes it too,*' said a voice-over. After the first showing canvassers reported comments along the lines of 'And her boyfriend has a great ass' and John was cut from repeat airings. He kept the $875 fee (less Cora's percentage) for his wasted morning.

Then he made a second appearance on *Solana Beach*. Hair ponytailed, he's in a volleyball game behind the Swann brothers in a confrontation scene. The volleyball players are brought into focus twice briefly, once with Jed Swann (the hunky one) left of screen, once with George (the chunky one) walking off screen right. John Howell (uncredited, of course), six foot one, lean and muscular in bulging Speedos, is on camera and in focus for perhaps a total of ten seconds.

Those ten seconds were the making of John/Jason. They generated one hundred and eighteen phone calls to TV stations across the country – most, but not all, of them from female viewers.

'Who's the new hunk with the ponytail?'

'Will he be in it some more? Are they going to make him a character?'

'What else has he been in?'

'Where does he live? Can I meet him?'

'He's got a great lunchbox! Tell him I'd like to –' (operator disconnected).

Cora met with the producers and came rapidly to the point:

'Are you going to give him a part? Lines?'

'Can he act?'

'Does it matter?'

'What's so special about – what's his name again?'

'John Howell. We may change his name. A hundred eighteen calls, that's what's special.'

'It's no big deal. We often get calls about extras. Do you know how many calls we get about Darla? Not to mention her mail.'

'I'd be more interested in how many calls you get about Jed.'

'We'll think about giving your guy a part – a small part.'

Cora didn't wait. She planted a story about the phone calls (now amplified to 418) in *Variety* with a small head and torso picture of 'Jason Howl'. On the morning the story appeared she called John. He was off work and somewhat off his head after a heavy night with a new doped-up beach-babe. He stumbled to the local 7-Eleven and bought *Variety*.

Back at the apartment the girl was still asleep, hanging half off her side of the bed. He ran cold water over his head and then called Cora.

'What's with the *Jason*?'

'It's cooler than John.'

'I guess it is. But they kinda spoilt it by getting my last name wrong.'

'No, I changed that too. Sorry I didn't talk it over with you first, but I wanted to meet their deadline while you're – you know – hot.'

He laughed. 'Is that what I am? Hot?' Cora laughed.

'Hot *and* cool! So you don't mind about the name change?'

'No, like you said, it's kinda cool. My dad would probably mind, except he doesn't give a shit about me anyway.'

'I thought you said both your parents were excited about you getting into television.'

'That's my stepfather. He's just happy to see me stop being a beach bum. Howell's my real dad's name back in Wyoming.'

'Well, H-O-W-L is a bit more California, wouldn't you say?'

The new Jason Howl laughed again. 'I don't know about that. They've got wolves in Wyoming – you know, in Yellowstone.'

Cora laughed again. 'Perhaps I should call you Jason Wolf – you being such a ladies' man and all!'

He chuckled. 'No, I'll *howl* all you want, Cora! By the way, I forgot to ask who made the extra three hundred calls.'

Still laughing, she said airily, 'Oh well, I made them. Agents have a bit of "poetic license" when it comes to publicity.'

'I sure do appreciate all you're doing for me.'

'Why, thank you, John – Jason,' she said in a cutesy voice. Gratitude was not what Hollywood agents usually heard down the phone line. Marlene's mother would have said it was his grandfather coming out in him.

'My mom's gonna pee her pantyhose when she sees this,' he said before they ended the call. He promptly called his mother and told her to go and buy *Variety* from her local store and look on page eight. Marlene screamed in the store and, as predicted, came home in damp panties. She clipped the article and pasted it into a scrapbook she'd started with fuzzy Polaroids of his TV appearances, including one of his feet in the credit card commercial.

A week later Cora called him again.

'We need to talk,' she said. 'But not over the phone. I'll come to the beach this afternoon.'

It was one of those days when the thermal inversion seems to oppress the ocean as much as the city. The surf was flat, the air hazy. Palm trees drooped. Flowers wilted. People walked with drooping shoulders.

They sat at an outside table of a coffee bar that was smarter than those he patronized with the guys and the beach-babes. Cora ordered iced tea, John a caffe latte. She broke the bad news:

'No more *Solana Beach*.'

'They won't give me a part with lines?'

'They won't even give you another walk-on. You're a bit too good-looking, Jason. My guess is, somebody – somebody whose name begins with a J – spoke to his agent and they spoke to the producers and they called me.'

Not yet affected by that hunger that most extras have, he shrugged. 'So – is it back to commercials?'

Cora took a sip of her cold tea. 'I could have put you up for a commercial every day last week. You'd have gotten two or three of them. But I didn't.'

Now he frowned. Three more commercials would have completed the payments on his Harley. 'I thought you said I was hot.'

'You are, Jason. Those hundred eighteen calls show you are. That's why I'm letting you go.'

'Like – I'm fired?'

She smiled. Used to her by now, he could see through her hard face to the softness that was occasionally on show beneath. 'I'm not firing you, Jason. It's time to move on. On and up. I've lined you up with the Grant Agency. Myra Mae Grant and me go back a ways. She used to work for us before she made it with her own agency. She mainly gets her people on TV – soaps, dramas, miniseries, TV movies – but also into for-real movies.'

'But that's the same as you.'

She gave him her hard smile. 'Yeah, but we only do walk-ons. Grant people get lines, they get parts. Myra Mae's up there with the big guys. Dolores Delano is on her books. OK, Dolores is getting past her freshness date, but she earns big bucks at Hunts and she makes six zeroes a year from those perfume ads – though I hear Myra Mae's fighting to stop them dumping her for somebody younger.'

Jason Howl felt the first faint stirrings of the hunger in his vitals. He grinned. 'So I'm gonna be the next Dolores Delano!' Cora shook her head.

'You might be the next Rudi Vallarte,' she said. The Latino star of *Eldorado* had been a favorite of Jason's mom's since his pretty-boy debut in *Falcon Crest*. Jason wasn't sure she wasn't teasing him.

'Can't I be the next David Duchovny?' His youngest stepsister had a poster of Fox Mulder in her bedroom. When Jason's stepdad announced that he'd been abducted and probed by aliens, Marlene threatened to give him some of the dog's worm pills. Cora leaned across the table.

'Jason, I'm gonna level with you. Christ knows the competition's tough. There's probably a million people in the States right now who want to be in movies. Most of them are in Hicksville amateur theater and high school pageants, but some of them are here in Hollywood and some of those are already on the fringe of the business – like you are. How many of them are gonna make the big time?'

She set about answering her own question.

'Myra Mae isn't gonna put you straight into movies. You'll come up through television. OK, Rudi Vallarte came up through television, the Swann brothers are coming up through television. But –' she stared into his cornflower eyes – 'there's a one-in-a-hundred-thousand chance of you ending up as big as those guys. Rudi Vallarte was in Italy last year making a picture for Isaac Hunt with Dolores and James Dean. It could be the making of him, although – with Isaac's history – it could do absolutely nothing for him or anybody else.'

There was now a film of dust on Cora's tea. She emptied the top third onto the pavement where it steamed; she drank the rest before resuming.

'LA's full of hunks like you, Jason. By the law of averages some of them are going to make it. There's maybe a one-in-a-thousand chance you could get to the level of Jed Swann or Rudi Vallarte. Most of Myra Mae's clients never make it anything like that big, but they make a good living from just playing small parts on a regular basis. You might have to settle for that.'

'There's something you've forgotten.'

'What have I forgotten, Jason?' He was beginning to like the sound of his new name, which his stepsisters had teased him with over the phone.

'I can't act.'

Cora laughed. 'Don't worry about that. How much acting did you see on *Solana Beach*, for Christ's sake? Myra Mae will fix you up with a drama coach. And you'll learn as you go. Television's the best acting school in the world.'

A man walked past. He was in his forties, overweight, his thinning hair going gray, wearing plastic sandals, saggy shorts and an orange tee-shirt faded from over-laundering.

'See that guy?' Cora said.

'Yeah, he's always down here. He's a drunk.'

'He was a client of Myra Mae's before she had her own agency. She got him into *Dallas* for a year. Big loverboy part.

God, I can't even remember his name today, but the first time I saw him – it was a Tennessee Williams play in Chicago, he was in his twenties – my heart turned somersaults. I thought I could give up pussy for him! Not just handsome, he was beautiful. It was as electrifying as the first time I saw James Dean. I thought he'd be the greatest actor of his generation. But it just didn't happen. Christ knows why. And look at him now. OK, he's a pisshead, but he's the other side of the coin we're flipping now. Some make it big, some make it not-so-big, some end up as beach bums.'

'A beach bum is where I was headed when you found me,' he said, his own candor surprising him. Cora was equally blunt.

'It can still happen,' she told him.

'I could of lived with it,' Jason said. 'Maybe not now, but I could of.'

4. LEARNING AND EARNING

The Grant Agency had offices in Century City. Older than Cora, Myra Mae Grant was a large and formidable woman with a formidable sexual appetite for 'dark meat' (the agency had more Black actors on its books than some that were run by Blacks), although none of her three ex-husbands had been Black. John Belushi was attributed a joke (off-camera) about Myra Mae: 'She'd like to be a foot-fetishist, but she's never managed to find a twelve-inch dick.' Jason, on hearing this, cracked that he could only offer her seventy-five percent of what she was after.

Jason, the new kid on the block, wasn't handled by Myra Mae personally. He was delegated to one of her team of Actors' Representatives, a smart Cuban-American in his mid-twenties called Vasco De Vasco, known as Vaz. Born in LA of middle-class parents, Vaz looked a typical Latino: darkish skin, gelled-back hair as black as Jason's, a gym-built body of medium height. Hair frothed from his shirt collar and the sleeves of his Rodeo Drive suit. Jason was reminded of an otter: sleek and slick.

'Get a haircut' was almost the first thing he said.

'The girls say it makes me look like Rudi Vallarte.'

'If producers want someone who looks like Rudi Vallarte, they'll hire Rudi. You know who you should look like?'

'You tell me.'

'Jason Howl, that's who. They have to want *you*, not someone you remind them of.'

Jason had been trading the Vallarte look for sex for over eighteen months, but he nodded. He realized that this was Day One of Acting School.

'And those clothes,' Vaz said with an extravagant gesture of both hands. Jason was dressed as *Eldorado*'s Raul Leon: chinos, pastel tee-shirt, Texan boots.

'This is what everybody wears.'

'You want to look like everybody else?'

'I don't?' Jason was catching on.

'You're catching on, Jason.'

Winfried Gott, his acting coach, was a German character actor turned Broadway theater director turned Hollywood coach. Sixty-five, small and dumpy with his thinning hair in a ponytail, Gott possessed a mobile face that had been his fortune, capable of molding itself, like Play-Doh, into an amazing range of expressions. He spoke like a caricature B-feature Nazi.

Emphatically not from the Stanislavski/Strasberg Method School, '*Only connect*' was his credo, borrowed from E.M. Forster (via Laurence Olivier). 'You can alvays find somethink in a part – somethink the character vears or says or does – that connects with somethink you have vorn or seen or done, and on that you build the rrrole.'

There were four in the class, all from Jason's age-group. They did not, as in *A Chorus Line*, confess and re-enact painful scenes from their childhood or adolescence. In his dining-room on 5th Helena Drive, Gott gave them scenes to play – anything from Shakespeare and Shaw to soaps and sitcoms – and made them do the scenes over and over, exchanging roles (sometimes transsexually) and extracting different shades of interpretation and intensity.

Jason proved adept at love scenes, even those that were tender rather than torrid. Travis was a born comic. Caroline could cry on cue. Sandy was a bit of a dud, but they all picked up some of each other's skills.

The sexual chemistry in love scenes between Caroline and Jason was so strong that he was startled when she declined to date him after classes. Sandy did not decline. Jason fucked her to spite Caroline, who was not spited.

He quit the beach and rented a small studio apartment in Santa Monica. He worked out regularly at a local gym and, avoiding junk food, fed himself low-calorie microwave meals, fresh fruit and diet drinks. Most weekends he lunched with his mother and stepfamily. Marlene usually slipped him a couple of hundred bucks as he was leaving which kept him in food and gas for the Harley and dating expenses. He still hung out with the beach crowd and still (apart from Sandy) fucked the interchangeable beach babes.

Sandy's parents were paying for her tuition, but the other two, like Jason, had agents who would recoup the cost from future earnings. Jason and Travis also took fencing and martial arts classes, although Travis dropped out of both after breaking a finger and joined the girls in singing and dancing. Jason, born neither to sing nor dance, persisted (although he deemed it faggy) with fencing, which was more about posture and movement than swordplay, and with martial arts which brought quick dividends.

Gott and their other coaches worked them hard. And even

as they learned their craft, they also practiced it at auditions across the city.

Jason had had his hair cut shorter and gelled back like his agent's. For auditions he wore (also courtesy of the agency's up-front financing) designer casuals from Neiman Marcus (Rodeo Drive would come later). The Raul Leon look had gone.

'Wow,' said Cora when she picked him up to escort her to the premiere of Dolores Delano's latest movie in July, 'I'm dating George Maharis!'

Jason watched the creases on his rented DJ pants as he got into her car. 'Who's he?'

'*Route 66*? I guess you don't watch the oldies on cable, Jason. When I was about half your age I thought he was the most gorgeous thing on TV.'

Over the months Jason, her favorite recent male discovery, had learned Cora's history. She'd been married twice, the first time – 'too young' – to a wife-beater like Sheriff Howell. Divorcing him before she was twenty, Cora moved to Silver Lake and took a job as cashier in a drugstore while she put herself through a night-school secretarial course.

Five years, four jobs 'and a lot of lousy lays' later she lucked into Special Extras where over the next decade she graduated from secretary to administrator to talent scout to partner. Along the line she married Lance, twenty years her senior and the sole survivor of the agency's three founders. Two years later (with Cora in her late thirties and lacking previous experience in this area) they fell almost simultaneously in love with two of their discoveries, Cora with a nineteen-year-old girl from New

York, Lance (who did admit to previous form) with a thirty-year-old Texan wrangler who would become the stunt double for several major stars.

Still married and still in Silver Lake, they now lived in separate apartments in the same condo, Lance with his stuntman, Cora with four cats and no permanent partner. 'Four cats is practically all the pussy I can handle!' she'd told Jason. 'There is a lady in my life, but I don't talk about her and she doesn't talk about me. Gay men have practically got their own union in Hollywood, but it's harder for gay women. I'm out and it's no big deal, but my friend is convinced that a single whisper of gay gossip would finish her career.'

'The advance word is that this is a real stinker,' she said on the way to the premiere in West Los Angeles. 'It'll be a strictly B-list event. Tom Cruise won't be there. Or Marilyn.'

Cora's tickets were a gift from Myra Mae Grant. Not even being on the B-list, Jason and Cora had to be in their seats before the celebrities arrived and stay in them until the stars left. They parked the car and walked toward the red carpet leading into the twelve-screen complex, a prefabricated structure in brushed concrete with a metal roof.

'Keep off the rug,' Cora said. 'You're not red-carpet –' she laughed – 'yet!'

Jason laughed. *One day...* he vowed.

B-list or not, there was a good-sized army of fans behind the ropes. Somebody wolf-whistled as they approached the end of the line. Jason wondered whether it was for him or for Cora, who wore a Country Music Awards-style scarlet pants suit, rhinestone-spangled.

The interior overcompensated for the bleak exterior with walls, carpet and seats in bold primary colors. Their seats were toward the rear, near minor production people. 'Myra Mae could have gotten us better seats than this,' Cora grumbled.

Skating and volleyball behind the *Solana Beach* stars was Jason's closest brush with fame. He didn't know where the A-list ended and the B-list started; now he began to see. Between thirty and forty well-known faces came in, all dressed to kill. Most were non-top-billed TV players. There were a few from the movies, including some older celebrities not seen on screen for a while – or only in character parts. From the music business a recent chart-topping duo and a fading Easy-Listening star with a new wife and a new toupee.

Silver-haired porn king Al Kazman came in with his new discovery, Pussy-Kat Kane. Jason had seen her in *The Bigg One* and *Pussy Power*. She was wearing a simple green dress with a skirt of rippling pleats. Thinking about what she had – or hadn't – got on underneath and recalling, like almost every male inside and outside the theater, every detail of her anatomy, Jason got a raging hard-on. Beside him Cora drew a sharp breath.

The crowd outside saved their biggest roar for a pair of Brits: supermodel turned actress Lorna Kirkham on the arm of stage actor Warren Harding who had a small role in tonight's movie. Ms. Kirkham wore a red silk Versace with more material below the knee than above, exposing two-thirds of her stupendous breasts and three-quarters of her ass. *I could fuck her*, Jason thought (and – a few years from now – the vagaries of casting would bring them together).

Last to arrive were the Hunt Studios executives and, of course, the stars.

'Oh my God, he's brought Liz Taylor,' cried Cora, as Isaac Hunt entered with a male nurse pushing a wheelchair in which rode a white-haired diamond-encrusted woman in a white top. But it was only Yetta Novak Hunt, the sometime Radio City Rockette. 'Looks like Yetta slipped on another bottle,' said Cora and talk-show host DeeDee Delfein in different parts of the auditorium.

James Dean was indisposed. ('Maybe he knows this is a stinker,' Cora said when the compère made the announcement.) Last to enter, with the outside roar echoed in a surge of applause from the seated audience, were a tuxedoed Rudi Vallarte with Dolores Delano on his arm in another designer dress, rose-colored and shimmering with diamanté. It was not as low-cut as Ms. Kirkham's ('Just as well,' DeeDee Delfein whispered to her escort, 'or we'd see scars!') but it had a mid-thigh skirt that was ill-advised on legs of the vintage of Dolores's.

Festooned with rhinestones (or were they also diamonds?) and towering above Rudi in a Dolly Parton-sized platinum wig and three-inch Manolo Blahnik stilettos, Dolores looked, as DeeDee observed loudly enough to be get guffaws from her neighbors, 'like a longshoreman in drag.'

With only a brief introduction from the compère, the movie began.

Claretta. Referred to as 'The Italian Job' by Executive Producer Isaac Hunt, it told, with considerable license, the story of Claretta Petacci, mistress of Benito Mussolini (James Dean, still Method-acting and employing a stock 'greaseball' accent). The screenplay was the work of Hunt's 'I'll-script-anything-and-everything' Ben Burns, who slumped lower in his seat as the long two hours and eight minutes went by and left the auditorium before the lights went up.

To make her sympathetic to a non-Fascist audience, Petacci is secretly spying for the Allies and conducting a clandestine affair with Lucky Luciano (Rudi Vallarte, on a 'sabbatical' from *Eldorado*), the Chicago mobster sent to Italy to mastermind the link-up between the American invasion forces and the partisans. At the end of the movie ageing Italian beauty Labbia Maggiore as Signora Mussolini pulls Dolores into the line of fire just as Rudi squeezes the trigger on his machine-gun. The bodies of Mr. and Mrs. Mussolini are hung in a gas station forecourt. In the final frozen frame Claretta is lying in Lucky's hirsute arms, her face untouched by bullets (but much retouched by the Makeup Department), while Rudi gives heavy-duty grief (or is it relief at the temporary death of Dolores?).

The advance word was right. It was a stinker. Jason dozed through a half-hour toward the middle. Cora let him sleep. He had a big day tomorrow.

'Break a leg,' she said when she dropped him off.

'Do what?'

'Good luck with Mulder and Scully, Jason.'

Yes, the first part for which Jason had successfully auditioned was on *The X-Files*, as one of a group of zombies marauding LA. So much for the George Maharis resemblance. The makeup took longer than the filming. Jason's first TV lines, if they could be called lines, were just grunts and a final 'Aargh' as he was shot in the head by the LAPD.

Most of the zombies were Canadian extras, strutting their zombie stuff on the streets of Vancouver, where production costs were lower, but Jason was one of a group filmed on Hollywood Boulevard to establish the LA background. David Duchovny and Gillian Anderson were with the main shoot in Canada.

On the strength of grunts and an 'Aargh', Jason's fee tripled from what he'd received for his two non-speaking scenes in *Solana Beach*.

Three months and seven auditions later he had six lines and two days filming in *ER* playing a biker with head trauma worked on by Dr Benton and Nurse Hathaway. Between scenes Julianna Margulies asked Jason about his background and aspirations.

On day two of the shoot he went into coma so that the lard-ass harridan playing his mother (an ex-Broadway character actress now better known for TV roles) can sob her consent for his organs to be harvested. As he was getting off the gurney, Nurse Hathaway came over and wished him 'Good luck'.

He auditioned for a barman on *Friends*. 'You're way too cute,' said the female casting director.

'Well, you are,' Vaz confirmed, 'but it was worth a shot. Think what it might have led to.' Jason thought of Jennifer Aniston.

He auditioned for another barman on *Melrose Place*. 'You're way too cute,' said the casting director's assistant (male). 'The job's yours.' Jason steeled himself for the infamous casting couch (*It's just another blowjob*), but got away with his butt being patted on the way out.

It was his best part yet. A dozen lines flirting with Heather Locklear who leads him on and then tells him to get lost. Before leaving the set he told her he'd enjoyed working with her.

'Get lost,' she said, still in character. Then she grinned and kissed him briefly on the mouth. 'Now get lost!' she said and sashayed off to her dressing-room.

Jason learned to cope with male as well as female admiration. Gay male casting directors were bolder than females, but he managed to stay zipped up and still get almost half of the parts Vaz put him up for.

Melrose Place was, for the moment, Jason's last brush with prime-time television. Over the next nine months he played small parts in daytime soaps and off-peak sitcoms, a Jackie Collins miniseries, a cops-and-robbers pilot that was pulled and a serial-killer TV movie in which most of Jason's part as a DA's assistant was left on the cutting-room floor.

There were no commercials. 'It turns producers off,' Vaz said. 'They don't want viewers thinking, 'Oh look, there's the Slush Puppy guy'.'

'What about Dolores Delano and her fragrance?'

'That counts as "celebrity endorsement". Not the same.'

Vaz parlayed Jason's martial arts training into his first three cinema parts as a kick-boxing thug up against, successively, Jackie Chan, Jean-Claude Van Damme and Steven Seagal. He'd phoned Cora when he got the first movie. He phoned her again when he got the third. 'You're on your way, Jason,' she said. 'But don't get typecast.'

It was, with a bit of help from his mother, a living. Jason didn't have to wait tables or stack shelves between 'real' jobs. And his debt to the agency was declining. Overcoming opposition from Vaz, Jason quit all his classes after nine months. Cora was right, television was teaching him all he needed to know and precious little of it was stagecraft as taught by Winfried Gott.

Basically there were only two parts anyway: good guys and bad guys. Makeup, costume and action were all that Bad Guy required apart from scowls and a cocky walk which Jason had seen a thousand times on the beach. For Good Guy he played himself, the All-American high school kid who joshed with the other guys and hit on girls.

Jason Howl possessed a big dick and a small talent. But he was a TV director's dream, quietly doing what he was told to do without any argument or insistent requests for 'motivation'.

He faded out of the beach scene and now dated other walk-on players and girls from makeup, costume and continuity. He might screw the same girl more frequently than at the beach, but romance did not blossom. These girls weren't looking for involvement, at least not with somebody who wasn't yet a Somebody. Everyone in the business wanted to date a star, but a well-hung walk-on was always good for a few fast fucks.

Then came *Eldorado* and Dave Crowe. The part which made Jason a name and, almost, a star.

5. DAVE CROWE: THE DICK OF DEATH

More than just another soap, *Eldorado* was a phenomenon. A revamped *Dallas* or *Dynasty* for the 1990s.

It had begun as a two-night miniseries pitched at the vast Latino audience that mainly subsisted on a diet of Spanish and South American imports. A flimsy plot centers on a boy/girl pair of wannabe dancers at an outdoor Miami nightclub called Eldorado, which ripped off Havana's world-famous La Tropicana. To avoid blatantly ripping off *Fame* as well, the writers recycled *Romeo and Juliet* instead (Shakespeare couldn't sue), emphasizing the dancers' families who are rival orange-growers. Since Latino society is matriarchal, the clans are headed by women. Hunt Studios loaned Dolores Delano to play 'Juliet's' mother in Alexis Colby-style overdrive and Shelley Winters did everything except swim underwater to get her 'Romeo' grandson into the big time.

The highlights were showcase appearances by Gloria Estefan and Ricky Martin, glimpsed rehearsing on the first night and then performing two full numbers each on the second. But although the music pulled in record ratings for Part Two, surveys indicated that the audience also identified strongly with the family drama.

And so *Eldorado* the soap was born. British viewers were

initially confused by the recycling of the title of a low-suds BBC soap from earlier in the decade, but the imported version quickly obliterated memories of home-grown dramas.

The miniseries ended not with the deaths of 'Romeo' and 'Juliet', but of the two matriarchs (if only Shakespeare had thought of this ending, he could have given us *Romeo II* thru *VII*). Shelley Winters suffers a coronary and Dolores gets pushed down an elevator shaft – both events of course happening on the night of the kids' debut as solo artistes at the club. But – 'My mom/grandma would have wanted it' – The Show Must Go On.

And it did. On and on.

Like the miniseries, *Eldorado* the soap is set in Florida but filmed in California apart from a few establishing shots of Miami. The producers dumped the nightclub in favor of a new *Dynasty*-style feud. The Romeo and Juliet grandson and stepdaughter were banished to careers on Broadway, and Eldorado now became, like Southfork or Falcon Crest, a piece of real estate. 'Papa Leon' (Ricardo Montalban), widowed by the death of Dolores, dies under suspicious circumstances in Episode One of the soap and leaves the Carrington-sized mansion and its vast acres of orange trees to 'Topaz' (Tawdra Thanatos), his Bride-From-Hell of three weeks.

In a lawsuit that drags on for most of the first series his remarried ex-wives, Broadway legends Chita Rivera and Wanda Winsome, contest the will (and each other) on behalf of their sons Daniel Baldwin and George Swann (George had walked off *Solana Beach* after the studio gave his brother a bigger raise – hunks are worth more than chunks).

The producers of *Eldorado* imposed stricter rules than other soaps had allowed; nobody gets out alive! No character walked through fire or fell into a pool and came out with a new face.

When Daniel Baldwin asked for time off to do *Mulholland Falls*, Ms. Rivera's favorite son is killed in gangland crossfire; two weeks later her estranged youngest son Rudi Vallarte joins the cast. When Chita herself wanted to go to Chicago for a revival of *Chicago*, a hurricane strikes Eldorado and guess who gets hit by a falling tree? Wanda Winsome wisely turned down an offer to play Norma Desmond in Taiwan. How Rudi Vallarte got six months off to film *Claretta* was a one-off mystery: it was hard to believe he was fucking one of the producers since the only female was a sixty-year-old Mormon and there were no gay rumors about Rudi, on his third marriage at twenty-seven. The writers sent Raul Leon on the run from a murder rap which he would beat on his return.

It was in its third year when Jason successfully auditioned for the role of a highway patrolman who stops Topaz Leon for speeding on the road to Eldorado. She flirts with him; he tears up the ticket. This trivial incident has far-reaching consequences since, half-a-mile down the road, Topaz does a hit-and-run job on Ms. Winsome's bicycling granddaughter (Jason's acting-class fuck-buddy Sandy in her first non-speaking role).

By now *Eldorado*'s weekly audience was up with the 'Who Shot JR?' episodes of *Dallas*. Latinos accounted for forty-three percent of viewers, gay fans of Wanda and Tawdra (and Rudi Vallarte's pecs) for an estimated three percent.

With no help from Cora telephone calls and emails about the blue-eyed patrolman ran over 600. Vaz didn't need to call the producers. The producers called Myra Mae. The writers were already working on Jason's return. As a bandaged Sandy breathes through a respirator, Topaz's jilted lover (George Swann, her stepson and third jilted lover this series) gets a tip-off from a bodyshop worker and calls the DA's office. Topaz claims the car was stolen on the night in question. Her current lover (Rudi Vallarte, another stepson – two consecutive *Phaedra* references) gives her an alibi. Can anyone prove she is lying…?

Cue Jason Howl.

Yeah, yeah, yeah. Let's not drag this out. We've all seen the show. The kid dies, so now it's a murder charge. At the end of this episode Jason, in a pair of tantalizingly bulging shorts, is watching the news in his apartment. His return is a silent one: the camera closes in as recognition dawns (Jason's performance lacks subtlety: 'dawning recognition' looks as if someone has jammed a revolver up his ass). His face fills the screen – ooh, those cornflower-blue eyes! Freeze and roll credits.

In the racing end credits for his previous appearance 'Patrolman … Jason Howl' was sandwiched between 'Waitress' and 'Valet'. Now his character has a name, 'Dave Crowe' and – wow! – is preceded by an 'And'. In the next episode Jason Howl's name features in the opening credits. Two months from now his face and name will become part of the opening montage.

The phone calls and emails reached thousands. Half of them praised his eyes, the other half rhapsodized – some graphically – over his physique. Jason was assigned a publicist who had to send out signed photos (signed by her) to over 400 fans who'd mailed a return envelope.

Teasingly, at the beginning of the next episode Dave Crowe is back in uniform. It's a big scene, reporting to an Orange

County Assistant DA that he remembers pulling Topaz Leon over on the night of the hit-and-run.

'She came on to me and –' Jason scowls, indicating guilt, anguish, remorse – 'I tore up the ticket.'

'This could land you in a whole heap of trouble,' says the ADA, a lardy actor who not so many years ago had his own series as a private investigator. 'It might be better for your own career if you kept this under your shirt.' (This line is telegraphing that a) the truth will out and, b) Jason's shirt will come off; shirts are frequently off in *Eldorado*, bad-boy Rudi Vallarte's more than most.)

'No, sir. I just gotta do what's right,' says Dave. Jason screws up his face to communicate the enormity of this triumph of virtue over venality.

Needless to say, we are not through with venality. After Dave/Jason leaves his office, the ADA gets on the line to Topaz who's got some handy dirt on him that has so far caused charges of grand larceny, arson and a prior hit-and-run to be loudly dropped.

There are other plot lines on the go, of course, involving other members of the land-stealing Leon clan and the Fernandez and Lopez pretenders. All three families, in this global 'otherworld' that is soap, keep discovering new siblings/offspring/exes. Topaz Leon and Esmeralda Leon Fernandez (la Winsome) regularly turn up at each other's homes/offices/love-nests/garden- and dinner-parties to kvetch or bitch or even, at least once per series (in that glorious tradition established by the Carrington women), get down to some dirty hand-to-hand stunt combat.

At the end of the episode Topaz turns up at Dave Crowe's door wearing a low-cut lemon-yellow dress with a short skirt and narrow shoulder-straps. Jason, just out of the shower, opens the door in a towel, his face and hair wet, his body hair trimmed to designer stubble.

'Aren't you going to ask me in?' Topaz purrs.

Jason does his gun-up-the-ass expression. 'Ma'am, I don't think –'

'That's right,' she snaps. 'You don't think.'

The camera briefly tracks down Jason from his scowling face to the towel-line (is something twitching down there?) before freezing on Tawdra Thanatos in one of those leering/triumphant looks that older viewers can trace back to Larry Hagman.

Something *was* twitching down there, which sharp-eyed viewers and those who slo-mo'ed their VCRs would catch.

For ease of continuity the rest of this scene was already in the can: forty-five seconds of screen-time plus a minute and a half of unintended footage that would lift Jason's career once and for all from the rut of kick-boxing stunts and six-line walk-ons.

'A nude scene?' Vaz had echoed. 'How nude?'

'Just my ass, they say. Do I have to?'

'Let me look at your contract and talk to Myra Mae.'

'A nude scene?' Cora said. 'We're just talking ass here, right?'

'Yeah. Do you think I oughtta?'

'Give them all the ass they want, Jason. It'll be the making of you.'

'It'll be the making of him,' said Myra Mae. 'Tell him to do the scene. Tell him to do one every frigging week.'

*

'Myra Mae says –'

'It's OK. I talked to Cora. They can have all the nude scenes they want.'

They wanted plenty. Not every week. Teasing was the name of the game. Sometimes – not often – he might keep his clothes on for a whole month.

And, inevitably, Some People (and their agents) weren't too happy about the shift of focus to this twenty-three-year-old nobody from Huntington Beach with the killer ass and, shortly to be immortalized on film, the Dick of Death.

We've all speculated – haven't we? – about nude scenes in mainstream TV and movies. How come you see tit and ass and, if you're lucky, pussy – but never dick? How do they hide it? What happens if the actor gets a hard-on? For Jason these questions would now be answered. On the day of the nude shoot he snorted a couple of lines to psych himself up.

Nude, he discovered, wasn't actually nude. Or wasn't meant to be.

'What's this?' he asked Tracy, the makeup girl, when he went back to his dressing-room after the towel scene. She was holding a triangular scrap of flesh-colored cotton.

'It's to cover up your – you know – down there.'

'Oh.' Jason's dumbstruck expression would have been useful on set. 'I thought I'm supposed to be naked.'

'Well, you'll look naked. But you won't actually be naked. Tawdra doesn't want to see your – you know.'

Jason took the piece of material from Tracy. 'How does it stay on?'

She held out her other hand. 'Surgical tape.'

He grinned. 'Are you wearing crotchless pantyhose?'

Ridiculously, considering the task ahead of her, Tracy blushed. 'Yes, I am. Why d'you ask?'

'Well – this looks to me like the hoseless crotch!' He laughed loudly at his own joke. The girl joined in. Then:

'OK,' she said. 'Drop the towel.'

Jason's grin evaporated. 'Excuse me.'

She retook possession of the cotton triangle. 'I have to fix this on.'

It was his turn to redden under the makeup. 'Can't I do it?'

'It's easier for me. I've done it before.'

'Who on?'

'We're not supposed to talk about it, but …' She named three well-known actors, looking round nervously and lowering her voice as if they might be within earshot.

'No kidding.' He thought about asking her who had the biggest dick but decided this might breach studio etiquette and ethics. 'We'd better get on with it, then.'

He dropped the towel. Tracy knelt in front of him and, as if on cue, that which had recently twitched on set now urgently surged and throbbed inches from her face.

'Jeesus,' she said reverently.

Jason went an even more lurid shade of scarlet under his makeup. The coke didn't seem to be working – or perhaps it was.

'Sorry about this,' he mumbled. It felt odd to be apologizing for what, since high school, had been his most prized asset.

Tracy stood up. 'I'd better get Kevin in.'

Kevin, short and plump, was Head of Makeup. By the time

he entered the dressing-room the problem had solved itself. Jason was still nude in front of the mirror which reflected a droll image, face and body made up except for his mid-section which was also divided into the area that was tanned and the area that was not. The tidal surge had fully subsided.

'They need you in porno, Jason,' Kevin said. 'A guy who can turn wood on and off.' As Kevin took the flesh-colored triangle and knelt where Tracy had knelt, Jason's 'wood' had never seemed such a sapless sapling.

And so it remained as Kevin applied surgical tape and then body makeup. Jason had to hold the towel clear of his ass so that it wouldn't smudge the makeup before he dropped it on-camera. Under the towel his gonads shrank to a pre-pubescent state as he walked barefoot through the studio and the clusters of cameramen, sound, lighting and continuity people, set dressers, the director and his assistant, two of the producers and even someone from the orange-juice company that sponsored the show. Since the scene was not going to be explicit, they weren't operating a 'closed set'. Jason was grateful for the scrap of cotton that would shield his inadequacy from the gossip columns when he dropped the towel.

Tawdra Thanatos, still showing plenty of cleavage in her lemon dress, gave him a cheesy grin that did not put him at his ease. They'd rehearsed the scene dressed; now they retook their positions on either side of the doorway.

'Let's try for a take,' said the director. Three cameras began to roll. The director called 'Action'. Jason remembered to hold the towel clear of his ass with his left hand out of camera sight.

Topaz enters Dave Crowe's living-room. 'I hear you're planning to testify for the DA,' she says.

Jason, dreading the moment to come, managed to remember his lines.

'Ma'am, you killed that girl,' says Dave.

Topaz opens her pocketbook. 'How much to forget you ever saw me?'

Jason (he practiced this in front of a mirror at home) furrows his brow. 'What kind of cop do you think I am?'

Thanatos raises her eyebrows. 'You tell me.'

Dave narrows his lips. 'Not the kind you can buy off.'

Topaz closes her purse. 'Don't screw with me, Patrolman. I can stop your career dead in its tracks.'

Jason does his cocky beach-guy look. 'Not from behind bars, you can't.'

'With my connections? You wanna take a chance on that?' She takes a step toward him. 'Come on now – *Dave*, isn't it?'

Jason nods dumbly and with visible apprehension.

'It doesn't have to be like this,' Topaz purrs. 'I was hoping we could be friends.' She pauses and licks her lips provocatively, a lip-smacking sight with which we are all happily familiar. 'Good friends.'

Jason backs off, looking (it was how he felt) like a cornered animal. Thanatos slips her left shoulder-strap off, then the right. The dress falls down and –

Despite his apprehension Jason felt another twitch starting beneath his towel and the scrap of cotton.

'Cut,' called the director as the dress, taped in place like Jason's miniature loincloth, stopped falling and actually covered more of Thanatos's chest than it had when the straps were up. Jason did his frown in genuine puzzlement. The twitching stopped.

'That was fine, Tawdra,' the director said. 'Jason, you don't need to look so scared. She isn't going to eat you. Not on-camera, anyway!' Laughter from the crew and another big grin from Ms. Thanatos. 'Nancy!' the director yelled.

'Here, Frank,' said an unfamiliar voice with a Texan twang. And another Tawdra Thanatos in an identical yellow dress walked into Dave Crowe's living-room.

Prior to being offered his first appearance Jason had only seen isolated episodes of *Eldorado* at his mother's house. He'd seen Ms. Thanatos in two nude scenes – back view only, of course, once with just a hint of breast on a partial profile shot. It had not occurred to him that the breast didn't belong to Tawdra Thanatos.

Her nude stand-in, Nancy, looked less like her than did Linda, her stunt-double whom Jason had seen in the canteen. Both were in their early twenties and the same size as Ms. Thanatos, but Nancy with a different wig and the right clothes could as easily have doubled for Rudi Vallarte. Beneath the 'Topaz' makeup she had broad cheekbones and a wide mouth with big teeth. She beamed Jason a four-inch smile.

'Here we are about to get down and dirty,' she said in a Lucy Ewing drawl, 'and we haven't been introduced! Hi there, Jason Howl. I'm Nancy Schlitz.'

'Hi, Nancy,' he managed to get out. He wondered why they hadn't rehearsed together and then realized that this scene was similar to the others she'd done – back view, bare ass. Were her tits covered below the cleavage? (Was that another twitch?) Would she be wearing something similar to him 'down there', as Tracy would say? (Oh God, it was a twitch.)

'OK, people, let's rock and roll,' said Frank. 'Jason, you've moved. That's it. Nancy, left a bit. Right a bit. Look toward him – yes. Head higher – there. Remember: left strap, right strap. Jason, got your moves ready?'

Jason nodded. He tried to focus on what he had to do, tried not to think about what he might be about to see, tried – desperately – to control the twitching. Tawdra Thanatos, her straps restored, was sitting next to one of the producers. She flashed Jason another smile. He smiled limply back, hoping, praying, that everything else stayed limp.

'Jason, focus on Nancy's chin,' Frank called. 'One take would be good for everybody, but don't worry if you fuck up. Cameras rolling? Lighting? Sound? OK, people ... And *action*!'

Nancy's face was out of shot so she didn't need to duplicate any of Thanatos's lip-licking. Her expression was deadpan as she repeated Topaz's moves with the shoulder-straps. The dress shimmered to the floor around her yellow spike heels, again identical to Tawdra's. Uncovered and unsupported, her breasts were, Jason guessed, bigger than Thanatos's, with small budlike nipples. Forgetting that he was on-camera he lowered his eyes to where she too had a scrap of cotton taped to her thighs and abdomen. A stray curl of blonde pubic hair was visible on one side.

'Jason, we're not making porno here,' Frank called (these scenes always play to an orgasmic swell of music; the director's voice would be wiped). 'Don't look at her twat. Look at her tits.'

Jason raised his head a fraction and focused his eyes on Nancy's large firm breasts with their small hard nipples.

'That's a great expression, Jason,' said Frank. Jason was no longer acting. 'Now drop the towel. Watch your makeup.'

Jason dropped the towel. And the career-defining moment arrived.

Notwithstanding the crowd of onlookers, the twitch beneath the cotton triangle taped to Jason's abdomen and thighs became a stirring. Nancy lowered her eyes without moving her head. Her solemn expression changed to a smile that was possibly five inches wide. 'Well, Ah can see you're pleased to see me!' she said in a Mae West voice. A gale of laughter greeted her observation.

'Ow.' Jason yelped as the surgical tape began to tug at the hairs on his perineum, but despite the sudden pain the process that had restarted continued inexorably until that which it had briefly constrained cast off the surly bond of cotton and surged into the full view of twenty-seven awestruck onlookers. Tawdra Thanatos's mouth opened but she did not speak.

There would be – courtesy of the internet – millions more viewers. As well as the cameras behind Jason and Nancy, a third cameraman was standing by to film head-and-shoulder profiles when Ms. Thanatos resumed her position. Not needed at present, he held his Steadicam at hip level. But it was pointing toward Jason and Nancy and had been running since Frank called 'Action'. A shot of hunky Jason Howl in just a codpiece would provide a tasty treat for Camera Three's boyfriend and their gay pals. He was getting more than he could have dreamt of. This ninety-second footage would be the most watched X-rated tape since Jed Swann's poolside bimbo blowjob and, arguably, the most watched performance of Jason's career.

Everyone on set stood as if frozen by a pause button. Belatedly, Frank called 'Cut! *Cut*, for Christ's sake.' Two of the three cameramen obeyed.

Ms. Thanatos's mouth closed. 'Call me when you've sorted this out,' she said curtly and walked off the set. As Jason realized that his career might now be hanging by a cotton thread, the 'wood' rediscovered some elasticity and slipped beneath its modesty panel, which was still adhering to his six-pack abdomen. He was trying to formulate an apology when the director got in first:

'Take him back to his dressing-room, Kevin.'

'Sure, Frank.' Kevin, grinning broadly, picked up Jason's towel. Jason wrapped it round himself with fumbling haste.

'I'm sorry about this, Mr. –'

'Call me Frank, Jason. And don't worry. You know what they say: shit happens. And sometimes wood. Wood is easier to handle than shit!'

There was more laughter and an easing of tension. Camera Three quietly switched off his Steadicam as Jason disappeared off set behind Kevin. A buzz of conversation broke out behind them.

'OK, big boy,' said Kevin inside the dressing-room. 'We have three ways round this *problema*. One, I tape you up inside a baseball-player's cup, which you might send flying across the set and give someone a nasty concussion! Or I leave you to jerk off and then we go back with the cotton on.'

'Jesus,' said Jason, realizing that everyone on set would know that this was what he had been sent here to do.

'The third alternative,' Kevin said, 'is me giving you a quick blowjob. Only kidding,' he added as Jason backed away. 'But I can get Nancy in if you want.'

'Are blowjobs in her contract?'

'Let's say you wouldn't be the first person to get one in the line of duty.'

'Other actors have had this – problem – with nude scenes?'

Kevin shook his head. 'It's usually done in the name of stress relief, like a session with the studio masseur. Don't ask who: my lips are sealed – unlike Nancy's! She gets an extra five hundred from the Hospitality Account, though I think she'd be just as happy to do them pro bono.'

'Pro *boner*, in my case!' said Jason, and they shared a dirty laugh.

'I'd better let you get on with it,' Kevin said. 'Time is money, as Mr. S. keeps reminding us.' Jason thought rapidly. His reputation was already shot. Did he also want to be known as a jerk-off?

'Get Nancy in here,' he said hoarsely.

Nancy's face is of course not seen in Take Two of the crucial scene, the version that aired two months later (by which time Jason's name – and dick – were well-known to those who surfed the celebrity porn sites on the Net). But her expression was now, aptly, that of the cat-that-got-the-cream.

During his not-quite two years in *Eldorado* Nancy Schlitz from Fort Worth, homely but hot, chorus-girl turned stand-in, frequently knelt to service Jason – and not only in the dressing-room ahead of his nude scenes with Topaz Leon and other members of the Three Families. 'You're not the biggest star I've done this to,' she told him once, 'except that you *are* the biggest!'

With his contract renewed during the summer break, Jason bought a cottage high up in Laurel Canyon. Nancy moved in with him, his first live-in lover since a brief shack-up at the beach when he was nineteen. He took her to San Diego for

Thanksgiving, a panty-wetting event for Marlene. Nancy told her friends (mostly in Production) that they made love a lot. Jason told his friends (mostly fellow cast members) that she was fucking his brains out.

6. TWO OLD BROADS

Financing the property on Lookout Mountain was easy. His salary on *Eldorado* had doubled when his first six-week contract was renewed and then doubled again. For the new season Myra Mae Grant had negotiated a full-series contract at $60,000 per show plus syndication.

As well as a decent income and a home in the Hollywood Hills Jason now had recognition, which plagues minor soap players almost as much as it does megastars. The novelty of being asked for his autograph wore off quickly, although requests (from guys as well as women) to get his dick out in public never lost their shock impact. Jason Howl and Dave Crowe had pages devoted to them on the *Eldorado* website. And Jason had his own website fan club, run by a girl in New Jersey whom he'd talked to but never met.

For shopping or going out with Nancy and their friends, he went back into his Raul Leon leather jacket and tee-shirts. He didn't buy a car: Nancy rode pillion on the Harley to the studio or shops or bars. On formal outings – a party at Thanatos's, a dinner with the producers – they took taxis or a limo.

Now that he was higher in the league of Grant Agency clients Myra Mae herself lunched him in restaurants patronized by the stars: 'New Wave' places like Stamp's or Stars & Snoops as well as ancient stalwarts like Spago, Ma Maison and Romanoff's. She also had him to dinners at her house on Mulholland Drive.

Much worked over by designers, the house and its contents were 'eclectic' – in other words, a mess.

He wasn't allowed to bring Nancy: Myra Mae would not let a stand-in sit at her table. She partnered Jason with unescorted female guests – not-quite-A-list actresses from not-quite-major movies with egos bigger than their résumés. The latest of these, a week after Thanksgiving, was the dragon who'd played his mother in *ER*. Following an Emmy-nominated supporting role in a TV movie, this lady's career had undergone a revival and her self-esteem, never modest, had gone into hyperdrive. Character players had, decades earlier and with justification, nicknamed her 'the Bitch of Broadway'.

'Be nice to the Broadway Bitch, Jason,' Myra Mae instructed him in her rasping three-packs-a-day voice. They were standing at her bar, an art-deco block of smoked glass with same-era stools that came from Ramon Navarro's house. 'She's running on empty.'

A new barman, young and Black with a shaved head and a gym-built hardbody, handed Myra Mae a glass of neat vodka. Jason had beach-bum tastes: he asked for a Bud Lite. The barman held his gaze a fraction longer than necessary. This Black stallion would not be gracing Myra Mae's black silk sheets.

'How nice do I have to be?'

'Well, you don't have to go down on her, for Christ's sake.' The barman nearly dropped the beer he was pouring. 'Unless you're into mercy fucks or zombie snatch. She's not going to do your career any good. The only big part she could get you into is walled in with cellulite!'

'She's old enough to be my mother. She was my mother.'

'This is niceness for niceness' sake, Jason. If you're feeling magnanimous you could let her cop a quick feel of your dick, but you don't need to get it out or anything.'

The barman's thick pink tongue licked saliva from the corner of his mouth.

'Only kidding!' Myra Mae added with one of her trademark gap-toothed grins. 'She's old enough to be your grandma ... But then, you know what they say: there may be winter chills in her heart but there's a summer brushfire up her snatch.'

Jason knew the joke. 'Yeah, and it's fall in her tits and not much spring left in her ass!'

The barman joined in Myra Mae's dirty laugh. She froze him with a glare.

Jason wasn't required to be nice to the Broadway Bitch during dinner. She concentrated on working the major celebrity on her other side. Her cloyingly musky perfume, as subtle as Drano, invaded the flavor of every dish.

In the rear of a homeward-bound limo she scuttled toward Jason like an over-painted and well-lubricated crab, waving bejeweled claws. Suffocated by her perfume, Jason gritted his teeth as she smeared lipstick over his face and copped the authorized feel. A pheromone rush took her over the edge, and the driver had to stop so that she could puke outside rather than inside the limo. Jason held her head while she projectile-vomited an assortment of beverages and a catered five-course dinner onto the sidewalk.

Surely this was niceness beyond the call of duty?

At Myra Mae's New Year's party he was introduced to his first movie producer – and his first studio head: Zola Gorgon. His agent sang a familiar song:

'Be nice to her, Jason. She could do great things for your career.'

Jason hoped that being nice to Ms. Gorgon wouldn't entail being coated in expensive lip-gloss and watching her throw an Olympic barf.

'Here she comes now – with Dolores. Zola and Dolores have something in common. They've both been fucked by Isaac Hunt. Fucked and fucked over. Look at that dress. Who does she think she is – a fucking prom queen?'

Criticizing another woman's clothes Myra Mae was on unfirm ground. Her own outfit tonight was a shiny black sheath that hinted at bondage and clung unflatteringly to her broad-shouldered bony frame which reminded most people of Jack Lemmon in his Daphne drag. Her hair, appropriate for both the setting and the season, was a sculpted silver helmet – with the wet-look sheath, very 1920s butch.

Zola Gorgon, seventy-some, wore a time-warp billowing lilac-taffeta number, pure Gloria Swanson. Above and below the billows she displayed mantis limbs, scrawny shoulders and a scrawnier neck. Lines canyoned a narrow face that, failing extensive tightening and collagen, needed more makeup than she had allowed, perhaps more than the human head can support. Her crowning glory was vast red curly Elizabeth-the-First hair that was very nearly a fright-wig.

As Myra Mae and Zola exchanged mwah-mwahs that threatened to entangle their hairpieces in a riot of silver and titian, Dolores smiled at Jason. Wearing a deceptively simple calf-length black dress and no jewelry, she looked radiant in this unchallenging company, every inch a star and (almost) young. If Dolores came on to him in the back of a limo Jason thought he might give her a tumble – if only for the 'star-fuck' kudos.

Myra Mae performed introductions and then whisked Dolores off to 'someone who's gagging to meet you.' Zola Gorgon ordered a white-wine spritzer from Black Beauty and escorted Jason to a white-leather settee.

'I want to hear all about my favorite TV show.'

'You watch *Eldorado*?'

'I'm an old woman, Jason. Television's my constant dining companion.'

All he knew about Zola Gorgon was that she headed a studio mostly noted for schlock and an occasional quality movie. Her questions about *Eldorado* were more those of a shrewd film producer than a gossip-hungry fan. In case she had plans to jump him during an unsupervised moment, he worked in a mention of Nancy – 'my live-in girlfriend'.

'Point her out to me.'

'She's not good enough for Myra Mae. Not for me either, Myra Mae thinks.'

'A stand-in? I'm inclined to agree. How serious is it?'

'I don't know.' He answered spontaneously, then realized that she might be testing her chances. 'Getting that way, I guess.'

'Getting married serious?'

'It's too early to say,' he hedged.

'Well, you won't welcome lonely-hearts advice from an old biddy like me, but where you are right now you should not get married unless it's to someone who can give your career a boost. Which kind of rules out Topaz Leon's stand-in, doesn't it? This would be somebody whose career is a couple of notches ahead of yours. I can think of some girls who fit that bill, and you're working with one of them: what's-her-name who plays Tawdra

Thanatos's other-side-of-the-blanket daughter. Marcilla.'

Topaz's bastard daughter was played by twenty-two-year-old Darla Dawson, whom Jason had skated past in *Solana Beach*. After Eduardo/'Eddie' Leon (Daniel Baldwin) died his heroic death and Rudi Vallarte joined the series as the Bad-Brother-With-Mystery-Past, Raul and 'Marcie' rapidly became a hot item; lots of sheet and shower action – with no stand-ins.

In the end-of-series plotline Topaz turned the tables on Dave Crowe and got his nuts in the wringer, so perhaps the writers might now give Jason some scenes with Marcie. He'd seen Darla Dawson on set and in the commissary a few times, but had not yet spoken to her. In the eighteen months since Darla left *Solana Beach* and joined *Eldorado* the tabloids had linked her romantically with a half-dozen major stars, including Leonardo DiCaprio and co-star Rudi.

Before they could discuss Jason's matrimonial plans any further, Myra Mae came up and parted them in the interests of circulation. Jason had arrived in Mulholland Drive with Vaz and the Grant Agency PA Vaz usually squired. 'We're not an item,' Vaz had told Jason months ago, 'but – you know how Myra Mae is about Nancy – we're not allowed to lower the tone of her living-room with low-rent dates'. The pair had left early to go on to other parties.

Escaping, after midnight, from a yesteryear star comic whose off-screen jokes were off-color and un-PC, Jason was on the point of phoning for a taxi. Zola Gorgon intercepted him.

'Myra Mae says you need a lift. You can ride with me.'

'I wouldn't want to put you to any trouble, ma'am.'

'If it was any trouble, I wouldn't be offering. Let's go, if you're ready.'

Her car was a sensible Volvo saloon, smoked glass the only concession to Hollywood. No chauffeur. Jason offered to drive, hoping she would get in the back, but she got in the front passenger seat before he could move round to open the door for her. Roiling taffeta flooded the front seats. Jason had to fish under it for the controls.

'You live in the hills, don't you?'

'Yes, ma'am, but I left my motorcycle in Westwood.' He turned onto Sepulveda which was almost as busy as the freeway had been earlier.

'You don't drive a car?'

'A bike beats the traffic, especially getting to the studio. My girlfriend wants me to buy a car.' He seized the opportunity to remind her of Nancy's place in his life. 'Says the bike ruins her hair. You know girls.' He grinned. Zola Gorgon's thin penciled eyebrows shifted fractionally but she did not smile.

'I want to talk about you, not your girlfriend,' she said. Jason braced himself. Just when he needed to put his foot down, traffic slowed to a crawl.

'Yes, ma'am.'

'Stop calling me 'ma'am'. You're not a valet or a bellboy. Call me Zola.'

'Yes, ma'am. Zola.' Now she smiled.

'I wish I could offer you some work – help your career along – but right now I've got nothing slated that would do you better than *Eldorado*.'

'That's OK –' he bit off another 'ma'am'. 'I'm doing OK.' *God, I sound dumb*, he thought.

'Yes, you've been lucky. Luckier than most actors. From half-a-minute on *ER* to a major role on *Eldorado* in – what was it?

– less than a year?'

'My first part was a walk-on – a skate-by – on *Solana Beach* eighteen months before *ER*.'

'And – pardon me asking – did you screw anybody to get any of these roles?'

Passing a quartet of shunted cars, the traffic picked up some speed. 'No,' he said.

'Be grateful you're not a woman. But here's some more free advice: don't let the grass grow under your feet.'

'Well, I don't feel I am,' he said. 'Getting into *Eldorado* so fast.'

'You need to get out of it just as quickly.'

He checked her expression. She seemed to be serious. 'It's only the best part I've had. And the most money.'

'Let me guess. Fifty grand a week? Fifty-five?'

He rewarded her acuity with another grin. 'Sixty.'

'You young people,' she said, 'The world's gone crazy. I had to bust my ass for sixty bucks a week when I started out and here you are on sixty grand. But then there are people in movies making six million, for God's sake.'

Jason chuckled. 'Well – I don't see myself as the next Jed Swann.' He and Nancy had attended a preview of Swann's first big-screen feature the night before.

'Then it's high time you did.'

The lights at Sunset were red. Stunned by her matter-of-fact pronouncement, he almost rear-ended a classic old Chevy that was snarling at the line like a dog on a leash and belching emission-standards-busting smoke signals. Jason held the Volvo on the footbrake to avoid another forage under the Gorgon's dress for the handbrake.

'OK, he's a few years ahead of you,' she persisted. 'But what's Jed Swann got that you don't? Apart from maybe a million bucks.'

'Talent?' he offered. 'Looks.'

'You're as good-looking as he is. Ask the people who watch *Eldorado*. You're attractive in the best possible way. One minute you're drop-dead gorgeous, the next you're the boy next door, cute but kinda awkward. OK, Swann's shaping up to be a halfway decent actor since he graduated from *Solana Beach*, but so can you, Jason. You're still learning and who knows how you'll turn out.'

The Chevy shot forward and almost clipped a motorcyclist who ran the red. Thinking that Zola Gorgon spoke the same language as Cora, Jason took the intersection at a more careful pace, pulled over for the left turn toward the Village and waited for the cross-light.

'A woman's got to have talent *and* looks,' she continued. She rattled off four star females' names: 'They'd be nowhere without their beauty and their talent. But it's different for men. I can think of a half-dozen men who are having major careers on the basis of seriously weird looks and seriously small talent.' Thinking of six, she named four, starting with Jedd Swann's brother George. And she hadn't finished.

'It's timing and luck that make men's careers. I guess Myra Mae had to push a few buttons to get you on *Eldorado*, but that pirate videotaping – yes, checking out porno websites isn't exactly where I'm at, but I know who's hot in this city – and why –' A gargoyle grin. 'That was luck, Jason.'

Jason had long passed the point of blushing about his filmed mishap. He gave his usual aw-shucks grimace as the cross-light changed and he made the turn. Three more turns brought them to Vaz's building, three storeys with a façade that didn't know whether it was trying to be Colonial or Deco.

'Excuse me,' he said and lifted the taffeta aside until he found the controls. He put the car in Park and yanked on the handbrake. He gave her what he hoped was a boy-next-door smile and not a Dave Crowe get-'em-down leer. Plainly she knew even more about the movie business than Cora. Was this old buzzard appointing herself his next guru? She was.

'What you need to do now is get yourself in the right place for your next lucky break.'

'And that means quitting *Eldo*, you reckon?'

'It's a dead end, Jason. Most television is like the production line in a car factory. What comes off the line is driven for a few years and then traded in for a newer model. OK, every now and then someone who came up through a show like *Eldorado* hits the big time, like Rudi Vallarte seems to be doing now. But for most of them it's a couple of late-night TV movies, if they're lucky, or a daytime soap for the trailer-trash and care-home viewers.'

Jason didn't know how to respond. He couldn't envisage quitting *Eldorado*.

'If my people come up with something, I'll be in touch with Myra Mae.'

'I'd love to work for you,' he said, meaning it.

'You can kiss me goodnight,' she commanded. 'I may be dead from the waist down, but the old girl still likes a smooch from a handsome escort. Watch the hair.'

He planted a quick peck on her cheek. 'Goodnight, *ma'am*.' He gave her a cocky Dave Crowe grin. She laughed. He got out and left the door open. She wriggled over to the driver's seat in a cyclone of taffeta. He leaned in and kissed her other cheek.

'Goodnight, Zola,' he said.

'Good luck, Jason.'

He closed the door and she drove off with some unsteady pressure on the gas pedal. Jason went to see if his motorcycle was still round the back of Vaz's building.

It would be five years before he made a picture for Gorgon.

7. WHO KILLED TOPAZ LEON?

He did not act on her advice to get out of the show, didn't even mention it to Vaz or Myra Mae. He was happy with *Eldorado*. The producers seemed to be happy with him. Unlike some cast members, he didn't throw tantrums or refuse to play a particular scene. He was a team player, really a dream player. And his fan mail testified that he remained a waking wet dream for female and gay viewers. The writers were told to beef up his part. Why jump off the gravy train?

Early in the new year came the episode wherein Patrolman Crowe rescues Topaz's kidnapped daughter Marcilla (Darla Dawson), in the process killing two men and turning over some explosive family rocks. Clan matriarch Esmeralda Fernandez pulls strings and Dave is transferred to the DA's office. 'Marcie' demonstrates her own gratitude in the way viewers prefer. More nude scenes, more dressing-room warm-ups with Nancy. And, inevitably, the natural progression from on-set faking with Marcie to off-set fucking with Darla.

Darla Dawson was more beautiful than Nancy but lacked Nancy's earthy appeal. She fucked like it was a studio scene, arranging herself for the best camera angles. 'Oh, yes,' she said, and 'Give it to me,' but the lines sounded scripted; when Nancy said them they were from the heart. But he fucked Darla a few more times, and escorted her to a Touchstone premiere – the red carpet, at last! – and to a couple of paparazzi-haunted restaurants. Knowing which stars she had previously dated, Jason felt that even if he was yet again 'driving a pre-owned vehicle', at least it was in the Lamborghini class.

Nancy wasn't happy.

'It's only for the publicity,' he told her.

'Does that include fucking her?'

'Yeah,' he said. 'It does, kind of. It doesn't mean anything.'

'It does to me,' she told him. Used to glycerin tears on the set, he was disconcerted to see real ones.

But it didn't mean anything. He hadn't told Nancy about Zola Gorgon's suggestion that he marry someone like Darla to help his career.

He had told Cora. Her reply was characteristically blunt:

'Don't go down that road, Jason. Marry for love – or because your hormones are on fire – or stay single.'

After a few tense weeks during which Nancy almost walked out on Jason there was another major development in *Eldorado*. Dino Lopez (chunky George Swann) meets his suitably unheroic fate, and into the Handsome Villain breach steps Topaz's smoothie cousin Tarquin from England, played by the unfortunately named Warren Harding. Another from the crop of rising British stage and screen stars trying to break into Hollywood (he'd had ten lines as a British army major in *Claretta*), Warren was impeccably – preposterously – British, somewhat blandly good-looking, a natural blond, thirty-six going on twenty-five (onscreen, at least). He'd unintentionally usurped the name of the twenty-ninth US president as a stage name when he prefixed his mother's maiden surname with a first name that reflected his hope of being a British Warren Beatty for a new generation. His unusable real name was Jim Carter.

Cousin Tarquin rapidly romances Marcilla, making an enemy of Dave Crowe – among others. Warren's first nude scene, which he played for embarrassed laughs, Hugh Grant-style, was not a success; he kept his clothes on for the remainder of his three-month contract. A plane crashes over the Atlantic and it's bye-bye, Tarquin; grief being in Soapworld even more transient than love, he is never spoken of again.

Warren was married to an actress trapped in a lower-class role in Britain's glummest soap. But on- or off-screen a married man is always fair game and, in Warren's third week, Darla did the dirty deed. Warren's personal hygiene wasn't up to US standards, so the deed was dirtier than she expected. Perhaps unused to Hollywood ball-busters, he also had a little trouble cutting the mustard, as Darla quickly reported to Jason and anyone else who would listen. Moving on, she'd given Jason the excuse to move back to concentrate on Nancy. And for Darla there would be other hitchhikers on the long and winding road to her Mr. Right.

And more deadly dramas were being lined up for the denizens of *Eldorado*.

'There's a rumor they want to ease Wanda out and get in some new talent,' Myra Mae told Jason over a springtime lunch in Stars & Snoops. 'I'm trying to talk them into taking –' she used the Broadway Bitch's real name – 'but they're not keen. Time was she had New York and London in her pocket, but right now she's no hotter than Monroe – and one Emmy nomination isn't worth what all those Kennedys gave Marilyn in terms of gravitas.'

Jason didn't know what gravitas was. But he did know what stars from *Eldorado* and other soaps over the decades all know: actors great and small live entirely at the merciless whim of the producers. And the writer giveth and the writer taketh away.

Myra Mae had heard the wrong rumor. Wanda Winsome was not about to shuffle off her soapy coil.

In the last episode of *Eldorado* Series Four, an unidentified pair of hands sends Topaz Leon flying off the terrace of her penthouse in a stunt that was too hairy even for Ms. Thanatos's regular stunt-woman Linda.

Whose hands were they? It was the biggest cliffhanger in Soapland since the shooting of JR Ewing.

Was Thanatos 'pushed' or did she jump? The lady wasn't saying. At the end-of-series party her behavior was more cheerful than most people last seen floating out to sea. Before Christmas she was back on the small screen as the latest incarnation of Lucky Santangelo in a new Jackie Collins miniseries.

Three versions of '*Who pushed Topaz?*' would be filmed after the summer break, and not until the day it aired would the cast and crew learn which ending the producers had selected. All of them were reminded of the Secrecy Agreement they had signed and of the punishment that awaited anyone who leaked information to the media: *You'll never eat lunch in this town again.*

One of the cameramen updated Jason on his sacked gay colleague who had posted the infamous footage onto the internet. He'd ended up working for Al Kazman; the porn industry wasn't so picky about whom it employed.

'Lucky dog,' said Jason. 'Imagine spending your working day looking at Pussy-Kat Kane's snatch.' (Prophetic words, Jason.)

With Topaz gone, Nancy became redundant. The producers gave her six weeks' severance pay. Despite appeals from Jason, Myra Mae refused to take her on. 'She may have D-cup jugs, Jason, but she's never gonna make the A-list.'

'Well, neither am I.'

'Maybe not,' said Myra Mae, 'though I wouldn't rule it out. But within two years I expect to see you at the top of the B-list.'

Cora took pity on Nancy, but most of the females at Special Extras were beach-babe bimbos or 'character' walk-ons. Despite her D-cup boobs Nancy wasn't cute enough for *Solana Beach* or old enough to do character. Cora's New York office got her into *NYPD Blue*, a 'street furniture' part, a hooker in a bust scene, one day's work, hardly worth the flight (which Jason paid).

One of the other hookers, another dancer, told her about a new production of *Cabaret* that was auditioning. Helped by a call from Myra Mae (seeing the chance to uncouple Jason from this going-nowhere chorine), Nancy got the part of one of the dance-hall girls. A three-month contract with the possibility of a year's run. She flew back to LA to collect her belongings.

'I'll be back,' she said, *Terminator*-style, when Jason dropped her at the airport. Chances were she would return to LA sooner or later, but it was less likely that they would get back together. Grass doesn't grow on busy streets.

'*Hasta la vista*, baby,' he replied in the same vein. They both laughed, but Nancy had tears in her eyes. She kissed him fiercely and then ran into the terminal with the tote-bag that was all she'd brought to Laurel Canyon and which was apparently all she needed to start a new life in the Big Apple.

Jason was sorry to see her go, he'd enjoyed her company as well as the sex, but like Dave Crowe he didn't seem to be ready for commitment. For the first time since his teens he took a 'sabbatical' from sex. It lasted two weeks.

His contract precluded him doing any other work during the summer recess without their say-so. They had vetoed the cheesy miniseries he was offered last summer, but this year they okayed an underwear commercial for Calvin Klein that enhanced his *Eldorado* persona. Orgasmic female panting accompanies the camera as it rises from a facial shot to an overhead view highlighting Jason's Calvin-clad buns and Mount Rushmore 'lunch-basket'.

Myra Mae negotiated the deal herself and settled on a puzzling $137,000 for what proved to be less than a full day's work for her client. Her financial adviser started Jason on a pension fund, but he splurged some of the money on clothes from Rodeo Drive and a black BMW sportscar. He also installed new decking and a hot tub on the cottage's terrace and took Marlene and Bill to Cozumel for their twentieth wedding anniversary. He had a two-night stand with a Brazilian divorcée who, her nationality notwithstanding, didn't believe in waxing: going down on her was like looking for a clitoris in an unmown lawn.

Jason's holiday fling made an inside page of *The Enquirer* ('*Soap-Stud Gets Sexico in Mexico*'), but he was happy enough to come back to his bachelor pad on Lookout Mountain. Lying alone (not for long) in his hot tub beneath the stars to a background of cicadas and the occasional coyote howl, it was not to Cozumel but to Wyoming that his thoughts returned. *We're a long way from Wicket*, he told John Howell.

The publicity department spent the summer milking '*Who Pushed Topaz?*' for all it was worth. Tawdra Thanatos reportedly made over $100,000 from interviews and personal appearances. Even Jason, in his more minor role, was getting up to five grand for a primetime cross-examination.

'*Who did it?*' was the question every interviewer asked every interviewee.

'I don't know,' was the standard response.

'You mean you're not saying?'

'No, I honestly do not know,' the interviewees honestly replied.

They didn't. But they did know that Ms. Thanatos wouldn't be the only star of *Eldorado* for whom the gravy train had hit the buffers.

Bookmakers were giving odds of three-to-one on Wanda Winsome, who at sixty-six was clearly expendable (and had never been winsome despite her stage name). At ten-to-one the corrupt ex-ADA graduated to Machiavellian State Senator indicated – hard to believe this – that politicians merited more respect than the nation's matriarchs.

Jason and four other junior cast members were at eighteen-to-one even though, so firmly were the wraps on, only two of them would make the final 'shortlist'.

'They may be about to kill you off,' Vaz told him bluntly.

'Shit. How?'

'You know they lock down the scripts between series. Maybe the killer'll get you too. Or it might just be a snow job, part of the suspense. But your new contract's gone back to six weeks. I'm sorry, Jason. This really sucks.'

Myra Mae had delegated the Bad News Bunny role. Vaz had taken him to Stamp's, the ultimate 'In' place to tell him he was on the way out. Richard Gere and Julia Roberts were lunching across the room: a new picture? Gere had waved at Jason when they came in and Roberts gave him a Nancy-sized smile. He'd never been introduced to them but they knew who he was.

He took a sip of Italian mineral water. 'So where do I go from here?'

Vaz smiled empathetically. He stretched out a pale-gray-jacketed arm and patted Jason's other hand. Jason was uncomfortable with all this touchy-feely stuff: women who stroked your pecs while they mwah-mwahed mouthwash into your face, men who took your hand in both of theirs and hung on to it.

'I know, it sucks,' Vaz repeated. His eyes held Jason's till Jason looked down at the table. 'It may be time to head your career in another direction.'

'Like what? *The Years of Our Lives*?'

'I'm not sure we want to go down the soap road any further.'

'What other road is there?'

'Movies.'

Jason's pulse quickened. He gestured toward the table where Gere and Roberts were deep in conversation with a young guy Jason didn't recognize, probably some rising producer. 'Like – their kind of movie?'

Vaz's dark eyes flashed in the direction of the other table and then back to Jason. 'Let's not get blown away here. We're probably talking TV movies. Or maybe a miniseries.'

'Wouldn't that give me less exposure than another soap?' He was too embarrassed to mention money, but there were payments on the cottage to be met and he didn't want to have to raid his new pension fund.

'Jason, please don't think I'm jerking you off. This is as much Myra Mae's idea as mine. You've had a good run in *Eldorado*. We need to show these cocksuckers that you've got more than one part in you.'

'Which cocksuckers are we talking about?'

'Producers, Jason. Casting directors. Who else?'

'So what are you gonna put me up for?'

'We're keeping our eyes and ears open. The studios contact us all the time. We contact them. We don't just sit around with our fingers up our asses.'

Fingers up our asses. Jerking you off. Cocksuckers. Vaz used these terms even more liberally than most Angelenos. The penny belatedly dropped.

'Vaz, are you *gay*?'

'Jesus, Jason, what kind of a question is that? After nearly three years!' He met Jason's challenging gaze, then looked away. Obviously Jason had seen more fags in the studios than he had at the beach. But it was odd to realize he'd had one for a close friend and not known it.

'Why didn't you tell me before? I thought we were buddies.'

'We are buddies, Jason.' He gave a smile that would have been wan but for his dark complexion.

'Don't you trust me?'

'It's not that, it's – I guess I don't trust anybody with this. Myra Mae would go ape-shit if she knew. She hates fags. Her second husband turned out to be gay – just using her to move his career on, you know.'

He managed to look Jason in the face again. 'Haven't you noticed there aren't any gays in our client list? Well, none that Myra Mae's cottoned on to, anyway. She's not all that good at spotting them – hence the husband, I guess. Remember that barman at her New Year's party? Black Maria – stood out a mile, but not to her. She has difficulty getting her mind round the idea of Black fairies. She sees a Black guy and all she can think of is a big Black dick. Well –' he laughed – 'she's not the only one who has that problem!'

He stopped, apparently realizing that he was beginning to babble. Then he added: 'Don't tell her, Jason. Please. Don't tell anybody. I live a very discreet life. I never go to gay hangouts, I mostly screw around with married men who've got as much to lose as I have. Mum's the word, Jason, huh?' His eyes pleaded. Jason grinned.

'The word is mother, motherfucker!' he promised. 'With Nancy gone there's nobody to tell.'

But there was. There was Darla. In the series Dave Crowe and Marcie Leon had been feuding and fucking again, and since both of them were between lovers they had resumed fucking off-screen. It lasted through the summer. He knew it would never get serious, but they were work-mates and fuck-buddies – and she was, like most soap ladies, a Gay Icon – surely he could tell her a secret or two. Confidentially, of course. In his hot-tub.

'Wow,' she said. 'Two closet cases this year. I reckon this is Warren's little *problema*. But does Wifey know? That's the million-dollar question.'

'You have to promise not to tell anybody,' he emphasized.

'I won't,' she said with lowered eyes, a you-can-trust-me expression that many actresses had borrowed from Princess Diana.

But, like Jason, like most keepers of most secrets, she told Just One Person. She told Kevin in Makeup.

'Jason.'

'Hi, Vaz, how's it hang-'

'Some fucking pal you turned out to be. You went and told Myra Mae.'

'I did not.'

'Somebody did. And she fucking fired me, just like that. Four-and-a-half years down the toilet. It's only three days since I told you. It can't be a coincidence. You told her, Jason.'

'I didn't. I may have mentioned it to Darla.'

'You told *Darla*? Miss Motormouth! Jesus, Jason. Why didn't you take a full-page ad in *Variety*?'

'I'll talk to Myra Mae. She'll take you back.'

'No, she won't.' He was now audibly crying at his end of the line. 'This is Myra Mae's version of the First Amendment: the right to kick the asses of those who suck cock.'

'Hey, man, I'm sorry. What else can I say?'

'Jason, I've dreamt of you fucking me since the first time you came into my office.' He gave a short laugh. 'And now you have. Boy, have you ever fucked me. Thanks a bunch, Jason. I really owe you one.'

'Vaz, I'm –'
But Vaz had hung up.

Myra Mae did not want oil poured on troubled waters.
'Don't ever mention that Cuban faggot's name again.'
'But –'
'D'you want to start looking for a new agent, Jason?'

Contrition was not Darla's middle name.
'Between us we got my agent fired,' Jason told her.
'Well, don't let's lose any sleep over it,' she said. 'He'll make out. These gays look out for each other. And Myra Mae will put somebody else on your case.' Her tone hardened. 'Agents need us more than we need them. We're the predators in this swamp. They feed off the bottom.'
'Vaz wasn't just my agent. He was my friend.'
'Straight men don't have gay friends, Jason. With one photo of you in the wrong company the tabloids can crap all over your career.'
'Yeah, like one word from you crapped all over Vaz's.'
'One word I heard from *you*!' she said with a careless laugh.
'You're all heart, Darla.'
'Grow up, Jason.' She hung up.
As a penance he stopped seeing her off-set. Darla didn't need a shoulder to cry on. By the weekend she was dating another rising star.

Not since high school (ironically, some fag-baiting of a kid who would die of AIDS at nineteen) had Jason been a party to ruining somebody's life. It didn't feel good. But with scripts to learn for the new series and then rehearsals he didn't get around to a bridge-fixing call to Vaz until the following week: too late. His home number and cell-phone were both unavailable. The girl at Grant's who'd been Vaz's date at parties and premieres told Jason that Vaz had got a job in publicity with a New York-based TV production company. She didn't have – or wasn't divulging – a contact address or phone number.

Myra Mae now handled Jason personally. Contractually prevented from putting him up for other work until his *Eldorado* fate was resolved, Myra Mae was nevertheless sanguine. 'You won't go short of work,' she told him. 'If they kill you off you'll be one of the hottest properties on television.'

'She's right,' seconded Cora who was also much more sympathetic to Vaz's shafting. 'If you're going to be big, you're going to be big this year.'

It was easy to forget the shitty thing he'd been a party to. He felt good about himself. He was – and he felt – hot.

Remember the first four episodes of *Eldorado* Year Five, reader? Of course you do! We held our breath for three weeks as the finger of suspicion pointed at almost every member of the cast until the killer of Topaz Leon was finally unmasked in the closing seconds of the two-hour Special that was Episode Four.

Practically the entire nation stayed home to watch the Special. The global audience almost eclipsed Live Aid and Princess Diana's funeral.

All three filmed resolutions ended with the same climactic shot: a blazing car somersaults off a cliff at the end of a high-speed chase that began in Miami. The cliff was, of course, in

California; how far from Miami the two cars would have had to drive before they found this kind of coastal location attracted, as the writers had predicted, not one complaint when the episode aired. Four different stuntpersons hurtled toward the Malibu cliff edge, one on her own, two together, one locked in a deadly struggle with Jason (who did his own stunts). Winches attached the three cars to the camera truck: the authorities wouldn't permit one of the state's prime beaches to be littered with wrecks. The editors used stock footage for the cartwheeling exploding vehicle. No fewer than seven dummies in different wigs and costumes were thrown onto the rocks – and retrieved to avoid litter and panic for joggers or dog-walkers.

All five actors in the two shoots were on six-week renewals; one (or two) of them was about to find out if there is Life after Soap-Death.

Shoot One revealed Raul Leon as the killer of his stepmother/mistress. Marcie confronts him with evidence that will seal his death by injection, but Raul KO's her in the car, only to lose control when his passenger slumps across his lap as if giving him a blowjob. After the critically mauled Mussolini picture Rudi Vallarte might be happy to move onward and hopefully upward, but Jason didn't think he deserved to be dispatched in such an undignified manner, although Marcie's behavior was in character for both her and Darla.

Shoot Two: a lame one-woman effort that had to be a red herring. Wanda Winsome babbles a confession on her cellphone before her stunt double drives deliberately to her death at 140 mph (close-up of dummy speedometer).

Shoot Three: Jason is lured into the car of the ADA turned State Senator who shows him a letter he has anonymously received in the mail, a blackmail letter from Topaz to Dave Crowe. Pursued in another car by the newest ADA (a twenty-five-year-old *Baywatch* 'veteran'), they fight for control of the senator's limo. Adding to the 'snowstorm', three different endings of this version had Jason and the senator separately leaping from the car as it skids off the road toward the fatal cliff; in Version 3.3 they both end up on the beach.

Ethics prevented Jason from placing a bet of his own, but his money was on the senator. Maybe Dave *and* the senator: more drama. His fellow players might shed a few crocodile tears for him, but they would relish the demise of the obnoxious lardy actor whose dummy had split gruesomely open the second time it hit the rocks. After the big summer build-up the producers wouldn't settle for axing only Jason – would they?

They would. They did.

Exit Dave Crowe, ending a summer of fevered speculation. Battered and bruised (until the next episode), the senator survives to muddy a few more ponds before his on- and off-screen ego finally does for him.

How are these things decided? Do the producers simply toss coins, roll dice, cut playing cards? They aren't saying. Whatever. We got over it, didn't we, gentle reader/viewer – even those of us who yearned for the lurid demise of Marcilla or the Senator or Esmeralda. (*Get a life*, for Christ's sake!)

Jason was now on two months' severance pay. In the next episode of *Eldorado* his name disappeared seamlessly from the credits. Dave Crowe and Topaz Leon are not mentioned. *Sic transit...*

Cora had warned him years ago about the evanescence of TV fame, and just last year Zola Gorgon was urging him to

quit and move on. Now he had to.
 But – *quo vadis*, O Jason? Whither do you go?

8. THE MAN FROM NOWHERE

Into TV movies, that 'sanctuary' for soap actors which all too often is just a staging post on the way to the glue factory. Low budgets, tight schedules. Jason did four in the next nine months.

He had co-star billing in the first, for ABC, which re-united him with George Swann. *The Beltway*: another weary variant on the Cain and Abel theme. Jason is the do-good social-worker brother who turns out to be a varmint, George the hard-headed lobbyist brother who ... you know the rest.

Their female co-star, another reunion for Jason, was Caroline Carfax with whom he'd studied at Winfried Gott's. The brittle brunette had become a sassy blonde. She plays the girl Jason steals from George and then loses to – guess who? There's some tit-action foreplay but no on-screen fornication.

Off-screen Jason finally fucked Caroline, spurned by George and seeing Jason as an alternative celebrity screw. After Darla (now linked in gossip columns with an Academy Award-nominated director – onward and upward!) Caroline was Little League, and a lousy lay. Jason missed Nancy, her energy, her humor, her sweaty unaffected sensuality. Darla's heat had been phony – just another part she played. Caroline had very little sensuality. Men wanted to fuck her; she let them, especially if they could help her career. It was a relief when the shoot ended.

Jason wondered who was the lucky bastard Nancy was fucking now.

Next: his first top-billed role, for Hunt TV, in *The Man from Nowhere*. The pilot for a western series, *Nowhere* crossed Lorenzo Lamas's Reno Raines with Clint Eastwood's unnamed avenger in the Sergio Leone spaghetti operas. Jason plays a turn-of-the-century itinerant horseman who saves a Texas town from a marauding gang who wouldn't be there if they weren't chasing Jason for a reason that the pilot never gets round to explaining.

It was filmed at the Hunt Ranch in Arizona where Yetta, Mrs. Isaac Hunt, spent most of the year. Winter temperatures were in the high sixties.

Twenty miles outside Phoenix, the Hunt Ranch boasted a complete western township and a variety of terrain, some natural, some enhanced. There was a dry gulch that could be flooded for river or lake scenes.

The crew were accommodated, cowboy style, in a bunkhouse. The director and the production people took over the ranch's guestrooms. Jason and his co-star had bungalow-sized two-bedroom trailers a short walk from the pool.

Billed as Special Guest Star, his co-star was Lorna Kirkham, the daughter of an English stockbroker who had graduated from modeling to movie roles that exploited her large endowment and, unavoidably, showcased her limited acting talent. In *The Man from Nowhere* she plays Madeleine, owner of the local saloon and a cathouse, a sort of (mercifully) non-singing Marlene Dietrich who dies at the end, paving the way for other women to enter The Man from Nowhere's life in future stories.

Since the series was pitched at primetime, the love-scenes were no raunchier than those in *Eldorado*, although one was nude.

Ms. Kirkham didn't require a stand-in.

'Let's face it, dahling,' she told the director, 'there's only about three square inches of me that I don't usually parade at premieres!'

'Dahling,' she told Jason, 'I hope you live up to the big things I hear about you!'

He grinned. 'I'll do my best.' In fact, he managed not to, at least not on-camera. He'd done enough of these scenes by now to have his earlier problem under control, although a topless Lorna Kirkham presented quite a challenge. There was chemistry between them onscreen, but although she was friendly enough off-screen she wouldn't let him into her trailer. She had dated A-listers on both sides of the Atlantic and was currently 'involved' with porn king Al Kazman's son Kyle, a New York investment banker.

'I think we have a hit on our hands,' the producer predicted. Wrongly.

Yetta Hunt, whom Jason had once glimpsed at a premiere with Cora, was a feisty old broad who almost belonged to the era they were filming. Generous with her hospitality around the pool and the barbecue, she proved that she could out-cuss and out-drink every man in the crew. Her reminiscences of Hollywood in its heyday included references to her husband's many mistresses. It was clear that much of the Golden Age's glitter was not even gilt.

They broke for Christmas and New Year's. Jason offered to drive Lorna to LA, but Kyle Kazman sent a Learjet for her.

After the dustbowl that was the Hunt Ranch Jason was glad to spend a couple of nights in his cool mountain eyrie.

Lorna invited him to a largely British New Year's party attended by stars he'd seen around the city, such as Joan Collins and Anthony Hopkins, and some, like Judi Dench, whom he only knew from the screen and TV interviews. People were making a big fuss around Diana Dors, an elderly British actress, now retired, whom Jason had never heard of: Lorna told him she'd been hailed as England's answer to Marilyn Monroe, who was older than Dors and still working intermittently and erratically. Dors had been a 'Bond girl' in one of the early 007 movies, which Jason hadn't bothered to catch up with; he preferred the CGI-heavy recent additions to the franchise.

He was at the bar when Lorna approached him with two of her guests in tow. Their hostess was pouring out of a knotted red satin top with matching harem pants.

'Dahling, here's someone who says he knows you.'

'Good evening, Officer Crowe,' said Warren Harding. 'Meet the missis.'

Vanessa Trench Harding was a buxom bottle-blonde, dressed in an overstated little black number from Knightsbridge. Her English, in contrast to Lorna and Warren's cut glass, was twenty-four-carat Tupperware, from a region that dispensed with aitches and g's. If Warren was a closet gay, as Darla had speculated, Jason wondered where his babe of a wife got her jollies.

There were a few Yankees at the court of Queen Lorna, including Jed Swann and Rudi Vallarte (Lorna had dated both of them), both looking cool and – stellar. Vallarte was in a hit Broadway musical, and Swann was in the running to be the next Batman. Cora, way back, had told Jason he could be the next Rudi Vallarte and Zola Gorgon, in her car, said he might be the next Jed Swann. He'd thought *Eldorado* was making him a star, but it proved to be a dead end (as the Gorgon had also predicted). Yes, he was bigger – and richer – but he wasn't, in that vital sense, *big*. He was still, essentially, the Man from Nowhere.

There was a latecomer to the storyline when they returned to the ranch in Arizona. Diana Dors had been lured out of retirement ('She does this every few years,' Lorna said) to play an eccentric Englishwoman breaking her journey to the gold fields of California. The writers – there were six of them – had gifted her some flirtatious lines. She stayed in character on Yetta Hunt's lanai that evening, patting the empty space on the couch swing next to her.

'Come here, Jason Howl,' she commanded. 'Let me get at you. I couldn't get near you at that party.'

'I couldn't get near *you*,' he said, obediently joining her on the couch. Unmade-up now, her skin was like over-tanned leather – she lived, mostly outdoors it was clear, on one of the Spanish Costas – but her seventy-year-old bust was almost as stupendous as Lorna's; Jason tried not to imagine how it might look unholstered.

'I loved you in *Eldorado*,' she told him. Her voice was rasping, a smoker's voice, he guessed, though she was not smoking now.

'You watch that?'

'I wouldn't miss it, though it's lost a lot of its appeal since they took you out of it.'

Much as he had with Zola Gorgon a year ago, he listened to another old broad recounting her favorite scenes from her favorite soap. Unusually for a star of her or any other generation, she didn't seem to want to talk about her own career. She smiled and laughed a lot. Their hostess joined them on the lanai; she and Dors had an *Eldorado*-style mock fight trying to charm the pants off Jason. The booze had ruined Yetta's complexion and her figure, but she still had a dancer's legs and a showgirl vivacity. Old age was a helluva long way off, but Jason thought it might not be so terrible as he and his beach pals had feared.

Ms. Dors flew out after they finished their scene next day. She didn't request a farewell kiss but he gave her one anyway. And after ten more days in Arizona the shoot wrapped. A goodbye hug from Yetta, his fourth old broad (he didn't include Myra Mae, who thankfully never expected to be kissed); his second old sexpot.

'Super to work with you, dahling,' said Lorna when Jason dropped her at the airport for her flight to London. She gave him a full-tongue kiss.

Back in LA he spent six weeks making *Nightmare at the Mall*, a late-nite slasher movie for HBO with two more former soap stars. *Nightmare* climbed onto the self-referential horror bandwagon but ended up ripping off late-era Joan Crawford movies that we all need to forget. Jason the security guard is clearly being set up as an alternative prime suspect to the ex-*Dallas* mall-owner, but the psycho murderer turns out to be the *Solana Beach* seductress, avenging a stingy divorce settlement. No sex-scenes for the leads, only for the teenage victims carved up in parked cars or (the movie's best scene) whilst supposedly testing mattresses in a furniture showroom in the mall.

*

TV critics sharpened their knives for *The Man from Nowhere*, savaging Ms. Kirkham, the writers, the director, even the wardrobe department. DeeDee Delfein in the *LA Times* called Jason '*a poor man's Joe Lando in this version of* Doctor Quinn, Bad Medicine Woman'. Hunt TV canceled the series.

This was the first of the three movies to air, so it looked as if Jason had slipped from lead to second and third billing when *The Beltway* and *Nightmare at the Mall* went out. The TV critics ignored both films. Meanwhile Jason had gone on to make what would become the most successful of this quartet – and the one that would most embarrass his mother (from Marlene's viewpoint much worse, was to come).

Reckless Endangerment would air on HBO immediately after a spicier-than-usual episode of *Sex and the City*. Namzak, the production company, was Kazman spelled backward; it was the porn king's soft-core TV arm. Two of Namzak's major stars, Maria Casablanca and Janet de Jong, were as well known to cable viewers as Pussy-Kat Kane and Peaches Snatch, their hardcore rivals from the top shelf of the video stores and the jerk-off booths.

Soft-core or hardcore, the women always get top billing in straight porno. But at least Jason's name preceded the title. *Reckless Endangerment* is a witness-protection thriller whose sources aren't hard to spot, although in none of its antecedents had Trojans been such a visible element of the protection on offer to the witness. Soft-core and hardcore both now preached the Safe-Sex message.

Although Jason, reprising Dave Crowe as the cop guarding drugland-slaying witness Janet de Jong, is seen reaching for the condoms and then in situations which expressly require them, he doesn't actually put one on on-camera. Nor would he have needed to.

These scenes were, finally, his first totally nude scenes, since there was no way to hide his customary codpiece from the overhead circling camera. He'd seen such scenes in raunchier mainstream movies before and had wondered if the stars were actually fucking for real. How else did they hide the weenie?

Well, as it turned out, a soft weenie can still be squashed or taped out of sight. A hard one might be harder to vanish, but a hard-on with Janet de Jong would have been hard to raise. She was in the breaker's yard of ball-busters. And despite the contrary video evidence of dozens, if not hundreds, of shrieking on-screen orgasms, she was also a hundred-percent frigid.

'Jeez, can't you use a milder mouthwash?' she complained after their first rehearsed kiss.

'Watch your teeth, bozo,' she insisted after the first take of Jason tonguing her augmented breasts with their permanently erect nipples. It wasn't the first time he'd encountered implants, although Janet's were firmer and more firmly in the public domain than those he'd worked on in *Eldorado*.

'Is that all there is?' she half-sang when he finally walked onto the set wearing nothing except makeup.

'It's all we need right now,' the director got in quickly.

Janet made a point of yawning in Jason's face when they had to do a re-take of their first clinch because one of his balls got in the shot. She chewed gum between takes of a mock blowjob. It was hard to reconcile this snotty bitch with the teasing threshing sex-machine whose scenes he and Nancy had sometimes re-enacted on their own bed. Any teasing or threshing she now produced was the soulless application of technique.

'Shift your ass, buster,' she demanded when the director called 'cut' on her last fifteen-second screaming orgasm underneath Jason. While he moaned and grunted into the camera for his own head-and-shoulder cum-shot Jason thought not of fucking her for real but of crushing her windpipe. A hand-job from Rebecca-Ann in the Hope Valley bleachers had been a more erotic experience than a pretend fuck with the Soft-core Queen.

'Don't get me any more work with Namzak,' he begged Myra Mae over lunch at Ma Maison after *Reckless Endangerment* wrapped in the week of the Oscars. His agent gave one of her eardrum-shattering laughs.

'Why, Jason, I thought it would be pure joy for you! Duty and pleasure combined.'

'The pleasure was not mine,' he said. 'Janet de Jong may have the biggest cunt on cable TV, but as far as I'm concerned she *is* the biggest cunt on television.'

'Cunt, shmunt,' said Myra Mae, who'd just ordered crudités as a starter. 'Women will be gagging for you when that goes out. Which I hear is next month. They sure edit fast at Namzak.'

'So what are we gonna give these gagging women next?'

'Actually, there isn't anything right now. But once these awards are out of the way everybody will start thinking ahead again.'

This time last year, as one of the hottest couples on and off the small screen, Jason and Darla had walked the red carpet into the Dorothy Chandler Pavilion, had even been briefly interviewed by Oprah and Letterman for their respective networks.

This year, in the last week of March, Jason watched the Oscars over beers and pizzas in Cora's apartment. He experienced a twinge of envy and regret as Darla walked the red carpet with horror-director Rodney Fire, followed not far behind by Lorna Kirkham with Kyle Kazman.

'Wow,' exclaimed Cora, 'there's nearly enough material in that dress to make me a bikini! I'd kill to have those tits – preferably about an inch and a half from my face. I bet she's hung like a stud donut. What can you tell me about her, Jason?'

'My lips are sealed,' he deadpanned, although he truly didn't want to dish dirt on the actress who'd been more fun to work with than anyone in his career so far. 'I can tell you a few things about Janet de Jong, if you like,' he offered in part-exchange.

'What's to tell? Plastic tits, plastic cheekbones, plastic calves – is her clit still original?'

He told Cora about his ball-busting shoot on the Namzak movie while, on the muted screen in front of them, Marilyn Monroe Kennedy, James Dean, Kathy Bates, Dame Helen Highwater and others who were going to be thrilled or disappointed in the course of this evening made their way up the red carpet which was no longer rolling out for Jason. Jason only recognized the major stars, but Cora seemed to know practically everyone in Hollywood, even some of the obscurer Brits and people from costume, music and special effects.

'What's Myra Mae lining up for you next?' she asked.

'Not a lot. Actually, nothing.'

'I know I put you on to her, but I'm kind of disappointed. After *Eldorado* I expected her to get you into better stuff than this schlock you've done so far.'

'Maybe this is all she thinks I'm good for.'

'Then she's wrong. You're not just blue eyes and a big dick. Well –' she laughed – 'actually, you are! But the same basic equipment has gotten some other actors a lot further than cable porno and crappy pilots.'

On the screen in front of them DeeDee Delfein was turning from Mr. and Mrs. Rudi Vallarte to beat Letterman to Isaac Hunt and Dolores Delano. Zola Gorgon glared at the camera as she swept past un-interviewed despite having a multi-nominated picture. The Gorgon had her red wig on, matching a red face and a red velvet gown that evoked the 1950s. Only a diamond choker and her grimacing yellow teeth stood out from the carpet. Her escort, one of her producers, small, tubby, bald, walked two paces behind her in a faded tuxedo, looking like the lapdog he was.

'Tell Myra Mae to give *her* a call,' Cora said. 'I hope she's not just sitting around with a finger up her ass.'

Fingers up asses. Jason thought of Vaz

After two worryingly quiet months Myra Mae got Jason a guest appearance in *Sex and the City* – more crypto-porn, but Quality Porn, Fun Porn. He plays the stud who turns out to be screwing two of the girls behind each other's backs. The screwing mostly took place under the bedcovers or with arms and legs blocking saucy glimpses of nipples and pubes, but the producers didn't miss the chance to get in a few shots of Jason's famous and much-loved ass. The final shot of him in a hot-tub with the full quartet must be one of the show's most memorable moments and was used as a bus poster in New York City until the graffiti artists rendered them too lurid for even the depraved denizens of Gotham and Gomorrah.

The shoot was little short of a riot with endless re-takes as the cast cracked each other up on camera. Jason would happily have fucked any or all of them for real, but although very friendly toward him they were all in relationships.

Halfway through the second day of filming he found a message from the agency on his cellphone: *Call me soonest.* (Myra Mae, in a throwback to the era of ship-to-shore telegraphy, was needlessly economical with her prose in the era of email and voicemail.) He returned the call.

'Big, big news, Jason,' her voice boomed into his ear. 'A big-big part in a mega-big movie for Isaac Hunt.'

Christ, thought Jason, *another shitty pilot*. 'What's the deal?' he asked with no show of enthusiasm. Myra Mae took an audibly deep breath before answering:

'Only a remake of Bette Davis's greatest-ever picture.'

'You mean *Whatever Happened to Baby Jane?*' It was the only one of her films he could recall seeing. Was there a Dave Crowe-type role in it? 'Didn't they remake that already, for television?'

'Jason, Jason.' Myra Mae attempted a tinkling laugh which tinkled like a Skid Row shopping cart on broken glass. 'I always forget how young you are. No it isn't *Baby Jane*.'

'So who's gonna be the next Bette Davis?'

'Only one of the greatest actresses working in Hollywood today.'

'Meryl Streep?' Jason guessed. 'Glenn Close? Michelle Pfeiffer?' Myra Mae sighed.

'No, Jason. Try thinking double-D.'

'As in tit-size?' Nancy had been a double-D, but surely Bette Davis wasn't remembered for her boobs?

'Double-D as in – Doris fucking Day.'

'Isn't she, like, about a hundred years old?' Another double-D came into his head – Diana Dors: was she older or younger than Doris fucking Day?

'*Dolores* –' Myra Mae practically screamed the name. 'Dolores Delano, for Chrissake.'

Cora had taken him to the premiere of one of Dolores's movies; it had sent him to sleep. And Myra Mae had seated him next to her only superstar client at a couple of her dinners on Mulholland. Dolores still had beauty, courtesy of plastic surgeons more than her genes, but she was no spring chicken. Is there a movie where Bette Davis had a son half her age?

'So – she's gonna be my mother, right?'

'Wrong, Jason. You're gonna be her love interest.'

Jason had a vision of a movie theater audience screaming with laughter as his much-admired bare ass bounced between Dolores Delano's upraised varicose-veined legs. Or would they use a stand-in?

Nancy Schlitz, where are you now?

****

To be continued . . .

Jason's story will be resumed in HOWL AND THE PUSSY-KAT, Part Three of David Godolphin's Hollywood Trilogy, but before that, cherished reader, we must introduce you to Katharine 'Pussy-Kat' Kane, his future co-star in Isaac Hunt's remake of a Bette Davis classic -----

BLUE-MOVIE GIRL

1. BATON ROUGE, LA

When the future all-time-hottest porno actress was born in 1978, her waitress mother was living in a trailer park in Baton Rouge and her garage-mechanic father was serving time for indecent exposure. The girl whose pudendum would one day be almost as widely photographed as Princess Diana's face was the daughter of a serial flasher.

Katharine Kane's life would be filled with ironies.

Born Joylene Duchat (pronounced 'Dew-shat'), she was what people used to call an *octoroon*; her mother Jaynette had a Black grandmother. Jaynette was paler than her daughter whose natural skin-tone was the color another Southern beauty, Ava Gardner, had to be made up to in *Bhowani Junction*.

From her mother Joylene inherited good cheekbones and a petite body to which puberty would add voluptuous curves. From her father she inherited a wide mouth that smiled easily and mid-blonde hair that in certain lights could seem almost reddish. Her eyes also changed with the light from jade to aquamarine; on film they sometimes seem two distinct shades of green.

'Ain't she a beauty?' Crooking the telephone between her right shoulder and ear, Jaynette held her six-week-old daughter up to the reinforced glass of the visitor booth at the Dixon Correctional Institute in Jackson, thirty miles from Baton

Rouge. This was her first visit since her confinement.

'She is too,' her husband agreed. Barton Duchat's own confinement still had three months to run. 'She don't look much like me,' he added.

'She's got your hair,' Jaynette said quickly.

'If you can call that bit of fluff hair.' Bart's suspicions were not easily allayed. 'What color eyes do you call them?'

'They're green, sugar. Kinda blue too, but mostly green.'

'Ain't nobody in my family got green eyes. Not in yourn neither, I reckon.'

'It must be somebody way back on your side or mine,' Jaynette said, trying not to wheedle. 'She is yours, sugar. I swear to God.'

The baby suddenly smiled at her father through the glass, a dimpled pink-cheeked smile that melted his heart.

'She's got your smile,' Jaynette got in quickly.

Bart twinkled his fingers at his green-eyed daughter who would one day melt the heart of her co-star in Hunt Studios' most daring remake, the presently three-year-old John Howell IV.

Barton Duchat felt entitled to question his daughter's paternity. Jaynette was third-generation trailer-trash and a second-generation tramp. Her mother had dropped out of both church and high school and gone through four divorces, ending up dumped by her most recent ex-husband in El Paso.

Bart was Jaynette's first husband – she was sixteen when they married – but she'd lost count of the number of guys she'd slept with, some of them on a cash basis. And she had an abortion and a miscarriage under her belt – two abortions really, since a fetus dislodged in a thirty-foot jump from a barn roof onto a hay-bale can hardly be said to have miscarried by accident.

She'd been pregnant when she married Bart but had lost this child, which might or might not have been his, to a genuine miscarriage that was perhaps an after-effect of the two previous terminations. But she'd stayed on the rails during the eighteen months of her marriage, the last six of which had seen her husband incarcerated. And the child whom the world would one day know as Katharine Kane was beyond doubt the daughter of Barton Duchat.

Twenty when Joylene was born, Bart was a two-time jailbird with prior arrests and fines. He wasn't a rapist, he just liked to show off his dick. To women. On porches, from shop doorways or from behind bushes, on buses and trains, Bart, every once in a while, opened his coat or his flies to reveal his pride and joy in all its (actually quite modest) splendor.

Small wonder, is it, that Katharine Kane would grow up with a shortfall in the area of personal modesty?

The prison psychiatrist failed to find some murky event in Bart's formative years to account for his exhibitionism. His ma could have told the shrink it had started in his baby-cart and that no amount of smacks from her and beatings from his father had made a lick of difference.

While he was a kid his victims had tended to laugh or cuss him out or clout him, but a few had filed complaints. Warnings from the sheriff had escalated to fines, probation and finally to a stay at the local Youth Correction Center. Despite her trailer-park background and her reputation Ma and Pa hoped Jaynette might stabilize him, but they didn't live to see this hope dashed in the fourth month of her third pregnancy. Just before Jaynette lost this baby, a favorite levee on which her parents-in-law were picnicking gave way without warning, engulfing them in a sudden shroud of mud and river water.

The year between this freakish tragedy and the incident that sent Bart to Dixon passed quietly. Bart's share of a modest inheritance enabled them to move into a newer and bigger trailer. An uneventful year culminated in Joylene's conception.

And then Bart went and ruined it all. Queuing for meat in the local Walmart he suddenly hauled out his own meat and walked through the store and up to a woman security officer by the exit with it poking through his fly.

'The urge just comes over me every now and then,' he told the shrink at Dixon. 'I reckon I'm doin' it before I even know I'm doin' it. I don't wanna do it, especially now there's the baby an' all. Can you help me stop?'

'I don't know,' the psychiatrist admitted. 'There are drugs that suppress your libido – we give them to the more dangerous types in here to safeguard the rest of you – but I'm not sure they'd work for your kind of problem.'

'I'd like to give 'em a try,' Bart said.

There was no way to tell if the medication was working since the Dixon Correctional Institute for Men afforded Bart no temptation. The test would come on his parole. One of his brothers owned a garage and gave him a job. Bart was the kind of mechanic who could resurrect an engine from way beyond extinction. His wife – or perhaps it was the baby – kept his wilder instincts reined in. He stopped taking the pills; Jaynette had a demanding appetite for sex.

*

God moves in mysterious ways. When, despite Jaynette, the irresistible urge finally overcame Barton Duchat after five months, the door at which he chose randomly to knock, two blocks from the garage, was a pretty pink, the color of most of his daughter's romper-suits. The lady of the house, who opened the door and its pink flyscreen, was herself a symphony in pink: pink mules, pink housecoat, pink ribbon in her strawberry-tinted hair. She wore no makeup but her skin was rosy from sitting in the sun on her back porch.

'Can I help you, young man?' she asked in a friendly voice.

Bart said nothing. He never did on these occasions. He unzipped the last few inches of his coverall to give the pink lady an exclusive view of what he'd paraded in Walmart early last year.

'My-oh-my,' said the pink lady. Her tone was still not hostile. And after a quick glance left and right and over the road she flung open the pink housecoat to reveal yet more rose-red, all of it skin apart from a small thatch of mousy hair. 'How'd you like them little apples?' she enquired.

'Them' were actually very small apples indeed. No apples at all. Her breasts had been amputated and not replaced with silicone. There was scarring of the washboard-flat skin over her ribs where it was drawn into two separate tucks that might have been, but plainly weren't, nipples. Bart could barely divert his gaze to the thatched area lower down. It was now his turn to turn red.

'Excuse me, ma'am,' he stammered, zipping up his coverall. It was the first time he'd spoken to one of his victims and the first time one of them had flashed back at him. Embarrassed and confused, he turned to go.

'Come back here, young man,' said the lady, covering her rosy disfigured flesh with the pink housecoat. Her tone was firm but in no way sharp.

Bart turned again and so turned a new page in his life.

The pink lady without breasts was Mrs. Grace Goodenough, the forty-year-old widow of a tree surgeon. 'Amazing Grace,' Bart took to calling her. She had achieved what harsh words, beatings, fines, Youth Detention and Dixon had not: Bart was cured. Her scarred flesh gave him some sense of that shock to which he'd exposed his victims (not a huge number: two dozen at the most).

No woman other than Jaynette and, once divorce and a marriage certificate legitimized an encore, Grace would ever again be confronted with the sight of Bart's sometime pride and joy, now – thanks to 'Amazing Grace' Goodenough – his shame.

Even before Grace became the second Mrs. Barton Duchat she became the second-biggest influence he would ever have. The very biggest influence was her best friend, to whom she introduced him that very day he flashed on her front porch for the first and last time. A friend whose name was Jesus.

Reformed sinners are apt to make zealous converts. Zealous and bigoted.

To Jaynette the new Bart, praying at the dinette table, singing hymns in the john, was a bigger pain than the one who'd had trouble keeping his pecker in his pants. Her life was focused on the small bundle of joy and beauty that had been gifted to her after the abortion and the miscarriages. Yes, she concurred with born-again Bart, this gift was probably from God, but she didn't feel the need to attend prayer meetings and Bible-study groups five nights a week plus two services on Sunday to prove her gratitude.

Jaynette, in her heart, remained a good-time girl. Before the year was out she was dispensing good times to men she barely knew, even some she definitely didn't. She'd wasted more than two years being faithful to Bart, at home and in prison. She had some catching up to do.

Bart prayed for her to find, as he had, redemption. Mrs. Goodenough prayed for her to find, as she had, healing grace. Practically the entire congregation of the Divine Church of the Resurrection And the Pentecost (local cynics and Catholics had coined the acronym 'Divine CRAP' for this assembly) spent one September Saturday evening on their knees begging the Lord to bestow, as He had on them, spiritual favor on Jaynette and other named sheep that had strayed. Their prayers for Jaynette were certainly wasted: she got more than usually drunk that night on whisky-sours at the Ace of Clubs and knelt on the poolroom floor to bestow secular favors on no fewer than four guys – a scenario her daughter would re-enact in her early movies.

A God-fearing man can only stand living with an unrepentant whore for so long; and sanctimony makes a hard bed for a party-girl to lie on.

Bart was not cut from the same cloth as Sheriff John Howell III, father of the future Jason Howl. He didn't beat Jaynette, no longer even laid a hand on her in pursuit of his conjugal rights. Divine grace had temporarily neutered Bart as effectively as the drugs at Dixon ('Amazing Grace' would later restore a natural balance). But Jaynette, a more spirited young woman than Jason's mom Marlene, liked to have a hand laid on her and might have tolerated a certain amount of vigor behind it. The new Bart was a born-again bore.

The parting, when it inevitably came, was not acrimonious.

'I'm leavin' you,' she interrupted his prayers over breakfast one morning soon after their daughter turned two.

'I'm not stoppin' you,' he replied with equanimity.

'And I'm takin' Joylene.'

'She's your daughter.'

'She's yours too.'

'Maybe she is and maybe she ain't.' Bart had taken to speaking slowly in normal conversation as if his every utterance came down from the Mountain. 'Where you gonna go?'

'Tucson. I've been talkin' to Ma. She says we can live with her till I get a place of my own.'

'When you plannin' on goin'?'

'Day after tomorrow. Can you give me some money to hire a car? I can't take all my stuff and Joylene's on a Greyhound.'

'Take my pick-up. Brew will give me somethin' else to drive.' Brewster was Bart's brother and his employer at the garage.

'That's kind of you, Bart. I'm sorry things haven't worked out for us. I'll see a lawyer when I get to Ma's.'

'I hope you find happiness in Arizona,' he declaimed in his solemn new voice. 'I hope you find salvation.' He lifted his hand. For a moment Jaynette thought he was going to administer a blessing but he only scratched his ear.

'Thank you, honey,' she said sweetly. 'I hope you get on all right too.'

'With God on my side, how can I fail?' he intoned.

'I guess you can't,' she said, managing not to smirk or tell him to blow it out of his self-righteous ass.

'God is watchin' you too, Jaynette. His eye is forever upon you.'

Jaynette cracked up. 'I'll try not to give Him too much of an eyeful,' she snorted.

2. THE SELDOM MOTEL

And so Jaynette and baby Joylene headed west in the nineteen-year-old Ford pickup (the same age as Jaynette) that Bart and Brew had salvaged from a breaker's yard. It snarled like a cougar at anything over fifty mph and required oil as well as gasoline at every pit-stop, but it made the 1,300-mile journey in three days without breaking down and was still running a year later when Jaynette sold it to a Navajo farmer for two hundred bucks.

Abigail, Jaynette's mother, had made this same journey in five stages over five years. When Jaynette was fourteen she and her two younger sisters had been left in the care of their Black grandmother in Baton Rouge when husband number three, a Texas 'oilman' who turned out to be a pipeline maintenance engineer, took Abigail to Houston. This marriage lasted barely a year, considerably shorter than the previous two. Husband number four was quickly in the frame: he owned a third-rate hotel in Amarillo which he soon sold to buy a motel outside Albuquerque that was going cheap and going nowhere.

Abigail, a demon housekeeper and something of a handyman, revamped the motel; once it thrived, her husband mortgaged it to buy another in El Paso that was totally derelict. Leaving Abigail to supervise renovations he returned to Albuquerque and took up with the new housekeeper. In the ensuing divorce

Abigail received the near-worthless hotel in lieu of alimony.

Around the time Jaynette was having her baby, Abigail was diagnosed with ovarian cancer. Luckily she had a health plan that paid for the hysterectomy. Six months later, broke and with the hotel only half restored, she went back to the hospital to begin radiation and chemotherapy for secondary tumors. The two Mexican brothers who were working on the hotel came up with the money to buy her out. After another six anxious months she was pronounced cancer-free. This was around the time her son-in-law in Baton Rouge was making the acquaintance of Grace Goodenough and her friend Jesus.

While Jaynette resumed her interrupted career as a part-time party-girl, her mother brought down the curtain on her own longer one as a full-time adulteress. Before – and after – her hysterectomy she'd been screwing the two Mexicans; it kept them on-site after her money ran out. But the secondary tumors had, in a very literal sense, scared the willies out of Abigail.

The money she'd got from the brothers wouldn't go far; it went as far as Tucson where she found a small motel (four cabins) on state highway 79 at a small unincorporated township called Seldom (population: 84 assorted whites, wetbacks and Indians), a farming community struggling against the water crisis. There was a general store, a ma-and-pa restaurant – and the Seldom Motel. What little business the aptly named motel obtained came from long-haul travelers avoiding the interstate, short-haul adulterers from Tucson avoiding those who knew them, and silent-movie buffs making a pilgrimage to the nearby desert memorial to Tom Mix (the two-foot-tall black iron silhouette of a riderless horse on a plinth of mortared cobblestones). Bald, thin and weak, Abigail somehow found the strength to apply paint to the walls and sew new drapes and bedcovers.

And it was to the Seldom Motel that Jaynette and Joylene came to seek a new life in February 1980. John Howell IV was in his first year of elementary school in San Diego.

Including the front office, the management cabin had about the same area as Bart's trailer in Baton Rouge. Abigail gave them her bedroom and made the teensy office behind Reception into a bedroom for herself.

It was a strange cohabitation of three generations.

At thirty-eight Abigail was still, now that her hair had regrown and her flesh filled out, a fine-looking woman, the color of oak, big-breasted with a wide strong-featured face and a cheerful disposition. While she worked she sang gospel hymns learned from her own mother and Soul songs from the easy-listening station on the radio.

Jaynette, half her mother's age and nearer the color of maple, was less voluptuous, but a pretty young woman nevertheless except when, as now, frustration and boredom often gave her a pouting sullen look. She sang along with Dionne and Aretha, but Bart had soured her taste for hymns.

At two Joylene, whose color was somewhere between that of her mother and grandmother, was a child of rare beauty with her long curly fair hair and green eyes. She was happy, lively and button-bright. In Seldom there were no other children her age apart from a pair of Navajo kids from one of the remoter farms. Joylene was much fussed over by the Mendozas who ran the general store, by Mabel and Pete in the ma-and-pa restaurant, by farmer's wives and the wives and mistresses of the Seldom Motel's infrequent clients.

Abigail, gradually inducted to climate change in her jumpy moves westward, had come to love the searing heat that laid shimmering mirages across the bleached landscape of southern Arizona. Joylene took to it instantly, romping like a puppy-dog in the sand in just her knickers. Jaynette hated it: hated the arid ochre creeks and washes, the dusty gray highway, the relentless aching blue of the sky. She yearned for the lush greens of Louisiana, and for rain.

Seldom was aptly named from her point of view since she only got laid four times in the first year (three truck-drivers and a farmer's eighteen-year-old son on vacation from agricultural school). She hoped her mother couldn't hear her vibrator through the thin walls of the cabin; it didn't wake the baby. The cleaning and laundry did not require two women, and once they caught up on the five years they'd been apart and commiserated over each other's marital misfortunes there wasn't much left to say. They watched a lot of television.

Under the terms of the Arizona divorce Bart was required to send maintenance for the child he didn't believe was his. Urged on and helped by Grace, he sent a bit extra that kept Jaynette off Welfare.

'This ain't workin' out for you, is it, sugar?' Abigail asked her daughter one morning in 1981 over their fourth cups of coffee. Joylene was outside, playing cowgirl games with her dolls.

'It's drivin' me crazy,' Jaynette confessed. 'I'm honestly minded to go back to Louisiana. Jaynice could maybe give us a bed. Or Granma.' The two sisters were named after their father, Abigail's first husband 'Jay-Jay' (John Jacob), a janitor. Jaynice lived in a tract house outside New Orleans with her bus-driver husband and two infants. Denise, their teenage half-sister by stepfather number one who took tourists on Lake Pontchartrain boat rides, was still in the Baton Rouge trailer park with their grandmother.

'Don't go back, Jaynette,' her mother said now. 'If you get a job in the city I can go on looking after Joylene and we wouldn't have to lose touch again. You can stay on here and drive my car to work.'

In the time it took Joylene to reach kindergarten age, Jaynette worked as a waitress in a series of bars and restaurants in Tucson. She fooled around with some more guys and was briefly married to the manager of one bar, a burly man almost twice her age who couldn't keep his hands to himself or to his new wife. There were no more babies and no abortions. She stayed on the Pill and left Joylene with Abigail, even during the five months that this second marriage lasted; an apartment over a topless bar was no place for a child.

The Seldom Motel prospered. Abigail added four more cabins to cater for a growing clientele of truckers who liked her homely style and the food at *Mabel's Luncheon Diner* which repainted its sign to *Mabel's Lunch 'n Diner* and now served early dinners. The out-of-town location kept the other side of the enterprise expanding also: cheating wives and two-timing husbands and a growing number of horny affluent high-school kids. The washing machine ran all day.

*

Their mothers couldn't have been more different but absentee fathers were something the future Katharine Kane and Jason Howl had in common and would one day discuss. Joylene had yet to experience living with a stepfather.

The money Bart sent increased incrementally each year and there was extra cash at Christmas and birthdays. But he never came to Seldom.

'Do they have banks in Heaven, Granma?' Joylene asked on her fourth birthday in 1982 when Abigail showed her the $50 from Baton Rouge. Her grandmother's ample flesh shivered as she laughed.

'I don't guess so, pussycat. But this here check's from your daddy in Baton Rouge. To your mommy and me that's more like Hell than Heaven!'

Joylene thought this through. 'Is Daddy in Hell, then? I've heard Mommy say he can go to Hell for all she cares.' Abigail laughed and shook some more. She licked her fingers and used the spit to reset a stray curl of Joylene's.

'Mommy just says that when she's feelin' mean.'

'Daddy's dead, though, isn't he?' Joylene had this way of coming out with eerily adult syntax. 'He's dead, but you and Mommy pretend he's still alive and living near Mommy's granma.'

'No, he ain't dead, pussycat. They just divorced, which ain't the same thing though it sometimes feels like it. My mom told me your daddy's studyin' to be a preacher like Reverend Oral and Reverend Jimmy on the TV.'

'Why doesn't he come and see me?' She was a child again; tears welled in her eyes. 'Even the Injun kids have got daddies. I'd like to have one too.'

Abigail hugged the child. 'I guess your daddy's a mite too busy right now, pussycat. What with studyin' an' all. But I'm sure he still loves you. He sends your mommy some money every month for your keep. So what shall we get with this fifty bucks he's given you for your birthday? Toys? A new dress?'

Joylene gave the wide smile that had once, in Dixon, melted her father's heart. 'A dress *and* some toys!'

'And a thank-you card to send to your daddy.'

'I guess so.' Joylene sighed a deep adult sigh. 'I appreciate the fifty dollars,' she said thoughtfully, 'but if he doesn't come and see me he might just as well be dead.' She paused before adding: 'That bastard.'

Her grandmother replaced her mother in Joylene's affections. When Mommy wasn't working she was apt to be feeling tired or just plain mean. Granma got tired too, but never too tired to find time for Joylene – and never mean. She played with her and taught her the alphabet and numbers up to a hundred.

By the time she was four Joylene was reading her first storybooks and could count the change from an ice-cream at Señor Mendoza's store or a soda and a cookie at Auntie Mabel's. Cookies, sodas and ice-creams were apt to be free, but Joylene didn't mind paying. She always had a stack of bills from the truck-drivers who couldn't resist giving the cute little girl a dollar when they checked out. Sometimes 'the fornicators' gave her money too, although they paid in advance and usually snuck away leaving the cabin key in the door.

Joylene had picked up on Abigail's use of 'fornicators' to describe this particular clientele although Granma was vague about its precise meaning.

'You know I sometimes sing songs about cheatin' men and bustin' up and women with broken hearts?' she began when pressed for a fuller explanation.

'Course I do. Mommy's had a D-I-V-O-R-C-E. Two of them.'

'Well, fornication is – kinda like lovin' the one you're with when you can't be with the one you're supposed to love.'

Joylene went off to discuss the ramifications of this lesson with Ken and his harem of Barbies and Sindy's. She later explained to Granma and Mommy which combination of her dolls was a happy couple and which were 'fornicators'. Jaynette and Abigail laughed till they ached.

Less amused, initially, was the thirty-something woman who sat outside in her convertible while the man she was with prepaid the cabin in Reception.

'Are you here for the fornication?' the entrancing four-year-old enquired. The woman stared speechlessly at Joylene who wagged a finger at her and uttered an admonition worthy of Reverend Jimmy Swaggart on TV (and, obviously, of Mister Ray Charles):

'Your cheating heart will tell on you.'

The woman joked about this with her lover in their cabin. But she ended the day by telling him she couldn't see him anymore. She went home to her husband vowing to give it another shot.

In later life Pussy-Kat Kane's video movies would provide a fixative – not always a permanent bond – to many a shaky union. They would of course do a lot more to stimulate adulterers and solitary masturbators. But here she was, four years old, talking like an adult and providing adhesion, however temporary, to a cracked marriage.

3. LE BAYOU

Almost overnight, it seemed, the weight began to fall off Abigail again. God was continuing to move in His mysterious ways: 'Too darned mysterious for me,' Abigail said. To hell with 'mysterious' – He was merciless.

She left Joylene with Mabel while she drove herself to the oncologists in Tucson for another round of tests and X-rays. They told her the cancer was now attacking almost every organ in her body. They gave her not months but weeks. They gave her pills for when the pain started.

Joylene was waitressing at one of the city's best restaurants; it was too good a job to quit. Glad to get out of the store, Mrs. Mendoza took on the motel's cleaning and laundry. Abigail devoted herself totally to the granddaughter from whom she was too soon and too cruelly to be parted.

The parting came in less than a month. Joylene was again left with Auntie Mabel while Mommy drove Granma to the hospital in Tucson on what would not be, this time, a round-trip. By an immense effort of will Abigail managed not to cry as she hugged for the last time this child who had filled her heart and her life for two and a half years in a way that four husbands and her own daughters somehow had not.

'Take care of your mommy while I'm gone, pussycat.'

'I will, Granma,' Joylene promised. 'And Auntie Mabel and

Uncle Pete and Señor and Señora Mendoza. Can I come and see you in the hospital?'

'You don't want to see me with all those nasty tubes and stuff like on the TV.'

'I don't mind that.'

'Best not, pussycat.'

'Come home soon, Granma.'

'Just as soon as ever I can,' Abigail assured her and had to turn her face away as Jaynette put the car into drive.

Joylene sent her grandmother a card every day of the next three weeks, during which the cancer devoured what remained of her flesh. It was a relief for Jaynette when the pain control knocked her mother unconscious four days before the end and a bigger relief when she got the call at work four days later, already dreading the evening vigil she would now not have to keep.

An overflowing car brought Denise and her grandmother and Jaynice with her husband and two children from Baton Rouge to Seldom for the funeral. Joylene was comfortable with the notion of her grandmother having moved to Heaven. On the day of the funeral she attached the wings from a Christmas-tree angel to her favorite Barbie and then ceremonially buried the doll under a yucca in the forlorn space that passed for a garden behind the motel cabins. She had cried a few times but, as small children do, she was already beginning to get over losing Granma. She missed being called 'pussycat'.

As the pastor reminded them at the crematorium, the Lord giveth and the Lord taketh away. What the Lord gaveth on this occasion was husband number three for Jaynette. They were already dating and screwing. He'd gone to the hospital with her twice on his days off. Drugged as she was with painkillers it wasn't easy to tell if Abigail approved of him.

His name was Ruiz. He was a chef at the Tucson restaurant where Jaynette was waitressing lunchtimes and some evenings. Aged twenty-nine and originally from a village in the southern Sierra Madre he'd been in the US for ten years, illegally for two, then in possession of the precious green card; two years ago he'd become a citizen. He was olive-skinned, black-haired, movie-star handsome and yet modest and almost shy. Jaynette had made all the moves. He seemed too good to be true, but good and true he turned out to be.

He wouldn't come to the funeral.

'This is for you and your family, *querida*.'

'But I want you to meet my family, Ruiz.'

'When the time is right. First I have to meet your daughter.'

'She needs a father, Ruiz. She doesn't remember Bart, and the bastard's never come to see her. She's gonna love you.'

In her will Abigail left her paltry savings to Jaynice and Denise. Jaynette inherited the Seldom Motel which she intended to sell and use the money to buy a small house in Tucson. Ruiz had a better idea. He'd been saving up to buy his own restaurant, and with some financing from a bank they bought the diner from Mabel and Pete who were ready to move to a retirement village outside Phoenix.

Southern Arizona is not short of Mexican eateries (is anywhere?). Ruiz's idea was for out-of-town French and Cajun cuisine. He was already a cordon bleu chef; from recipe books he taught himself the culinary secrets of New Orleans. Jaynette was more of a freezer-to-microwave cook.

They moved into the apartment over the restaurant, which was roomier than the management cabin. While Jaynette managed the motel Ruiz converted *Mabel's Lunch 'n Diner* into *Le Bayou*: blood-red textured wallpaper and velvet drapes, dark heavy Mexican furniture which in the dimly-lit interior could just about pass for period French.

Le Bayou put Seldom on the map; it got written up in newspapers and travel magazines. By the time Joylene started kindergarten in Catalina, twenty miles south, the restaurant was not only a hot favorite with diners from Tucson and Phoenix, it was attracting business from Flagstaff and even from out-of-state. They had to add another four cabins to the motel for overnighters.

A plump gay cousin of Ruiz's moved in to manage the motel, Javier, who also answered to the name of Carmen. His lanky and languid lover Leonard (aka Leonora), out of New England via Baja California, waited tables in Le Bayou and wowed the more sophisticated diners with droll verbal asides in the voices of Bette Davis, Joan Crawford and Katharine Hepburn. The sound of not one but three Judy Garlands or Barbra Streisands often emanated from the management cabin.

Jaynette dressed up in Southern Belle costume to greet and seat the diners. Apart from this she didn't do much except run Joylene to and from kindergarten and supervise the cleaning women, illegals from south of the border who also cleaned the motel cabins. Ruiz shopped and cooked.

Her sedentary life meant that Jaynette's costumes had to be let out every few months. Luckily Javier was a drag-queen's dream of a seamstress. He made her wedding-dress when Ruiz finally got Jaynette in front of a justice.

Thanks to Abigail and now Ruiz, Jaynette had been fully extracted from the trailer park; but the trailer park had not been fully extracted from Jaynette. She didn't cook, sew or garden; she didn't go to church or even to the movies; she read magazines rather than books; she watched television rather than make conversation or bond with her child.

She never did take to life in Seldom. To a girl from Baton Rouge cactuses and yuccas and creosote bushes did not constitute greenery. The trailer park rats had been a more tolerable form of wildlife than rattlers and scorpions. She hated the hot desert days, the cold desert nights. But if she didn't like it, she got by with lumping it. Basically, all it took to keep her happy was to be regularly fed and fucked. Ruiz didn't seem to mind that his wife and maîtresse d' was getting larger by the week; nor did he lose a near-insatiable appetite for her expanding flesh. It took Jaynette two years to get pregnant and then she had an early miscarriage. They continued trying for a baby for several more years before giving up.

Having had a loving grandmother for two and a half years, Joylene now had a loving stepfather whom she called Daddy. Jaynette could not – quite – be called a bad mother, but she wasn't generous with her affections in the way that Abigail had been. Ruiz and Javier and Leonard were profligate with theirs.

Joylene adored her two new uncles. And, as her mother had predicted, she loved Ruiz. She loved him with a passion that might have seemed unhealthy in an older girl. He provided a yardstick against which she would measure all the other men in her life. Not many would measure up.

Let's fast-forward through elementary school and rejoin Joylene Duchat (much as she loved her stepfather, why be one of two dozen Hernandez's when you could be the only Duchat?) in junior high.

It's 1990. Joylene has started puberty. And, aged twelve, she is getting ready to start an active sex life of her own.

'Joylene, have you been at my Kotex? They're not for playin' with.'

'I needed them, Mom. I had my period.'

'I guess I should talk to you about boys an' babies, huh?'

Joylene laughed. 'Puh-lease! I've known all that stuff since I was, like, six or seven. And yes, I do know about condoms.'

'Jesus, girl, is this where I start worryin' about you getting knocked up already?'

'No it's not, Mom. And condoms aren't just about not getting pregnant. They're about not getting AIDS.' Her mother's mouth fell open.

'They teach you about AIDS in school now?'

'Of course they do. God, Mom, you're so, like – not cool.'

At the Catalina Junior High School sex education was firmly on the agenda. This was the 1990s: the Safe Sex message needed to be hammered home to a new generation of pubescent fornicators. Teachers couldn't afford to be prudish. Prudery used to pave the path for pre-teen mothers; now it carried a death sentence.

At twelve Joylene had not only heard about condoms, she'd been the first in her giggling class to take one out of its foil and slip it onto a rubber penis modeled on gay porn-stud Ty Topman. (In her later incarnation as Pussy-Kat Kane she would one day fit a condom to the prototype.) The dildo gave the seventh grade boys – and girls – aspirations few of them would ever reach.

Joylene was the beauty of her year despite competition from some of the rural Hispanic girls, one of whom – Maria Hernandez (no relation to Ruiz) – already had breasts, which Joylene didn't. Maria, whose father farmed thousands of acres and employed more than a hundred other Mexicans, also claimed to have already 'done it'. ('It' in this context only meant masturbating a member of the opposite sex.) Joylene hadn't 'done it' but she'd seen a couple of 'them' during games of dare behind the toilet block and offered the first private showings of what would one day be the world's most public pudendum.

'Is that all there is?' she'd commented on seeing the first one a year ago. The crushed owner was the same age as Joylene – eleven.

'Small fuckin' deal,' she'd observed of the second one. She was already cultivating a laconic style. The twelve-year-old proprietor returned tit for tat:

'Well, yours isn't much, either. Maria Hernandez has got hair on hers.'

Eleven years old and Katharine Kane was feeling the heat of the sex war.

'Joylene, will you be my date for the Prom?'
'Did Maria turn you down, Jimmy?'

'I didn't ask her. I'm asking you.'

'I'd love to be your date,' she said and gave him a quick kiss on the cheek which already sprouted a few bristly black hairs. Jaime – Jimmy – Hernandez (no relation to Maria or to Ruiz) forced his thick tongue between her lips. Joylene pressed her tongue against his. This was her first kiss involving tongues.

Maria might have hair down there and breasts, but she didn't have Jimmy, the handsomest boy in the seventh grade. Actually, she did. Jimmy was the boy she'd 'done it' with.

For the Prom in July Joylene wore a new spangly top and silver high heels (twelfth birthday gifts from her Daddy) with black Lurex pants. Jimmy, whose father managed a gas station in Catalina, wore a loose-fitting tuxedo handed down from his sixteen-year-old brother. Maria Hernandez wore a yellow flamenco dress. Her date was Chris Lee, the seventh grade's number-one WASP, a blond jock-in-the-making whose father owned a used-car lot.

There was fruit-juice punch and a finger buffet contributed by parents and a restaurant-owning stepfather. There was dancing to a live band, a group of slumming seniors. Later, not too late, parents or older siblings arrived to collect them. A goodnight kiss and it was over. Jimmy tongued Joylene's throat.

Five years from now some of these kids would have their own cars and would make out in desert lay-bys and in the cactus 'forests'. Joylene's dates would be expected to do a lot more with their tongues.

Katharine Kane did not wait till senior school to begin making out.

March 1991, two months after Joylene turned thirteen.

Jimmy Hernandez cycled the twenty-five miles from Catalina to Seldom on the hard shoulder of the highway. Joylene took him 'exploring' with the intention that what they would explore was each other.

A mile from the highway they were out of view of anything except low-flying aircraft from Davis-Monthan Air Force Base. They climbed onto a gravity-defying rock shelf protruding from a creek wall. Already the desert was a cauldron. After a check for scorpions and rattlesnakes, they sheltered below the shelf. Joylene hadn't dared bring a give-away blanket but she had a discarded cot sheet in her rucksack and this she now spread on the sand and shingle. They lay down and tongued each other's mouths. Joylene registered Jimmy's erection pressing against her.

'I'm gonna come,' he gasped, breaking free.

'But we didn't do anything.'

'Near enough. D'you wanna see it?'

Joylene went laconic. 'Well, I didn't come out here to look at wildflowers.'

Jimmy pushed down his shorts. What he revealed was much darker than the rest of him and throbbed to a pulse of its own. It had hair. As during the dildo/condom demonstration, Joylene saw that the two boys she'd inspected behind the toilet block had been seriously short-changed in the genital lottery.

'Wow,' she said, no longer laconic. 'Can I touch it?'

'Yes. Only –'

She stretched out a hand, and it was all over. All over her hand.

'Gross,' she said, succinctly, then dipped a finger of her other hand in the fluid and sniffed it. Le Bayou's kitchen provided a frame of reference: the smell was somewhere between béchamel sauce and prawn gumbo.

Oral sex had not been on the school curriculum. Joylene knew it was not a route to pregnancy, but what about AIDS? She figured that at thirteen-and-a-half Jimmy was not a huge AIDS risk and brought her finger to her tongue. The taste was more redolent of seafood than white sauce and not too gross. It was Jimmy's turn to be impressed. Maria had not gone this far.

'Can I see your tits?'

'I don't have any.' She did, of course, but they were still at a formative stage.

'Show me anyway.'

She pulled off her halter-top and padded bra. Jimmy prodded the soft flesh around her nipples. 'They're sprouting,' he pronounced. 'My sister's used to be like that and you should see them since she turned fourteen. They came up in just a few months.'

'Your sister shows you her tits?'

'I peek when she's in the shower, but I think she knows I'm peeking.'

'Brothers,' she said, as if she had some. Her 'uncles' were more like sisters.

In most respects Joylene was a normal thirteen-year-old. She was only a year or so younger than John Howell's Rebecca-Ann who started jerking boys off under the bleachers at Hope Valley High at fourteen, three years ago.

Was Arizona ahead of Sodom-and-Gomorrah California in adolescent sexuality? Was Katharine Kane a freak? If so, can it be attributed to the dark African rivers that ran in her blood or to the overheated Latin climate in which she was developing? Or were other thirteen-year-olds in other environments also beginning to experiment with sex in the hedonistic Nineties – in, say, Alaska or Iowa or Rhode Island?

There were redneck kids in Catalina who sneered at the wetbacks. Having a Mexican stepfather (and being herself one-eighth Afro-American), it didn't seem a big deal to Joylene that her first boyfriend should be Hispanic.

Jimmy cycled out most weekends. Joylene continued to handle his adult-sized organ and he continued to ejaculate instantly. He fingered the buds that were her breasts and he probed between her thighs where there was sometimes a delicious tingly sensation, which was even stronger when she touched herself there.

Joylene and Jimmy and Chris and Maria became a foursome that lasted into high school. They switched partners from time to time, much as many of their parents' generation were doing. Chris was blighted with zits, but he grew to be handsome, tall and broad and represented the University of Arizona in varsity league football. Later still he would represent his district in the state legislature and would be a strong advocate of immigrants' rights. He would marry a Hispanic, but not Maria Hernandez.

Jimmy was destined to stay in Catalina and become a car mechanic working for his pa. He dated Maria even after she too went to university. He would be driving the truck in which they died on AZ-79, a few miles from the Tom Mix Memorial, at the age of twenty, by which time Joylene's metamorphosis into Katharine Kane would be almost complete.

*

In her movies Pussy-Kat Kane gives spectacular head. Joylene cast around for a 'mentor' in this area. She chose Leonard rather than Javier who was more likely to blab to her stepfather. Joylene pretended the advice was for a gay classmate; Leonard pretended not to see through the subterfuge.

'Honey,' he drawled, 'I'm just a one-guy gal these days, but from what I hear your friend would be better off being a boy who can say no.'

'Yeah, but if he's keen on somebody special, how safe is – you know?'

'Well, back when your Aunt Carmen and I were upbeat uptown girls I seem to recall that people were buying special flavored condoms for – what your friend wants to do. Speaking personally –' he turned into Mae West – 'if Ah'm taken out for a nice steak dinner, Ah'm not sure Ah want my meat to taste of strawberry!'

They shared a conspiratorial dirty laugh.

Joylene couldn't bring herself to ask a second question that was contingent upon the answer to the first: what to do when a guy comes in your mouth.

Slumber parties were single-sex affairs. Those at the Seldom Motel were among the most popular. Javier gave Joylene and her classmates a large cabin and dressed up as Carmen Miranda to get them in the mood for some merriment. Having a drag-queen for an uncle gave Joylene a rare distinction.

Sex talk – talk of oral sex – was on the slumber-party agenda, although not all the girls were yet doing it. On the burning second question, those who were doing it divided themselves into 'hawks' and 'swallows'. Maria, who'd started 'doing it' with

Chris once she knew Joylene and Jaime had beaten her to this next phase, was a 'swallow'; perhaps she knew she would not live long enough to find out whether it was unsafe. Joylene, most of the time, was a 'hawk'.

Extra-curricular life was not all slumber parties and blowjobs. There was homework and sport and cheerleading. Joylene took homework seriously but she despised all sports except swimming and refused to join the cheerleaders. Chris Lee was disappointed.

'It's so demeaning,' she told him when he pestered her on this issue. Chris stood naked in the creek with his muscular arms stretched up to the overhang like Atlas holding the Earth. Joylene, topless exposing bigger buds that promised to be proper breasts, knelt in front of him. She licked his balls, a zit-free zone and the only thing of his that she preferred to Jimmy's. Jimmy's balls hung low in a sack thicketed with dark hair that got caught in her teeth; Chris's were attached to the base of his penis and covered only by a peach-skin fuzz. Joylene liked the way his scrotum tightened just before he came.

'What's so demeaning about it?'

She raised her head and looked up his tanned torso which already had the definition that would soon make a star athlete of him. 'Girls in tutus,' she sneered, 'doing a stupid pompom routine to make boys feel important. It's so sexist. And definitely demeaning.' She went back to work.

'You don't think this is demeaning?'

She frowned up at him. 'In what way?'

'Aren't you making me feel important right now?'

'No more important than Jimmy or any other boy I could be

doing it with. Who do you think is in control here: you or me?'

'Who's getting his dick sucked?'

'Who's doing the sucking?'

'You are.'

'Not any more,' she said. She stood up, put her top back on and walked off. 'Still feeling in control?' she asked over her shoulder.

4. ALL THE WAY ... AND THEN SOME

There was one other out-of-hours activity in which she took an interest and developed skills which would serve her well in later life: drama. A born actress, she had already taken key roles in plays and pageants in junior high. At her new school, J. Edgar Hoover Memorial High in Oro Valley, it began to look as if Joylene might have a future in the dramatic arts. Which, as we shall see, she does – sort of.

The plays were stock (schlock) specially written for schools. At Hoover High some imaginative pageants were created by Mr. Dunne, who taught history. Teddy Dunne was in his mid-thirties, tall and lanky with long flopping blond hair. He wore glasses and an earnest expression and, being unmarried, was the object of many a teenage crush. Joylene reckoned he was gay.

'Have you thought about what you'll do after graduation?' he asked her during a break in rehearsals for the Christmas revue.

'I'm not sure,' she said. 'Teach history?'

He caught on to the tease and laughed. 'Think about acting,' he counseled. Joylene thought about it.

'Yeah,' she said. 'Why not?' She wasn't serious and didn't think Mr. Dunne was either.

Jimmy had replaced Chris again. He was keen to 'go all the way'. Joylene was more than a little curious about this small step for a girl that was a big step for womankind.

'Chris wants to do it too,' Maria told her, 'but I'm scared of getting pregnant. My mom would pitch a fit if I asked to go on the Pill.'

'We have to use condoms anyway.'

'My sister Inez swears she was using condoms but she still got pregnant. I think they can get holes. Or come off.'

'Talking of coming off,' Joylene said, 'do you?'

'Do I what?'

'Come off. With Chris.'

'I don't think so. Not like in books and movies. Do you with Jimmy?'

'Nah. I try to get him to use his finger more but he just doesn't do it right. Maybe it's better to be a lesbian. I hear they give each other great head.'

Maria made a face. 'No way.'

'I'm gonna go for it,' Joylene said.

'With a dyke?'

'Nah, stupid. With Jimmy.'

Joylene embarked on a 'training program' involving carrots and zucchini purloined from her stepfather's kitchen. For lubrication she experimented with various hand and body lotions, all of which shared a tendency to rapid absorption; there was one scary occasion when she had to limp to her mother's kitchen in a wide-legged John Wayne gait to acquire a spoon and extricate a carrot suffering from dry skin.

'Going all the way' took several attempts. Not because Jimmy was a bigger boy than ever at fourteen. The problem wasn't one of access but of velocity. The first three times he came while she was applying the condom. The only solution was to wait half an hour and then try again. Jimmy was just as chili-hot to trot as thirty minutes before and she managed – just – to get him into position, lying on the sheet in the shade of the rock shelf with her legs wrapped round him, before he came, this time inside the condom, inside her.

There was no blood; presumably she had surrendered her virginity to a vegetable. Neither was there much sensation, although Jimmy's shrink-wrapped organ had, even when rigid, a pliability that zucchini lacked: it felt nice sliding, however briefly, to and fro inside her; it felt right. So, even if she'd failed to achieve some kind of sexual 'transfiguration', there was a small sense of achievement. She had finally, in the spring of her fifteenth year, *done it*.

She did it two or three times a week with Jimmy throughout that summer semester as the heat built up and turned their creek into a pizza oven. His sweat poured over Joylene during their brief couplings beneath the rock slab whose upper surface now seared their skin if they touched it.

Not to be left behind, Maria overcome her qualms and did it with Chris. It was, she reported, a bloody and painful business. Joylene had not shared with Maria the secret of her vegetarian rehearsals in case it became classroom gossip if they ever fell out.

Penetrative sex brought with it a closer feminine alliance.

'We are both women now,' Maria said, sounding as if she meant it.

'Yeah,' said Joylene, unconvinced. 'Did you come?'

'I don't think so. Did you?'

'Not that way.' Joylene hesitated to admit that orgasm still eluded her, unless that occasional mild tingle was all that the myth amounted to. 'Maybe we should fix Chris and Jimmy up with a couple of hookers.'

'What for?'

'So they can learn how to please us properly. From professionals.'

'Hookers get AIDS. All those men. And they do drugs and stuff.'

'Or maybe they need to practice with older women, you know, like in that old movie. *The Graduate*. Or maybe –' the thought came to her – '*we* should practice with some older guys who can show us what to do.'

'Seniors, you mean?'

'Men, Maria. Not boys.'

'I'd like to get in some practice with Brad Pitt,' Maria sighed.

Joylene laughed. 'I'll take Richard Gere.'

Maria made a face. 'He's too old. Leonardo DiCaprio.'

'He's too young. Jed Swann.' They'd heard about, but not seen, the notorious home movie of the *Solana Beach* mega-hunk getting a poolside blowjob from teen bimbo Darla Dawson. As they giggled their way through a catalogue of movie and TV stars, it was clear that Joylene was already separating the men from the boys.

The last history assignment of the summer was on the JFK-inspired theme of W*hat I Can Do for My Country*. The boys' papers struck a uniformly gung-ho note: join the army, the navy, Top Gun; assassinate Gaddafi or Saddam; stamp out the last traces of Communism in Cuba, Korea, China.

If the boys wanted to conquer the world, the girls wanted

to save it. Their role models were Princess Diana or (for the Hispanics) Mother Theresa or (for some of the WASPs) Hillary Clinton: bring relief to the homeless, the indigent, the dying. Service and sacrifice were common themes, as was making the world a better place for US-style democracy.

Joylene took a provocative position and turned the question on its head. She wanted to know *What My Country Can Do for Me*. She too invoked the name of the First Lady but cited her as an example of how few women were permitted to achieve positions of power and then only as second fiddles in the male orchestra. Joylene pleaded the Feminist cause, calling for an America in which her generation of women would find no door closed to them. '*Then*,' she concluded in a nod to the original question, '*when I know what my special gifts are, I can be confident that my fellow citizens will not be denied the opportunity to see them at their fullest stretch.*'

Mr. Dunne gave her an A-minus. She was one of three students required to read their papers to the class.

'I know what I'd like to see fully stretched,' said one of the back-row jocks. A few years from now Al Kazman would grant him his wish.

'In your wet dreams, jerkoff,' said Joylene.

'So what exactly are these "special gifts" you think you've got?' demanded the brightest of the Hispanic girls, the future Mrs. Chris Lee.

'You tell me,' answered Joylene, in whom prolixity was limited to the written word.

'Giving head,' murmured a plain WASP in the front to her neighbor. Beans had plainly been spilled. Joylene gave her the finger. Teddy Dunne frowned.

*

She'd decided he wasn't gay. If his attention occasionally lingered on anyone in class or during rehearsals, it wasn't on Chris or Jimmy: it was on some of the Hispanic girls, and on *her*.

She didn't flirt with him. Some of the others were doing that and it was plainly not working. Joylene went for entrapment.

For this year's pageant – '*The Camelot Legacy*' – Mr. Dunne invited Joylene to be co-producer as well as leading lady (Hillary Clinton in a spoof Lady Guinevere costume). Co-producing combined the duties of all-purpose gofer and deputy ass-kicker; plus, she had to stay on after rehearsal, supervising the return of the auditorium to morning assembly status and then going over with Mr. Dunne the notes for the next rehearsal.

Freeing her mother or Leonard to drive her home from Oro Valley in the early evening was inconvenient for Le Bayou. When she pointed out to her stepfather that Seldom was only a small detour from Mr. Dunne's route to his home in Florence, north on AZ-79, Ruiz asked the teacher if he would mind dropping her off.

The first two evenings in his car, a Jeep Cherokee, they just discussed the production. Mr. Dunne came into Le Bayou and had a drink with Jaynette and Ruiz whom he'd he met at PTA meetings. He told Jaynette, who now weighed in at around 200 pounds, that she was giving him ideas for a *Gone With the Wind* theme for next year.

On the third night he inadvertently sprang Joylene's trap.

'So,' he asked as they turned north at Oracle Junction, 'have you thought any more about what "special skills" you're going to contribute to our great "New Society" after you graduate?'

'Mr. Dunne, I think you already know the answer to that,' she replied, eyes demurely lowered.

'Do I? Oh yes: you're going to teach history!'

Joylene laughed, pleased that he hadn't forgotten last year's tease.

'Or Hollywood,' she said. 'Which was your idea.'

'I don't believe I specified Hollywood. It could always be the Great White Way.'

'Excuse me, sir?' He'd never made such a flagrantly racist remark in class.

'Broadway. As in the theater.'

'Oh. Well, I think my "special skills" will be more use in Hollywood than on Broadway.'

'Don't put yourself down, Joylene. A lot of pretty girls break into TV and movies, but I think you've got what it takes to become a stage actress.'

Joylene didn't want to discuss her acting prospects which right now seemed less realizable than those in the teaching of history.

'I was thinking more about my other special skill, sir.'

'Which one's that?'

'The one Loretta mentioned when I read my term paper.'

'I don't remember that she said anything.' Had he truly forgotten or was he avoiding embarrassment? They were two miles from Seldom on a deserted highway. *Go for it*, Joylene told herself.

'Giving head,' she said matter-of-factly. Mr. Dunne didn't lose control of the steering. He laughed.

'You've been reading too many trashy novels. I think you'll find that the movie business is more about looks and talent than about giving head to producers.'

'But it might come in handy. And I am good at it.'

'Joylene, I don't think we should be talking about this.'

'You're right. We need to be doing it.' She reached over and groped him. He had a hard-on inside his chinos. Now he nearly lost control of the car. He decelerated to avoid a potential skid. In the twilit distance the Seldom Motel's neon sign winked its welcome to the tired and the horny.

'Joylene, I –'

'Stop the car,' she said, co-producer authority in her voice. Even before he brought the car to an obedient standstill on the gritty hard shoulder she had unzipped his chinos and freed his rigid organ from inside his jockeys. Bigger than Jimmy's, it was roped with prominent veins; its head was like a golf ball.

'Joylene Duchat, stop that right now,' he said in his classroom voice.

She leaned over, opened her mouth and engulfed the golf ball. Teddy Dunne gasped. Fumbling for the seat lever, he tipped his seat onto the horizontal. Joylene stayed with him, gagging and slurping. The Jeep shook as a truck thundered past. Teddy threshed on the seat and moaned incoherently. His hands seized her head and held her down on him. He exploded, prodigiously, in her mouth. Joylene briefly imagined how cheap and unladylike it would look if she opened her door and hawked on the ground. *Oh well*, she thought, and swallowed. Licking her lips she smiled triumphantly in the dashboard light at Teddy Dunne with his flopping lock of hair and now flopping, dribbling penis. He adjusted his clothes and returned his seat to the vertical. His expression was guilty, apprehensive.

'We shouldn't have done that,' he said.

'But I bet you're glad we did!'

'It can never happen again,' he insisted.

'Well, probably not before Thursday,' she said in a confident tone. Thursday was the next rehearsal. The slipstream of another truck rocked the Jeep as it rumbled past.

'Joylene, you're fourteen years old. I have a duty of trust to the children in my care.'

'Your duty is to fuck me Thursday night,' she told him bluntly. 'Bring a condom.'

'Joylene, I could go to jail.'

'Only if I tell. And I won't. I won't even tell Maria who's my best friend. This is something I plan to keep to myself.'

'*Please.*'

'Look,' she said, 'you teach me history and you coach me in drama. Now I want you to coach me in sex.'

He laughed harshly. 'Why me, for God's sake?'

'I reckoned you might be good at it.'

'Why not pick on someone your own age? I thought you and Jaime Hernandez were getting serious.'

'We are, I guess. But he's useless at sex. He comes off in five seconds flat.'

His laugh this time was rueful. 'I believe I just did too.'

'More like twenty! But I kinda took you by surprise. I reckon you can hold out for longer. And I reckon you can teach me some stuff that might hold Jimmy off too.'

The rear lights of the truck faded as it rounded the curve in the highway beyond Seldom. Teddy Dunne took hold of her hand and looked into her eyes, deep aquamarine in the encroaching darkness. His own eyes, hazel-brown inside his big-framed glasses, had the look of a cornered animal. Joylene wanted to kiss his wide full-lipped mouth but now was perhaps not the moment. Kissing Mr. Dunne, like fucking him, was something to look forward to.

'Joylene,' he began, 'you're a lovely girl. I'm flattered by what you're suggesting and by – what you just did. If you really need to add giving head to your career qualifications, I'd say you're on your way to being a top star! But you are still a child and I'm not in the habit of having sex with children.' He let go of her hand. She continued to meet his troubled eyes.

'You have no choice,' she said.

'I believe I do.'

'You do not. I won't tell anyone – my mom, my daddy, Maria, Jimmy, the cops – as long as you give me sex lessons. But if you don't, I shall tell them you got your dick out in the car tonight and forced me to give you a blowjob.'

He looked as if he might start crying. 'You're a little young to be a blackmailer,' he said.

'Yeah, maybe I am. But this isn't gonna cost you a cent. I don't even expect higher grades. And you get to get your rocks off on a regular basis. This is a win-win situation.'

Teddy Dunne sighed as he re-started the engine. 'Joylene, I have to say I'm extremely disappointed in you.'

'Get over it,' she told him.

He avoided looking at her during Wednesday's History period and he was edgy all through Thursday's rehearsal. In the car afterward he was more than usually loquacious; was he trying to distract her from what she had outlined on Tuesday? There was an electric storm over the Catalina Mountains, driven hundreds of miles inland by a hurricane in the Gulf. No rain fell on the desert, although the sky darkened threateningly. But no storm – or Teddy Dunne's verbal diarrhea – was going to distract Joylene.

She allowed him to get closer to Seldom than on Tuesday before giving instructions. 'Slow down. There's a track just ahead.'

'Joylene, I –' But he was already decelerating.

'Turn down the track. There.'

He braked and turned off without signaling. The track led eventually to an avocado farm that the bank had long ago repossessed and found no buyer for. Joylene and Jimmy had checked it out on their mountain bikes; the semi-collapsed buildings teemed with scorpions and rattlers. After half a mile, out of sight of the highway, she told Teddy Dunne to pull over beside a fifteen-foot saguaro and stop. He did so. She was already removing her top beneath which she was, tonight, bra-less. She kicked off her sneakers and wriggled out of her jeans.

South of them the sky was rent by non-stop jagged streaks, the crackling sound of which carried clearly to the Jeep. In the fast-fading light Teddy Dunne watched as Joylene reclined her seat and pulled down her panties.

'Did you bring a condom?'

'Joylene –'

'Did you?'

He smiled ruefully. 'Yes.'

'Take your clothes off. I want you naked.'

He tipped his seat back to give himself more room to strip behind the wheel. His skin was smooth, untanned; his flesh lacked the definition of Chris or Jimmy, but it was, plainly, the body of a man rather than a boy. His cock, when he removed his shorts, was rock-hard; there was a bead of moisture at the top. He fumbled in the pocket of his discarded chinos for the condom.

'Do you want me to give you some head?' she asked.

'Do what you like,' he replied. His tone belied the excitement signaled by his twitching erection.

'Put the rubber on,' she said harshly. 'Let's get to the real action.'

She took off his glasses. Then she climbed over and began lowering herself onto his sheathed erection. This was a way she had seen it done in movies, but just the sight of her hovering body made Jimmy shoot before he could get inside her. With Teddy Dunne there was a different problem: the condom was insufficiently lubricated and (the golf ball comparison again came to mind) it took a minute or more to achieve her intention. To a Wagnerian accompaniment of vivid lightning flashes and rumbles of thunder she slid down until she was sitting on his stomach. Teddy put his hand between them to stop her from crunching his nuts and pressed her clitoris against his cock which then rubbed her clitoris as she rode him. Suddenly there was plenty of lubrication. The familiar tingle in her groin became the strongest it had ever been – it was like an urgent need to pee, only exquisitely different.

'Jesus,' she moaned. 'Oh God. Give it to me. Jesus fucking Christ. Give it to me, Teddy.' It was the first time she'd called him Teddy. Talking dirty added to her excitement and she was sure it would add to his.

'Don't talk,' he told her. 'We're not making a porno movie here.'

Joylene shut up. She was conscious of his knuckles under her as she rode the golf ball high and hard, high and hard, and still his fingers pushed her burning throbbing clitoris against the turgid shaft of his latexed cock.

Teddy came with a series of convulsions and louder grunts, but he stayed rigid inside her and she continued to ride him until the burning throbbing sensation reached a crescendo and for a moment she thought that she had peed.

She subsided on top of him and, now at last, kissed his wide mouth with its full lips and big gapped teeth. His tongue filled her mouth. Air turbulence pushed ahead of the storm rocked the Jeep.

Flipping her onto her back he resumed fucking her. How different he was to Jimmy: tireless. She planted the soles of her feet against the roof and arched her back as he pounded between her painfully parted thighs. On some of his thrusts his cock came all the way out and then plunged all the way back in to an accompaniment of plopping and sloshing sounds which would amuse her later, in replay mode. His tongue filled her mouth and his golf ball-headed cock filled her hot dripping cunt. Joylene felt filled and fulfilled. She tore her mouth free, gasping for breath as they came simultaneously. A lightning-flash seared the Jeep's interior and there was a roar of thunder, closer now.

'*Fuck*,' Teddy said, breaking his own no-dialogue injunction.

'Yeah,' said Joylene, laconic even in extremis. 'Like, fuck.'

She'd found her vocation. Not that she knew at fourteen that Teddy Dunne was pointing her down a career path. But she knew that this was something for which she had a natural aptitude and a healthy – unhealthy, even – appetite.

It was not, now or ever, an obsession. She didn't think about it all day to the detriment of school and homework and other obligations. But she looked forward to it the way a bookworm might look forward to a new novel or a wine buff to an untried vintage that would blow his taste buds away.

In the last week of the semester rehearsals were daily. Desert sex became a nightly event. They didn't talk much before, during or after the action. Sometimes he would instruct her to shift to a certain angle or to apply her tongue in a particular way, to a specific spot.

He applied his tongue to Joylene, to her breasts, to the inside of her thighs, to her clitoris. She thought she would die. Her orgasms became so intense that she had to scream.

Instead of escorting her into Le Bayou he just dropped her outside. Ruiz was the first to comment on this:

'Your Mr. Dunne doesn't want to have a drink with us?'

'He needs to get home. He has stuff to do. You know.'

'Joylene's the teacher's pet,' Jaynette pronounced. Her mock-crinoline gown overflowed the large dining chair in which she sat enthroned like some Hanoverian consort. 'Mr. Dunne's got her eating off the palm of his hand.'

No, Joylene wanted to tell her mother, *actually I've got him eating out of my pussy.*

The techniques she was learning from Teddy Dunne failed to keep Jimmy in check. He still shot his wad in five seconds flat – no more than thirty if she got him back for a re-run (he couldn't manage an instant encore like Teddy).

He wouldn't give head. 'Christ, Joylene, that's like asking me to clean the bathroom floor with my tongue.'

'But I'm supposed to stick your toilet brush down my throat.'

'That's different.'

'It is not.'

'I don't make you do it.'

'You do too.'

'Well, stop doing it if you don't like it.'

But she did like it, so she didn't stop. She loved what Teddy did, what he made her do, but she also adored Jimmy's younger, firmer, darker flesh and his smooth velvety cock which was the same size all the way down – not like Teddy's golf ball on its gnarled shaft.

She didn't love Teddy Dunne. She loved Jimmy Hernandez. Jimmy was her boyfriend. Teddy was what she had asked him to be: her sex instructor. He never told her he loved her although she was sure that he did. He could not get enough of her – nor she of him.

The sex instruction did not end when term ended.

That summer Joylene replaced her mom as Le Bayou's host. Jaynette's bulk made it hard for her to navigate between the tables. She also had trouble with the stairs, and the apartment floor, which was the restaurant's ceiling, often creaked ominously as she moved around. They chose this time to swap homes with the boys. The management cabin had expanded since Jaynette lived in it with her mother: there was a proper living room and a full-sized second bedroom for Joylene. And there were decorating accents that only a dedicated fan of 1940s movies could truly savor.

Not so much a couch potato as the equivalent to many sacks of potatoes, Jaynette sat all day in front of the TV on a severely challenged sofa, munching an endless stock of snacks out of family-sized packs or from the microwave. Ruiz, when he was not shopping or cooking, danced attendance on her, washing her, dressing her, feeding her, pottying her, undressing her. Occasionally there were noises through the partition walls that suggested he was screwing her, although this was not a prospect Joylene cared to dwell on.

Joylene didn't wish to be another Southern Belle, so Javier and Leonard turned her into a more contemporary foxy lady modeled on Michelle Pfeiffer and Sharon Stone: slinky dresses, dramatic hairstyles, makeup that emphasized her cheekbones.

Ruiz only required her from 6 to 8 p.m. (most diners were ensconced by 7.30). After work she ostensibly went jogging in the desert to limber up her growing bones. Various routes took her across four or five creeks to the track where Teddy would be waiting in the Jeep to give her the exercise she most craved.

Maria had been right. That summer Joylene became a woman. That year she grew two inches in height. Her waist expanded: she had to buy jeans – and brassieres – two sizes bigger. Was it a normal adolescence or were the hormones unleashed by Teddy Dunne causing this phenomenal spurt of growth?

In mid-August he told her he had to visit his mother in Florida. He did not return. Joylene got a 'disconnected' announcement when she called his home. On the pretext of 'an idea for the Christmas show' she called the Principal.

'Mr. Dunne won't be coming back next semester. He's looking for a job in Ohio to be near his mother. She's had to go into a care home: Alzheimer's.'

'That's too bad,' was all Joylene could think of to say.

'What's your idea for the show?'

'A burlesque of *Gone with the Wind*,' she improvised.

'Well, keep it in mind. I think Mrs. Morales will be taking over our drama activities. I hope she can count on your support, Joylene?'

'I guess.' She flirted with the idea of telling him about her desert trysts with Teddy which would of course become the sordid tale of an older man seducing and debauching a fourteen-year-old child. He had lied to her and maybe to the Principal too: was his mother in Florida or Ohio? And was she really sick?

Joylene knew that she was the reason the bastard had cut and run. What power she had! If she ratted him out, Teddy would go to jail, get gangbanged by the other prisoners, catch the AIDS virus. Before he died he would learn that it was one thing to fuck Joylene Duchat and another thing to fuck with her.

Nah. Who needed all that exposure? Who needed Teddy Dunne, the asshole?

'Next time you hear from him, please tell him I enjoyed all the drama we did together,' she said, generous and stoical in her abandonment. 'And tell him I sent best wishes for his momma.'

'That's very thoughtful of you, Joylene. I can see you're growing into a nice sincere young woman.'

Joylene wanted to reply: *Actually I'm growing into a nymphomaniac hard-ass bitch*. But she injected coyness into her voice and trilled a flirtatious laugh borrowed from her mother's routine at Le Bayou:

'Why, thank-you sir, Mr. Padilla. Thank you most kindly.'

Come December she was a shoo-in for the part of Scarlett O'Hara.

Over the course of her remaining three years at Hoover High Joylene played many parts in plays, revues and pageants. But the role at which she shone, on and off campus, was what her grandmother (who'd been there herself, although not starting at age thirteen) would have called the role of Jezebel.

Granma had told the infant Joylene the story of the Biblical Jezebel, wife of King Ahab, who encouraged the ancient Israelites to worship false gods; she was thrown out of a palace window by her eunuch slaves and her body was devoured by stray dogs. The female fornicators who conducted their adulteries at the Seldom Motel were Jezebels in Abigail's lexicon. If she'd had a name for the women's partners in sin, Joylene had forgotten it. *Jezebel* was also the title of a 1930s movie in which Bette Davis played a woman, not a fornicator, whose only outrage was to wear a scarlet dress to a New Orleans ball. Kate had watched the movie three times with Javier and Leonard. Leonard had had them in stitches with his impersonation of Miss Davis.

Early in her sophomore year Joylene broke up for a fourth or fifth time with Jimmy Hernandez who was still at best a thirty-second wonder. She dated Chris Lee again; he was handsomer now that his zits were fading but he had developed a typical jock personality: Mr. I'm-the-football-captain-and-don't-you-forget-it. He'd broken up with Maria who was now going steady with Jimmy. Joylene dated a few seniors, but if they weren't jocks they had Jimmy's problem. She allowed the future Mrs. Chris Lee to go down on her a couple of times but found herself incapable of reciprocating the favor. To the disappointment of her many gay-lady fans, lesbianism would never be Katharine Kane's ballpark.

All the same, Joylene was intrigued to find that her beauty gave her a hold on women as well as men. Sex was all about empowerment. Joylene made sure that even in submission she remained on top in every sense.

In her junior year she dated more seniors, a Seattle truck driver at the motel, a trainee pilot from Davis-Monthan, her swimming coach and a State University student working at a drive-thru McDonald's outside Tucson. The student was in Teddy Dunne's league; they went steady for three months. Joylene stopped seeing him when he got into a druggy crowd. Promiscuity was a danger in itself, but she'd taken onboard the message that drug-taking, like unprotected sex, was a shortcut to an early grave. Sex was the only stimulant she needed.

In her senior year she fucked a couple more truck-drivers, some more (unremarkable) college boys, another history teacher (only once: he wasn't in Teddy Dunne's league) and – in the small hours of Christmas Day – her stepfather.

On Christmas Eve a group from the airbase took over Le Bayou. The motel was closed for the festive season; Javier and Leonard went to Mexico. Joylene acted as waitress and maître d', hoping to find a replacement for her pilot from last fall, a total hunk who'd transferred to Hawaii at the end of his training. She was out of luck: they were all couples, although as the evening and the drinking wore on several of the guys ignored their glowering wives or girlfriends and flirted with the green-eyed hostess in her foxy red gown.

After the desserts were served Ruiz let the rest of the staff go. He peeled off his kitchen coat to reveal a dress shirt and fancy waistcoat in which he helped Joylene serve coffees and liqueurs; then he loaded the dishwasher while his stepdaughter took care of the final round of drinks. When the last three couples piled drunkenly into their cars, Ruiz and Joylene cleared the tables. They put the credit card receipts in the safe under the bar.

'I'll cash up tomorrow,' he said. His speech was slurred. The Air Force guys had forced a few drinks on him. 'Thanks for your help, baby.'

'You're welcome,' said Joylene who'd accepted no more than a couple of glasses of champagne. 'It's after midnight. Happy Christmas, Ruiz.' She'd stopped calling him 'Daddy' a year or more back, although she referred to him as 'my dad' at school. The Reverend Barton Duchat was often seen as guest preacher on evangelical TV and the monthly checks continued to flow into Seldom, but it was hard to believe that this prophet of hellfire and brimstone was her natural father. She had told Hoover High School that Rev. Duchat was not a relation: it was a common name in Louisiana.

'Happy Christmas, pussycat,' said her stepfather who often used Granma's pet name for her. He kissed her, as was his custom, but Joylene didn't allow him to escape with the usual brief contact. She embraced his neck with both arms and forced her tongue between his lips. Wrapping one slit-skirted leg behind his knees, she pressed him to her and felt him harden as the kiss became longer and deeper.

Next thing he had the top of her dress down and was moaning incoherently as he mouthed her breasts. Joylene practically tore the clothes off him and went down on his cock which was sleek and velvety like Jimmy Hernandez's but massive. Then she pushed him onto his back on the floor and rode him to a rapid climax, pressing her clitoris against his cock as she rode it. Just before he came he came to his senses, but Joylene would not be stopped and perhaps Ruiz was too far gone, too close. But tears filled his eyes and afterward he begged her forgiveness.

'It's OK,' she said, sated and triumphant. 'I love you, Ruiz. It's what I always wanted. This is better than any Christmas present you could ever give me. Don't worry. Mom will never know.'

At a more tender age Ruiz had set Joylene a standard of love and of male beauty. Now his body was thickening, lines and puffiness were eroding his fine features, he was drunk and teary with guilt; and yet he added another dimension to her idea of the perfect sex partner. But he made certain that it never happened again, however much she wanted it to; he took care not to be alone with her for more than a few unavoidable minutes. When he was not in the restaurant he took his meals with Jaynette. Joylene ate with Javier and Leonard, although the novelty of their bitching and banter had begun to wear off.

She found another college boy to fuck.

She wasn't neglecting her studies.

Her family accepted that Joylene's aspirations and maybe her future lay in acting, but she knew that her chances of success were between slim and zero. The gulf between Scarlett O'Hara at Hoover High and even a bit part on *Solana Beach* – or what Leonard called 'a tit part' – was vast. Leonard told her about wannabe stars waiting tables or working as hookers to pay

Los Angeles rents. It was as well to have a second string, such as (would Teddy Dunne have shared his successor's sense of the irony of this?) a degree in History and a teaching credit. Another possibility was politics: a congressman's gofer or a lobbyist, perhaps even a political career of her own in due course.

Jaynette wanted her daughter to go to the State University in Tucson. UCLA was Ruiz's idea, putting some mileage between them, to which his wife reluctantly came round. The Rev. Duchat agreed to Jaynette's written request for a college fund.

Joylene jumped at the chance to go to California. Tucson was too near, too safe. And if she wanted to be 'discovered' or – which seemed the likelier route – to screw her way into movies, it wasn't going to happen in Tucson, was it?

Indeed it wasn't. It was going to happen in Seldom.

Leonard went with her to Los Angeles when she was interviewed by a member of the history faculty at UCLA. They stayed with Javier's sister in Huntington where John Howell had just begun his last job as a lifeguard.

They did the tourist stuff: Beverly Hills, Sunset Boulevard, Disneyland, Universal Studios. Joylene screamed her lungs out in Gorgon's House of Horror. When they saw Linda Evans going into a store on Rodeo Drive, Leonard died and went to Heaven.

Unasked and unexpected, Teddy Dunne's replacement purchased Joylene's silence about their Halloween tryst with an exemplary grade in History in her final exam. Coupling this with exceptional grades in English and Math, she came top of the class. Her place at UCLA was secured; she would study History and Politics there in the fall.

She was Valedictorian for the Class of '95. The Yearbook listed some of her dramatic triumphs but fortunately not her conquests among the student body or the faculty. Also excluded was what her peers truly considered her '*the girl most likely*' to be or do, which would have made for an eyebrow-raising read.

Graduation Day coincided with Mr. Padilla's fiftieth birthday. Eyebrows shot up when Joylene, seventeen going on eighteen, inaugurated proceedings in a platinum wig, heavy-make up and a replica (created by Javier) of the see-through sheath into which Marilyn had been sewn (Javier used Velcro) to serenade JFK at a famous bash in 1962. Joylene's breathy rendition of 'Happy Birthday, Mister Principal' in that dress had some of the younger boys creaming their shorts and some of their moms peeing their panties.

Changing into a severely tailored two-piece from Neiman Marcus, Joylene returned to the podium to deliver her valedictory speech. She pledged the developing talents of the Class of '95 to the service and betterment of both State and Union. Pissing off her largely Republican audience, she worked in a plug for Bill Clinton's re-election next year; and she praised Hillary Clinton, pissing off Chris Lee's mom who vociferously wished the First Lady in Hell.

'We're proud of you, princess,' Javier and Leonard chorused, kissing her on both cheeks after the ceremony. They wore sober shirts and slacks; only an excess of Navajo silver screamed the fact that they were gay.

'I'm proud of you too, Joylene,' said her stepfather with a

quick peck on one cheek only. Since the incident at Christmas Ruiz had rationed his kisses.

Jaynette no longer left her cabin except on milder days to sun herself on the porch in a two-seater garden bench that creaked its relief when she prized herself free. Javier continued to make her dresses, vast gaudy muumuu tents.

'I wish Granma could have been there today,' she said when they came home. 'She would have been so proud. I'm so proud, baby. And I'm so sorry I wasn't there. I have to do something about all this weight.'

'That's OK, Mom,' said Joylene. 'I still love you.' She felt a brief flare of guilt at what she'd done on Christmas Day.

'It's not OK,' Jaynette said and burst into tears. Joylene climbed onto the bed on which her mother lay like a beached whale, propped up with cushions and pillows. They hugged and cried.

After a year of cajoling Ruiz had paid for driving lessons for Joylene's seventeenth birthday. Now as a graduation gift he bought her a two-year-old Toyota RAV. Her evenings were committed to Le Bayou, but she spent the daytime cruising the Tucson malls and cineplexes with her co-graduates.

She acquired a new boyfriend, Scott, a sophomore from the State University working in mall security. His family in West LA was far from wealthy but in other respects he was a typical golden boy from the golden state, sporting the currently fashionable amounts of hair and pectoral development. Mall security was one of two ways in which he supplemented his scholarship. The other was modeling. As in nude modeling. As in magazines: gay magazines.

'No kidding?' said Joylene when he told her. 'Does this mean you're, like, gay or bi?' They'd been screwing for the past six nights in the desert where she had fucked Mr. Dunne (and his career in Arizona), so it could only be bi.

'No way, Jose,' Scott was quick to reply. 'They don't need 'em gay or semi-gay. They just want 'em cute. A big dick comes in handy, too.'

'Amen to that,' she laughed. 'But you don't have to – you know – do stuff with other guys?'

'Nah. I only do solo shoots. They pay more for the action stuff and a heck of a lot more for movies, of course, but I don't want to get into any of that.'

'How did you get into this business?'

'A guy at the mall introduced me to this talent scout. There's dozens of guys doing it right here in Ay-zee. Girls too. You could do it,' he teased her.

'No thanks!' said Joylene. 'My mom would, like, shit her bloomers and I doubt my stepfather'd be too happy about it either.' She didn't so much as spare a thought for the Reverend Barton Duchat whose Grace Here & Hereafter Ministry had now achieved as high a profile as any other televangelist mission.

In recent years Barton and Grace Duchat had usurped the long-running national campaign against smut. In his televised sermons Bart fulminated against the great tide of foulness that passed for culture on US TV and in cinemas, theaters, art galleries – and books. Outside the headquarters Church in Baton Rouge televised book-burnings were staged; a flagrant violation of the First Amendment. Literary works whose authors included Pulitzer and Nobel Prize-winners were consigned to the pyre alongside pulp fiction, top-shelf magazines (*Mayfair* and *Creamme* and their imitators) and adult (and mainstream) videos.

'We Shall Overcome,' sang Rev. Bart's followers around their campfires whose contents had been hot even before they were ignited.

'Yes, Lord,' Bart promised his Boss, 'we shall overcome the peddlers of pornography, those who defile and degrade Your Promised Land and seek to corrupt the children of This Great Nation of Ours.'

A large proportion of the children of this great nation of ours were skiving off not only church attendance but also homework and sports practice to watch movies about horny teenagers getting laid – and in some cases, eviscerated – in beds, cars, woods and classrooms. These videos were added to the pyre.

Book publishers protested. Pornography was, after all, protected by the Constitution. But the studio heads, mainstream as well as porno, warmed their hands on the bonfires. People would buy replacement copies of these cremated movies. The televised burnings, like Bart's sermons, tended to reach the already converted, but there was a bonus in free publicity, especially when a particular book or movie was singled out for more than usually vehement condemnation.

Such as would happen to a number of videos starring, under an alias, a less sainted daughter of Baton Rouge.

But don't let's get ahead of ourselves.

Joylene took the video of her Marilyn impersonation to Scott's room in the dorm.

'Wow,' he said, 'can I make a copy of this to remember you by?'

'You've got me to remember me by.'

'Yeah, but when you're a big movie star and I'm teaching high school in Pissboro, Idaho, I'll be able to tell my kids I once dated a girl who looked like Marilyn Monroe.'

'Those kids might be my kids too,' she said. But he knew she was putting him on. He shook his perfect head and smiled.

'You're gonna go places, Joylene. I kinda know that I'm not.'

'But you're the one doing porno. I'm just the one doing high school pageants in Shit Creek, Ay-zee.'

'No,' he said. 'My life is gonna peak somewhere in the middle, but you're going to the top.'

'Like, in what?'

'In whatever. In anything.'

She laughed, pleased with his confidence in her.

Tall, blond, smooth, muscled, Scott was the opposite of Ruiz or Jimmy, the two Latinos who had touched her heart. And he wasn't a pain-in-the-ass jock like Chris Lee. She came close to loving Scott. He was gorgeous; he was hung; he was a good lover, good company, a good person. He would make some girl a great husband. But he was right: it wouldn't be her. Maybe she wasn't cut out for love, or was not ready for it.

She made him a copy of her Marilyn tape.

Which brought Duane Schofeld to Seldom to midwife the birth of Pussy-Kat Kane.

5. KITTEN KANDY

Solo diners were a rarity at Le Bayou, apart from the occasional truck-driver treating himself/herself to an upmarket meal. This one was a bit below medium height and a bit above medium girth. His thinning hair was blond going gray.

'Good evening, sir,' said Joylene, tonight wearing a low-cut mini-dress from the malls where most of her wardrobe was now sourced.

'You must be Joylene.'

She smiled her best maître d' smile but went on guard. The world was full of perverts and predators. 'I don't think you've been here before, have you?'

He shook his head and gave her a flash of megabuck dentition.

'So how come you know my name?'

'From Scott Davison. He works for me.'

'At the mall?'

'No, not at the mall.'

Joylene met his eyes coolly, appraisingly. She was right to be on her guard. The guy was a pervert. 'Let me show you your table.' Her stepfather emerged from the kitchen with one of his Specials for a center table.

'Can we talk?' the pervert asked.

'Later, sir, if you wouldn't mind. The man in the chef's hat is my dad.'

'OK, Sugar. Later is fine.'

'Don't call me Sugar.' She smiled to take the edge off this admonition.

'What do I call you?'

'You call me Miss.'

'OK, Miss.' He grinned, plainly enjoying her crisp behavior.

He watched her throughout his meal. Nursing a succession of bone-dry martinis, he ate slowly and outlasted all but four of the other diners. When she offered to bring his check he said: 'Can we talk now?'

'You'd be wasting your time.'

He looked up at her, grinning. 'That's what Scott said you'd say.'

She looked down at him, not smiling. 'Scott can look forward to getting his balls busted.'

The man laughed. 'He told me you were feisty as well as gorgeous. He showed me your Marilyn tape.'

'Scott can look forward to getting his balls stir-fried in front of his face,' she said calmly, meaning it.

'If you don't mind, I plan to show it to the lady who sang for JFK.'

Joylene blinked. 'You know Marilyn? You're dicking me around.'

He shook his head. 'She and me go back a ways.'

'No shit?'

'No shit.' His stare appraised her. Hookers must feel like this, she thought.

'What color eyes do you call those?' he asked.

'I call them green.'

'The camera will love them. And your skin: is that a tan or have you got some Black blood?'

168

'I'm one eighth Black.' She thought of adding: 'And you can kiss my twelve-and-a-half-percent Black ass.' She went ahead and said it. He laughed again.

'Believe me, Sugar, I'd adore to.' She liked 'adore' and let that 'Sugar' go by, but decided it was time to put the creep in his place once and for all.

'Whatever it is you're offering, the answer is no.'

'What I'm offering,' he said slowly, 'and you might want to think about kissing my twenty-four-carat white ass, would get you out of this speck of fly-dirt on the roadmap and into the kind of life you dream of at the multiplex.'

'You think I dream of a sleazy motel in the San Fernando Valley?'

'I think you'll find you can live a little better than that on one-point-five million dollars,' he said. Joylene teetered slightly on her high-heeled wedgies as if a strong wind had just blown through Le Bayou.

'Now I know you're dicking me around.'

'Sit down,' he told her, 'before you fall down.'

Joylene looked round. The other four customers were lingering over coffee and liqueurs. She sat down opposite the balding blond pervert who claimed to be dangling one-and-a-half million bucks under her nose. He introduced himself.

'My name's Duane.'

'You're not from round here, I reckon. LA?'

'Yeah, but I do a lot of my work in Tucson.'

'Are you telling me I can earn one-point-five million dollars without leaving Arizona?'

He shook his head. 'No, for the big bucks you'd have to move to LA.'

She almost came out and told him she was going to UCLA in the fall anyway. Scott might have already told him this.

'And I can make that kind of money doing the kind of photo shoots Scott is doing?'

'No, Sug-, Joylene. For that kind of money you'd have to get down and dirty.' He looked her in the eyes. 'All the way down and pretty dirty.'

'What makes you think I'm that kind of girl?' She tried not to look prim as she spoke these prissy-sounding words. 'My Marilyn gig? Or did Scott tell you I'm that kind of girl? I'm really gonna bust his balls. And his ass.'

'All Scott said was you might be interested in posing for a few pictures.'

'But for the real money we're talking adult movies, right?'

He nodded.

'Who do you work for exactly?'

'Mostly I work for the studio that shoots your friend Scott with his shorts off, but I've got contacts all through this business. If you're willing to go with this I'd take you to one of the top guys. *The* top guy.'

'Who is?'

'Al Kazman. Right now he's the biggest of the big guys in porno. Peaches Snatch works for Kazman. Have you seen any of her movies?'

Joylene had seen the famous Peaches Snatch – and Peaches's famous snatch – at slumber parties, the videos sneaked from schoolfriends' parents' extensive collections. 'The Snatch' was toward the extreme end of porno.

'Yeah, I've seen her. She's pretty gross. More gross than pretty, I'd say.'

'Gross gets the grosses, Joylene. One-point-five million is about what Peaches has made out of porno so far.'

'I couldn't do half of what she does.'

'I think you can do twice what Peaches does. Wait and see. Don't rule anything out. Peaches is pushing forty now. It takes more and more makeup to hide the scars from all her lifts and lipo. And that worn-out cunt of hers is beginning to look like a worn-out cunt. How old are you, Joylene?'

'Eighteen,' she lied. No adult – not even Teddy Dunne or a truck-driver – had ever thrown the c-word in her face like that.

'Eighteen. And you've got those eyes, that skin tone.' He sighed as if her beauty saddened him. 'The secret in this business is to make a killing and then move out. Peaches just won't quit. Of course she loves the work.'

Ruiz came out from the kitchen and waved at Joylene. She got to her feet.

'I'll think about it,' she promised. She was already thinking about it.

According to Leonard some major Hollywood stars had started out in porno – even a goddess like Joan Crawford. Marilyn Monroe's famous calendar shots had made her a star. And what about Jed Swann and that video? Porno was more likely to help your career along than stop it in its tracks.

'Can I call you?' Duane asked. Her stepfather waved again.

It wasn't the money, she told herself. Sure, it would be great not to be dependent on the Seldom Motel and Rev. Duchat, but no way could she do heavy action in movies with guys – and, yuck, other women! – who must be riddled with every sexual disease from chlamydia to AIDS. What did tempt her was the thought that a few shots of her tits and pussy – maybe even an 'adult' movie, just one, nothing too gross – would get her noticed a lot quicker than campus reviews at UCLA or waitressing on Sunset Strip.

'Yeah,' she said. 'Why not? I'll give you my number with your check.'

She didn't bust Scott's balls – or stir-fry them. She swore him to secrecy on Duane's proposition. 'I'm not planning to tell Ruiz and my mom about this,' she said.

'You don't tell on me and I won't tell on you,' he promised.

Duane summoned her to a test shoot. He picked her up from Scott's mall and drove her not to the scuzzy industrial-zone warehouse she expected, but to a suburban hacienda-style property. The interior was *Playboy* bachelor-pad: off-white shag carpeting, white leather sofas, parchment lamps on brushed aluminum end-tables, a white marble coffee table. Duane was dressed to match the décor in white chinos and off-white shirt and loafers.

The photographer, Danny, was a nondescript underweight thirty-something from Phoenix wearing dark slacks and a white shirt; he looked more like a pen-pusher than a porn-pusher. A Latina makeup girl, Teresa, took Joylene to a guestroom to undress and applied a light all-over foundation that covered her few blemishes, which were mostly some scratches from screwing Scott against canyon rocks or trees in Saguaro Park.

Joylene stayed nude as Teresa escorted her to the basement studio: more white walls and off-white furniture with theater-sized spotlights, some ceiling-mounted but most on rollers. For the first time outside of a medical exam she was naked in front of two men, neither of whom she hoped to have to screw. The foundation and her skin-coloration hid her blushes. The Mexican girl stayed on as chaperone, sitting over by the stairs. Duane handled the lights and talked to put Joylene at her ease while he got her to assume a variety of poses, none of them too lurid. The photographer went through six reels of film but did not use a video camera, although there were several in the room.

'OK, that'll do for now,' Duane said. Handing Joylene a white silk robe, he ushered her upstairs to a bleached bamboo bar between the living and dining areas. The others stayed in the basement. Was he now going to jump her? Joylene sipped mineral water while Duane mixed himself a pitcher of martinis.

He showed her some of the magazines in which her images might appear, clones of *Playboy* that weren't too tacky and other publications which had less prose and cruder photos. There were worse than this, Joylene knew – boys had brought hardcore magazines to school – but Duane evidently planned to keep her at the shallow end of the porno lake. He didn't jump her.

Before they left the house he handed her five hundred dollars.

'This is for your time today,' he said. 'There'll be more when I sell the pictures.'

'Yeah,' said Joylene, now chewing gum and reverting to mall-speak. 'Like, thanks, Duane. We're cool.'

She felt a lot less casual than she sounded. Five hundred bucks for two hours of her time! Right now Duane could have gotten a blowjob from her if he wanted one. He grinned at her as if he knew what she was thinking.

'Yeah,' he echoed. 'We're cool. We're the coolest, Sugar.'

For five hundred bucks he could even call her Sugar.

*

He phoned a week later to ask if she had any preferences for a name to accompany her photos. 'I'm guessing you don't want to use your own name.'

'As if.' She could think of several good reasons not to be Joylene Duchat, porno model.

'Some of them use their real names, but most artists use names with some kind of innuendo – like Peaches Snatch.'

Joylene smirked at the notion of this morning's work as 'art'. 'You mean that's not her real name?' she mugged.

Duane chuckled. 'No, Sugar. She's originally from Britain. Her real name's Nellie Batt. You're young and sweet. How about – Kitten Kandy? That's Kandy with a K.'

'Like, whatever,' said Joylene in mall-girl mode. Young, yeah. But – sweet? As if.

And so Katharine Kane's first alias came to be Kitten Kandy. Magazines featuring her seventeen-year-old poses under this sobriquet would one day become almost as collectable as those early calendars of Marilyn.

By the time the first of these magazines hit the top shelves of the news-stands Joylene was in California. She came, she was seen, she conquered.

6. PUSSY-KAT KANE

As promised, Duane had sent her pictures to the main man of the main men of porno.

'He wants to see you,' Duane told Joylene, phoning her on her second day in LA at what Leonard called her new 'apartmentette', a small room with a tiny bathroom and closet kitchen in a Silver Lake house owned by two of Leonard and Javier's gay friends. Living in a dorm would cramp her new lifestyle.

'Like, when?' she asked Duane.

'Like today. I'll pick you up.'

'You're in LA?'

'Like, obviously. Give me your address.'

Duane had driven his silver BMW to California. He took her to a thirty-room mansion in Beverly Hills that had once belonged to Danny Kaye. The Kazman house was Joylene's first confirmation that millions really could be made in porno. The high-walled garden boasted enough nude statues to fill a small museum. Inside the foyer, into which they were admitted by a uniformed maid, the walls were hung with original artworks. Joylene reckoned she knew a Picasso when she saw one and right now she could see five (one was actually a Braque and another a Miro). Picassos in his foyer – what was in his dining-room, for Christ's sake? (A Matisse and a dubious Renoir.)

At the rear of the foyer a vast marble staircase rose to the upper floor. At the foot of the stairs stood a man who was either a cross-dresser or had just come down the mountain with the Ten Commandments.

The porn king wore a full-length brown-and-white striped robe made of a heavy-duty cotton that you couldn't see through. Joylene didn't know what, if anything, he had on underneath; but it was plainly a garment he could lift to his waist and jump her in before she had time to say '*Unholy Moses*'. On his feet he wore Gucci loafers rather than Mount Sinai sandals. One hairy wrist sported a diamond-encrusted Rolex; the fat pinkie of the opposite hand sported a pyramid diamond ring that could be broken down into a bracelet for Joylene's more slender wrist.

Al Kazman was in a business that was gross in both senses of the word. He himself was big rather than gross: a short, broad-chested, broad-beamed man with a long swarthy face dominated by hooded eyes and a nose like a toucan's beak. His gray hair, highlighted with silver, was long enough to add to the Biblical look of the robe. The hair at his wrists and neck and on his fingers was also gray, and there was a great deal of it. His teeth would – in fact, did – look good on many a leading man. Joylene put his age between sixty and sixty-five (he was sixty-six). Obviously he was Jewish (she was wrong about that too, but Omar Sharif is almost the only Arab in the history of Hollywood not to be mistaken for a Jew).

'Miss Kandy. It's a pleasure to meet you.' His English was guttural, heavily accented. It was the first time Joylene had been addressed by her new name.

'I've been thinking about this,' she said, making an effort not to be dazzled by his diamonds and his artworks. 'If you don't mind, I'd rather be Pussy-Kat Kane. That's Pussy-Kat with a K and a hyphen and Kane with another K.'

'Anything with pussy in it is perfect for this business,' said Duane. 'Did you get it from *Goldfinger*? What's her name who played Pussy Galore? Shirley Bassey?' Oddly for a man whose business, as Joylene would shortly discover, included bondage, Duane didn't know his Bond-girls.

'Kind of,' Joylene said. She'd actually taken it from the pet name her granma had given her, which Ruiz had stopped using since last Christmas. The Kane was from Sugar Kane, Marilyn Monroe's character in *Some Like It Hot*, one of Leonard and Javier's many all-time favorite movies.

'Duane is right about you,' Kazman said. 'You are very beautiful. Only I think you need bigger breasts. You will let me pay for this?'

He certainly didn't believe in beating about the bush (which she'd shaved only this morning).

'You mean, like – silicone?'

'Well, a padded bra doesn't really do it for Al,' Duane said dryly.

'No surgery,' Joylene said emphatically. 'My boobs stay the way they are.'

Kazman scratched his big nose. 'This could be a problem. Men want big breasts.'

'Then I'm not your girl.' She hoped she wasn't blowing her big chance, but no way did she want plastic tits at seventeen.

'Maybe she's OK just as she is,' Duane opined. 'The Russ Meyer boobs have probably peaked. It might be time to go back to the Sandra Dee look.'

'Sondra Dee. Who is this?' The name was equally unfamiliar to Joylene.

'Sandra. Before your time, Al.'

'She is in porno?'

Duane laughed. 'More at the other end. Somewhere between Princess Diana and the Virgin Mary.'

'I must see you naked,' Mr. Kazman said matter-of-factly. He was not looking at Duane. With his weird accent and werewolf fur he was a major-league creep. Her skin crawled at the thought of his eyes – or any part of him – on her.

'You already did,' she said. 'You saw my pictures.'

'Pictures is not the same. I must see you moving.'

'You mean, like – now?' She had a vision of this ending up as some kind of grisly three-way fuck-fest, which even for another five hundred bucks was not her idea of easy money. 'Where's the cameraman?'

Duane caught on that she was uncomfortable. 'Maybe not today, Al. How's about we do a test shoot at the studio? I think Joylene – Ms. Kane – oughta see the studio anyway.'

'You have seen my movies?' Mr. Kazman asked her. He didn't seem to mind that she hadn't stripped to order.

'I guess so. I've seen a few porno videos, including one with Peaches Snatch. That'd be one of yours?'

'I will give you some videos,' he said. 'Now we will drink by the pool.'

The pool was nothing special, a blue-tiled rectangle surrounded by more naked statuary, but to a girl from the desert any pool was hard to resist.

'Can I swim?'

'Please. There are some towels and costumes in the cabana.'

The cabana had a musty odor and a pile of towels that might have come from a thrift-store. He could afford Picassos and diamonds but not decent towels? Not liking the thought of who might have worn the costumes, she swam nude, granting the producer's earlier wish. His vulture eyes followed her up and down the pool. She took care to leave the water at the end farthest from where he and Duane sat over cocktails brought out by the maid.

'You like martini?' Mr. Kazman offered when she rejoined them in her Ralph Lauren pale-blue sundress which she'd chosen over nipple-revealing halter-tops or tee-shirts: the mall-girl look rather than trailer-trash.

'Just a Diet Coke, if you don't mind.'

'Your swim, it was good?'

'Yeah, sure.'

'For me also.' He flashed his Robert Redford teeth at her and she thought she might get to like the fat hairy creep after all.

When she left he handed her a brown paper bag containing a half-dozen video-tapes with lurid covers and even more lurid titles. He also gave her five hundred dollars. 'For your time – and the pictures.'

'You took pictures?' She almost added 'jerk-off'.

'Here.' He tapped his forehead with one hairy finger. 'The pictures are here.'

The tapes ran the gamut from solo masturbation to gang-bangs. Joylene was immediately sure she wouldn't be able to get beyond an embarrassing-enough-in-front-of-the-camera finger-job. The group action included sodomy, bondage, spanking and so-called 'water sports' (requiring neither skis nor surfboards).

She was relieved that there was nothing involving animals or people taking a dump, both of which Scott claimed to have seen on film.

The women had shaved crotches and silicone-enhanced breasts (often ludicrously over-inflated). Many of their vaginas appeared worn out from over-use. Exactly how much action was too much, and could it happen off-screen as well as on? Joylene didn't want to end up with a pussy like a frayed hearthrug.

Peaches Snatch was the Queen Bee of the porno hive and despite what Duane had said about her she looked in better shape than many of the other women. There were screen-filling close-ups of her vagina, which didn't seem unduly tattered. Also of her rear portal, which on the other hand did.

The Peaches Snatch movie in the selection Al Kazman had given Joylene was entitled *Cl-ass Action 9* (no roman numerals in Porn!). Lest anyone somehow missed the point of the hyphen and the helpful cover shot of Peaches's bared behind (with the first fatal folds of cellulite), *Cl-* was in a smaller font and a different color from *ass Action*.

Her adopted surname notwithstanding, ass was where Peaches was at, her major at the college of pornography. And there was no denying (was there, reader?) that when it came to Ass Action, Peaches was a Class Act.

Deep Throat's Linda Lovelace had taught America how to give and receive head. Cheerleader Debbie, doing *Dallas* and other locales, had taught America, the viewing universe, how to take cock properly (Rev. Duchat and others would say *im*properly) in at least two of the available orifices. Peaches Snatch had moved the emphasis from topside and frontside to rearside. She took it endlessly, tirelessly and loudly, up the ass. Hence, presumably, the sorry shape of her sphincter in *Cl-ass Action 9*. She also took it frontally, often at the same time as taking it up the rear: what the trade calls 'double penetration'.

(It's ironical, isn't it, Reader, that evangelists like Rev. Duchat railed from their pulpits against homosexuals whose sexual practices were, according to the Book of Leviticus, 'an abomination'; and yet some of their flock sat uncomfortably in their pews having only the night before dwelt in the tents of Sodom – if not those, whatever this might entail, of Gomorrah?)

Decades back, fastidious heterosexual middle-American women had cursed Linda Lovelace for legitimizing the blowjob as their husbands and lovers and boyfriends waved (not always) stiff misshapen organs in sundry sizes under their protesting noses. Over the last ten years some of these same women and a larger number of their daughters had berated Peaches Snatch as fulfilling their husbands' and lovers' sexual requirements became, all too literally, a pain in the ass.

Joylene had given head – plenty of it. She'd screwed in every position an inventive 1990s US teenager could conjecture, in a variety of locations indoors and out, in every kind of weather except a snowstorm. She had (with Teddy Dunne and one of the truck-drivers) taken it up the ass, although she wasn't keen on this: it hurt like hell and the preliminary douching gave her stomach cramps. Watching *Cl-ass Action 9* with the volume turned known in case her landlords thought she was hosting an orgy they could crash, Joylene knew she'd been right to tell Duane back in Seldom that she'd never be able to do half of this kind of stuff.

Funny the way life turns out, isn't it?

Her screen test took place the following afternoon. Duane again collected her. They didn't drive inland to the Valley but headed for the coast.

The studios were located two blocks from the beach at Santa Monica in a narrow-fronted building that from the outside could have been the office of a minor freight operation or a courier company. A small square of white plastic with black lettering quietly announced: *Kazman Productions*.

The lobby was far from plush, although the blonde manning the laminated desk was better upholstered than most receptionists. Her teeth as well as her boobs had been surgically enhanced.

'Hi, Duane. How's it hangin'?' The shrill voice of a hooker on Sunset.

'Can't you see it's stickin' right up when I look at you, Sugar?'

Her laugh was a grating cackle. 'Ooh, Duane, you're gettin' me all wet – again!' Joylene wondered if she edited scripts for Kazman Productions during quiet periods on Reception. She radiated a simpering smile at Joylene.

'And you're Kitten Kandy. I've seen your pictures. You're gonna be a big big star – after you get your boobs fixed.'

Joylene's return smile lowered the temperature a few degrees. 'If big jugs are all it takes, how come you're still busting your ass out here, "Sugar"?'

Sugar's smile faltered but she did not return tat for tit. 'I'm happy where I am, Honey. My old man'd kill me if I went in front of the camera. I did use to fluff.'

'Yeah?' Hard to imagine that misreading your lines was an obstacle to a porn career, although it was increasingly apparent that 36C boobs might be.

'You-all'd better go on in. Rocky's waiting for you.'

Scruffy and littered with papers and unboxed video-cassettes, the office of Rocky Coxman, Kazman Productions' Executive Producer, was one of four off a short corridor behind Reception. Coxman was another big mess, so fat that his popped navel was visible between his rucked-up food-stained tee-shirt and the Porsche belt-buckle on his sagging jeans. His receded gray-blond hair was yanked farther back into a greasy ponytail.

In the car Duane had shown Joylene some stills of a younger Rocky, beefcake star of such early 'classics' as *Cum-fight at the OK Corral*. The years had not been kind. But if he was unappetizing in his person, his persona was both gentle and gentlemanly. He cleared some papers off chairs for Joylene and Duane to sit down, and then regaled them in a Texas accent with stories about his own and others' misadventures in sex movies. Never once did he use f-words or the vile c-word: 'pussy' and 'giving it to her' were his favored euphemisms.

'You've seen some of our product?' he finally asked.

Joylene nodded.

'Well, now I'd better show you some of our production.'

A door at the end of the corridor opened into a larger warehouse-style building with partition walls up to a crisscross of girders some fifteen feet below its metal roof. A blaze of light reflected up in one corner and the caterwauling of a woman being torn to pieces contributed clues that a new Kazman feature was in the pipeline.

'There goes our Peaches,' Rocky said.

'Who else comes off at that volume?' said Duane rhetorically.

'She sure knows how to fake an orgasm,' Joylene allowed.

'That's not faking it,' Rocky told her. 'We sometimes have

to tone her down for the soundtrack. We'll leave her to finish this scene. Let's go in here.'

He ushered them into a dressing-room that had *Dick Bigg* stenciled on the door; the name belonged to a rising star of porno, one of the male leads in *Cl-ass Action 9*. The makeup table below a brightly-lit wall-mirror held only a box of Kleenex and toiletries. As well as a sink and a wardrobe there were two swivel chairs and an out-of-place movie-set brocade couch. A window opposite the mirror offered a view of the adjoining room which, unlike this one, had no ceiling.

The view took Joylene's breath away.

A spotlight on a crossbeam illuminated three naked people on a rumpled bed: two big-breasted blondes and a dark-haired muscular male. Joylene recognized Peaches's *Cl-ass Action 9* co-star. One of the blondes was sitting on his face, the other slavered at his groin. The rising star was having trouble rising to the demands of this scenario: as of this moment Dick Bigg was Dick Not-So-Special. The woman sitting on his face was chomping gum: she looked like a cow on the cud. The other blonde lifted her face from his groin and similarly rotated her lower face as if to ease lockjaw, unless she too was masticating gum as well as Dick. Joylene could see neither cameramen nor cameras.

'Where are the cameras?'

'That's not a movie they're making,' Rocky Coxman explained. 'We only film in there when we're extra busy. They're fluffing.' The same term the receptionist had used; it didn't appear to relate to getting the lines wrong.

'Excuse me?'

'Fluffing. Those girls are helping him – excuse me, Ms. Kane – get wood.'

None of the men in Joylene's life had needed any help 'getting wood'; rather the opposite: Jimmy Hernandez was not the only sapling in whom the sap had risen a little too readily.

'But you don't use – what they're doing – in the movie?'

'Those women aren't in the movie,' said Rocky. 'They're fluffers. This is what they do. All they do.'

'They're paid to "fluff"?'

He nodded. 'Two hundred a day.'

'It's less than they could make as hookers,' said Duane. 'Which some of them are, of course. But, hey, there are women out there who would pay a lot more than two hundred to suck on Dick Bigg's big dick!'

'Let's not get crude,' Rocky Coxman said primly.

'Let's not get prissy,' Duane retorted. 'Pussy-Kat ain't here to pass round the hymn-sheets.'

Rocky threw a switch that obliterated the view of the other room; the window became another mirror.

'If you'll excuse me, Miss Kane, I have to go and make the arrangements for your test. There's a refrigerator in the wardrobe. Help yourself to a Coke or a Dr Pepper. Duane, there's something we need to discuss.' He waddled through the doorway after Duane.

Joylene's throat was dry but she didn't dare drink anything ahead of her screen test. She was practically peeing with nervousness as it was.

The door reopened but it was not Mr. Coxman and Duane returning. It was the star of next door's tableau, still naked. Thanks to the ministrations of the blondes Dick Bigg was currently Dick Medium-Plus. Joylene, with an effort, focused her attention on his handsome wide-mouthed face.

'Hi,' he said cheerily. 'You must be the new kid in town.'

'Yeah. Pussy-Kat Kane.' The name sounded more ridiculous with each repetition.

'Love that name. Can't wait to see all that goes with it. I'm Dick Bigg.'

And right now, in a tribute to her presence, he was living up to his name.

'Excuse me,' he said. But he wasn't apologizing for his throbbing hard-on. He spat in the sink, then gargled with mouthwash. 'God, don't you hate the taste of these vaginal deodorants?'

Joylene's generation deemed genital hygiene to be beyond godliness. 'I wouldn't know,' she said. 'I've never tasted one.'

'You haven't eaten pussy?' She'd never gotten into this kind of conversation on so short an acquaintance. But neither had she sat fully dressed in front of a man wearing only some fake tan and a rampant erection. She shook her head.

'No way.'

'Well, you've got some surprises to look forward to.'

'I'm sure I have, but that's not one of them.'

'Don't discount your chickens, Pussy-Kat, that's my advice.'

'Do you do blow-jobs?'

'Hell no, I'm no fucking queer.'

'My point exactly.'

It was hard not to stare at his hard-on. It – everything about him – was perfect. And not just perfect for porno: perfect for a horny teenager. Joylene was getting horny. She didn't know what Mr. Coxman had in mind for her audition but she hoped it involved Mr. Bigg.

He was reading her mind.

'Are you ready for a little warm-up?'

'Aren't you due in front of the cameras?'

'They can wait. Who wants to fuck with Peaches Snatch and her sagging ass when there's jailbait like you around?' (At seventeen Joylene really was jailbait, but Mr. Kazman, like Duane, had taken her word that she was eighteen. No one had asked to see her driver's license.) 'Let's get you out of those clothes and onto that couch,' he continued.

His erection prodded at her from all sides as he circled her, deftly removing the Prada blouse and skirt she'd splashed out on with some of yesterday's five hundred. Her Veronica's Closet bra and panties were also eased – teased – away. He pushed her onto her back on the brocade couch, parted her thighs and lowered his face between them. Joylene hoped her deodorant wasn't too heady for him. Evidently not:

'Wow,' he said. 'That is one fine pussy. And that's a superstar clit if I ever seen one.'

Teddy Dunne and some of his successors had accustomed her to near-silent sex (although Scott, among others, was inclined to utter intermittent 'yeah's' and 'ooh, baby's'); but porno was the Talkies and Dick Bigg would talk the clitoris off a donkey. He kept up a near-non-stop patter of 'your pussy is so sweet/so good/so hot/so wet – you want that/like that/love that, don't you?' etcetera, etcetera. Joylene felt obliged to offer more than her usual restrained quota of 'hmm's and the occasional 'oh, yes'. Hadn't his mom ever told him not to talk while he was eating?

But he was good. Nobody had worked this well on her since Teddy, the now-dethroned cunnilingus king. Her clitoris burned. 'Ooh, yes' she found herself saying, unbidden.

He stood up, stood over her. His massive organ – it had to be close to nine inches long and proportionately thick – throbbed above her head.

'You want it, don't you?' he snarled, as he had snarled at Peaches Snatch in *Cl-ass Action 9*.

'Well – yeah,' she said, trying to catch the mood of the moment.

'What do you want?'

'You tell me,' she prevaricated.

'You want to suck on that big cock, don't you?'

Did she, though, just after it had been down the blonde fluffer's throat and who knows where else? Every penis was like a used car, but used cars were usually valeted before you got into them. Her mind filled with images from *Cl-ass Action 9* - Peaches Snatch and, double-yuck, Peaches's ass. Swallowing back this line of thought, she sat up and attempted to swallow what was on offer. It was immediately apparent that she was biting off more than she could normally chew.

'Careful,' he said. 'Watch your teeth.' Which probably wasn't in his regular scripts. Then, as she adjusted to the enormity of the challenge, he turned back into Mr. Gabby and reminded her how much she wanted/liked/loved his eponymous appendage. He repeatedly and redundantly urged her to do what she was already doing. He diverted her attention briefly to his balls, his belly-button, his nipples, then back to his prize asset. 'You love it, don't you?' he insisted on knowing.

'Hmm,' Joylene gurgled noncommittally.

Now he took hold of her ankles and folded her in half. She was open to him, wide open. He made to thrust himself into her.

'Wait,' she said. 'Where's your condom?'

'Christ. Aren't you on the Pill?'

'That has nothing to do with safe sex.'

'I don't have AIDS – or anything else – if that's what you're worried about. We all get tested once a month.'

Didn't he know that a negative HIV result was like a bus ticket, only valid for one journey?

'What about those women you were just with?'

'The fluffers? They get regular check-ups too.'

'Duane said some of them are hookers.'

'Who's Duane?'

'The guy who brought me here. He's one of Mr. Kazman's talent scouts.' It was strange to be having this conversation while he pinned her feet against the wall behind her head and his erection, declining a few degrees off vertical, pointed at her midriff like a divining rod.

'So what if the fluffers are hookers some of the time? They're not stupid. They practice safe sex with the johns.'

Joylene doubted he could be certain of that. It was said that hookers and hustlers would do unprotected sex if the price was high enough (what price do you put on a life-threatening disease?). Why was he arguing about it? In *Cl-ass Action 9* the men had worn condoms for all penetration acts. Some of Joylene's contemporaries at Hoover High had even insisted on condoms (the flavored kind) for oral sex. She didn't see the necessity for that as long as you were a 'hawk'. Where was the fun in giving head to a plastic bag? Leonard had finally told her that most gays considered the risk to be between negligible and non-existent.

'I'm not taking chances,' she told Dick Bigg. 'Not with you

or anybody.'

'Christ,' he grumbled again, 'you're only here for a test and already you're Elizabeth fucking Taylor.'

But he let go her feet and padded over to the makeup table to produce a pack of Trojans from the drawer. When he returned Joylene went out of her way to atone for the inconvenience she had put him to, voluntarily raising her legs to their previous altitude and bracing them against the wall. Calling to mind last night's movies she even treated him to some recycled dialogue.

'Yeah, come on, big boy, give it to me.'

The glistening Trojan visibly expanded.

'You really want it, don't you?'

'Oh yeah, I surely do.' She could hear herself lapsing into the role of an NC-17-rated Scarlett O'Hara.

'What do you want?'

'You know what I want.' In any case he was already giving it to her. No longer pretending, she gasped and grunted and briefly screamed as he gave her all that he had to give. Joylene ran out of script but she did not run out of soundtrack special effects. And Dick more than made up for her shortcomings in the dialogue department.

Despite his overwhelming size advantage he wasn't in the Teddy Dunne or Scott league when it came to screwing. He wasn't angling his thrusts so that they rubbed her G-spot, nor did he use his fingers to press her clitoris against his shaft. Perhaps because he was used to cameras he seemed to be concentrating on keeping their bodies apart as much as possible to allow for viewing angles. But if orgasm was not in prospect for Joylene, it was for him. With a Calgary Stampede yell he pulled back, whipped off the Trojan and gave the supposed cameraman the usual gooey cum-shot with which every sequence in every porn-film must culminate – the proof, so to speak, of the pudding.

It was a relief to get her legs horizontal again. She hoped she'd get the chance to shower before the makeup for her screen test. She felt bruised and sore and was no longer sure she wanted to do her test with the grueling Mr. Bigg – or anybody else. She felt – she felt fucked.

He threw her a towel to mop herself dry with.

'Welcome aboard,' he said.

'Excuse me?'

'Welcome to Kazman Productions. You're hired.'

'You can hire me? You mean – that was an audition? I thought I was getting a screen test?'

'Pussy-Kat, you just did.' He flipped a wall switch and the second mirror became a window, a window behind which stood a gangling man with a camcorder. The supposed cameraman for whom Dick had been providing good angles was all too real. Duane and Rocky Coxman stood on either side of him, grinning through the two-way mirror that was now another window. Duane had a heavy sheen of perspiration across his face.

Joylene blushed. 'This thing –' she gestured at the mirror/window – 'works from both sides?' Dick nodded.

'The trick's in the lighting.'

'You set me up.'

'At least you didn't get stage-fright,' he said.

'I thought I'd have to wear makeup.'

'Not with your skin tone.'

'Well, screw you,' she said, only half mad at him for the

deception now that the ordeal was over, with only a mild backache and a sore vagina to show for her adult movie debut. Dick Bigg laughed, another wide display of teeth that were beyond perfection.

'Screw you, Pussy-Kat. The pleasure was nearly all mine!'

Back in his office Rocky Coxman was all smiles and plaudits. He handed her a check for two thousand dollars.

'We pay the fluffers in cash,' he said. 'But the stars get checks.'

The stars! Just like that, she was a star!

'It's up to you to deal with the IRS,' he went on, 'but I should warn you, Mr. Kazman plays a very straight game with them. In this business we walk a lot of fine lines, but we don't fuck with the taxman. Pardon my French.'

'Do I owe you some of this?' Joylene asked Duane. He shook his head.

'I get what's coming to me direct from Rocky or Al,' he said. 'Don't you worry about me. I reckon I've just found me a new gold mine.'

'We all have,' Rocky Coxman confirmed.

The Bigg One, Dick's next release and his first 'starring' title, included the dressing-room scene: '*Introducing Pussy-Kat Kane*'. Another collector's item, irreplaceable. There is no 'back list' on Dick Bigg. Some of the women in yesteryear porno (Linda, Debbie, Peaches, Pussy-Kat) live on in memory and a million fantasies, but the men, literally, come and go. Just a few years later, Dick Bigg is largely forgotten. And, of course, dead.

By the time *The Bigg One* was released, in Joylene's second month at UCLA, her 'Kitten Kandy' stills had appeared in three jerk-off magazines. Nobody in the History Faculty connected these pictures to the gorgeous green-eyed freshman from Arizona with the designer wardrobe. But Pussy-Kat Kane was never going to be anonymous. The cover of *Creamme*, coinciding with the release of *The Bigg One* in October, blew Joylene Duchat's cover. Her face, tits, pussy and ass imprinted themselves instantly on the consciousness of millions of red-blooded males and their outclassed wives and girlfriends. The centerfold adorned lockers and bedroom walls from UCLA to the UAE, from Peoria to St Petersburg.

Creamme, owned by Al Kazman's publishing arm, was raunchier than *Playboy* or *Penthouse* but not so hardcore as to be deemed unacceptable by the nation's news-stands and bookstores. Monthly sales exceeded 1.5 million.

Joylene was paid $2,500 for this second photo shoot. There was another five grand when *The Bigg One* was released. She had gone back to the studio to dub in some lurid dialogue to replace her discussion with Dick of AIDS, the fluffers and 'Elizabeth fucking Taylor'. Her contribution to the new soundtrack included a high-decibel orgasm. The first of many: all fakes.

'Hi, baby.'

'Hi, Mom. How're things?'

'Same as always. I lost four pounds this week.' Four down: 150 to go. 'How's college?'

'Bor-ing. Like school.'

'Are you dating anybody yet?'

'Nah, they're all jocks or nerds.'

'Haven't you made any new friends?'

'It's OK. Patrick and Steven took me to a party Saturday.' Her landlords.

'A gay party?'

'Yeah.' A dozen drop-dead superbods who already knew all the words to every track on Celine Dion's new album.

'Well, I guess you can't come to any harm hanging out with gays.'

'There's the risk I may turn into Bette Davis!' (Prophetic words, as we shall see!)

'Are you doing any acting?'

'Nah. I'm kinda busy with books and stuff.'

Stuff like spending money in the malls. And making another movie. *Cl-ass Action 10*, with a '*Special Appearance by Pussy-Kat Kane*', would be out in time for Thanksgiving. Masturbators would, indeed, give thanks.

Pussy Power, her first starring feature, would be out by Christmas.

Cl-ass Action 10 was Peaches Snatch's swansong, the last and most popular of the entire series. But *Pussy Power* would outsell anything Peaches had done by a factor of three.

Rocky Coxman directed her early appearances himself. Her two scenes in *Cl-ass Action 10* were filmed in the studio proper. To ease the newcomer into her new career he barred from the shoot everyone except the quartet of cameramen and one lighting technician. But it was still mortifying to have a half-dozen guys watching her do stuff she had heretofore done only in private.

She stuck to her guns about not doing ladies or giving ass, so in *Cl-ass Action 10* Peaches Snatch as usual supplies the ass and Pussy-Kat Kane a certain amount of what within the limitations of the genre might be called 'class'. In one of her scenes Joylene is in a standing position getting eaten by Dick Bigg who is simultaneously giving a prone Peaches her tenth (ho-hum!) anal pounding. In her other scene Dick puts in some routine oral and pussy action with a now-horizontal Joylene, but with this movie Kazman and Coxman wanted to do no more than stoke up the fire she had lit in *The Bigg One*.

Her scenes only account for nine minutes of screen time, but each took half a day to film with retakes to allow for camera angles and blocking moves. Mr. Bigg, on these two days, didn't require any servicing by the fluffers. Watching the finished product it was amazing to see all the stop-starts edited into two flowing sequences.

Apart from the regulation corny sex-talk Joylene had expected filming to be conducted in an atmosphere of devotional silence, but in the absence of a formal script and rehearsals Rocky Coxman, no longer prissy, gave non-stop instructions to the cast and cameramen:

'Eat him, Pussy … are you getting her boobs? … take your hand away … more light on her twat … tell him how good it is … zoom in and out slowly … now deep-throat him … close-up on that ….'

And the cameramen contributed their own basketball babble of complaints and prompts:

'Her right arm's blocking.'
'I've got a shadow.'
'Her legs are too high.'
'Her legs are too low.'
'I've only got one tit.'
'I can't get a twat shot.'

'Peaches, your head's blocking Dick's dick.'
'Move your ass, Pussy.'
'Open your pussy, Sugar.'

After the second day's filming Mr. Coxman gave Joylene a check for $10,000. Closet space in the 'apartmentette' was limited; after one modest spree on Rodeo Drive she forced herself to stop buying clothes. She opened a savings account at the bank.

Cl-ass Action 10, Peaches's swansong, also featured the crossover straight 'debut' of mega-hung gay pornstar Ty Topman. The finale – Dick Bigg and Ty rhythmically duetting in Peaches fore and aft, English expat Hugh Mungus deeply down her throat while with one hand she jerks off Algerian stallion Yuyu and with the other finger-fucks an uncredited fluffer – may not be original but it undeniably reaffirms just how much fun six people can have at a party. And Peaches has her loudest-ever ear-bleeding orgasm.

Watching the edited movie with Duane Joylene asked him: 'Her orgasms – they're not the real McCoy, are they?'

'According to her they are.'

'She must have an extra G-spot up her ass.'

Did Peaches jump or was she pushed from the top floor of Kazman Productions? No one was saying. She retired to Jamaica and bought a colonial-style bungalow a mile from Ian Fleming's old home, *Goldeneye*. Peaches's property came to be known as *Goldensnatch*, *Goldenass*, *Goldfingering* and other predictable variations on this theme.

*

Straight or gay, a Kazman production normally boasts a cast of eight to fifteen performers. The *Cl-ass Action* series mostly have three scenes with Peaches: one lesbian, a one-to-one anal and an orgy. Two or three other duos and/or threesomes supply the remaining sequences. The fluffers fill in walk-on roles – motel maids, waitresses, etc. – appropriately dressed or undressed.

So, *Pussy Power* is unique for its time in having no other female performer, just Joylene with a series of men: Dick, Ty, Hugh, Yuyu and a couple of Latinos who were virtually plucked off the street. Having given the viewing audience a 'taster' with her appearances in *The Bigg One* and *Cl-ass Action 10*, Kazman and Coxman now gave them a Pussy-Kat Kane fuck-fest.

There is one other female in *Pussy Power*, uncredited. Rocky Coxman insisted there had to be an anal scene: 'Your public expects it.'

Now she had a public!

'My public can just kiss my ass,' Joylene told him, all mall-girl sass.

'Sugar, they'd form a line from here to Anaheim for the privilege,' said Duane, who now hung around the studio almost fulltime.

'I'm not doing it,' she said. After Dick and Ty, and especially after Yuyu (not the biggest star, but size-wise the biggest by a considerable margin) Joylene had begun employing post-natal exercises and creams to maintain her main base of operations in prime elasticity and 'photogeniality'. Having seen what bad shape a vagina could end up in, she wasn't about to court a prolapsed rectum.

'I'll give you an extra ten grand,' Rocky offered. He'd already announced that her fee for *Pussy Power* would rise to ten thousand now, ten more on release and another ten for each multiple of 20,000 copies it sold.

'Not even for fifty.' Joylene stuck to her guns.

'Half the women in this country are doing it.' This was almost certainly an exaggeration, although a taboo-busting sitcom on cable-TV would soon be bringing anal intercourse into the living-rooms of Middle America.

'Well, I'm in the other half.' Joylene's mouth set in an expression her mom would have recognized.

'Can't we use one of the fluffers?' Duane suggested.

'A stand-in? This is porno, buster, not *Eldorado*. She's not Tawdra fucking Thanatos.' A rare expletive from Rocky off the film-set.

Her landlords were in on her little secret and had seen the Kitten Kandy stills and a pre-release copy of *Cl-ass Action 10*. They let slip in conversation that a friend of theirs wore a butt plug. Joylene didn't want to expose herself as a rube but she wondered whether this was worn as a form of stimulation 'on the hoof' or was a prophylactic against incontinence brought about by overzealous use of the butt it plugged. And what if their friend farted at a nude pool party: were his fellow skinny-dippers in danger of being hit by the equivalent of a rogue missile on a Star Wars range?

From Leonard and Javier she already knew about gays being divided into 'top men' and 'bottom men'. Now she told Patrick and Steven about the pressure on her to be a 'bottom man' and her anxieties.

'Don't do it, babe,' Steven said. 'We have a golden rule:

nothing's too gross if you want to do it, but you shouldn't do stuff you're not comfortable with.'

So, the anal scenes in *Pussy Power* and its successors are not Pussy-Kat Kane: they're her stand-in. She *was* Tawdra (fucking) Thanatos!

Rather than make up a white girl to Joylene's skin tone – body makeup was apt to run or smear during the heavier action – they used a Black fluffer and cranked up the lighting to tone her color down. This accounts for the whiter-than-usual look of the white men in Pussy-Kat Kane's ass action sequences – and the absence of any zooms and long shots.

Some dialogue that's not in the released version of *Pussy Power*:

Ty Topman (famously the gabbiest of the gabby guys in gay porn): 'Lick them balls, bitch.'

Pussy-Kat: 'Those balls, for Christ's sake. Can't you speaking the fucking Queen's English?'

Ty: 'Ain't you heard? I've stopped fucking queens!' (Laughter on set.)

As Rocky Coxman had said, the adult movie public expected ass action.

And they got it. Every one of Pussy-Kat Kane's features would, like Peaches's, feature ass action. None of it supplied by the star herself. Brandy, the Black fluffer, stood in for all these scenes and was increasingly well paid for doing so, though she remained uncredited.

Brandy, like the other fluffers, was a girl who'd taken many a walk on the wild side. She dressed as if she was auditioning for an Andy Warhol retrospective. After three years her ass, plainly not as robust as Peaches's, finally collapsed under the strain of endless on-camera assaults by the likes of Yuyu and Hugh Mungus, but following reconstructive surgery it's as good as new. She recently married a famous track star and started a third career with a Gospel Choir who know nothing of her past.

The one area in which Joylene required no understudy was (not to put too fine a point on it) her cunt. Thanks to a regime of exercises and creams and physiotherapy she retained the most photogenic vagina in the industry.

At her impromptu audition Dick Bigg had remarked that she was blessed with 'one fine pussy' and 'a superstar clit'. No truer words were ever said at an audition. Those over-intimate close-ups which on so many female pornstars look like an inspection of household as much as human plumbing are, on Pussy-Kat Kane, Impressionistic glimpses of the clefts and passageways of which every viewer dreams and day-dreams. She possesses the cutest little love-button where some women (including Peaches) have nothing that the camera can detect and others something that resembles a miniature penis. Redneck American wet-dreamers do not want the studs that they fantasize being – many pounds slimmer, many times handsomer and at least twice as well hung – to be closet cocksuckers.

Joylene's photogenic love-bump rarely provided her with an orgasm on camera, even when the likes of Dick Bigg were giving her expert head. But she faked with the best of them; her orgasms sound no less genuine than Peaches's in a medium where over-the-top tends to be an understatement.

Her self-consciousness never entirely went away. Not just the cameramen, the lighting guys and the director were watching, but also the makeup girls, some of the fluffers, Mr. Kazman, Duane and sometimes other visitors to the set. It wasn't a vast remove from high school drama.

Joylene had wanted to be an actress, and now she was.

7. KATE COMES CLEAN

It's time to stop calling her Joylene.

Joylene was the girl who received weekly calls from Seldom and lunched once a month with Javier's cousins in Huntington, hoping these good Catholic folk and their teenage kids had not seen *Cl-ass Action 10* and *The Bigg One*.

At the studio she was Pussy-Kat, often abbreviated to Pussy.

At UCLA she'd been Joylene Duchat. But after the photo shoot for *Creamme*, which was clearly not going to pass unnoticed on campus, she dropped out. One of her fellow freshmen even approached the *National Enquirer* but got nowhere: college kids moonlighting in porno was not news. Had the *Enquirer* followed up this approach they might have uncovered this college kid's links to crusading televangelist Barton Duchat, but they missed that story.

Getting used to being Pussy-Kat, she no longer thought of her stepfather and her grandmother whenever the name was spoken. Ruiz and Seldom had begun to feel a lot more than 450 miles away. On the phone with Jaynette she maintained a fictitious life at UCLA.

She still aspired to becoming a serious actress and had conceived the name Katharine Kane for her straight career when – if – it came. When – if – she met a guy she felt serious about, he too would call her Katharine – or Kate.

She didn't go out on many dates and never with anyone from the studio. She went to movies and parties with her landlords. Now that she was screwing for a living, the thought of some horny college kid trying to fulfill his jerk-off fantasies on her did not tantalize.

Having a pornstar for a tenant, for a friend, gave Patrick and Steven a new status in the Silver Lake gay community. Everyone wanted to know what Dick, Ty and Yuyu were 'really like'. Could she bring one of them to a party? (No.) Especially Yuyu. (Especially not Yuyu.)

In this circle she had debuted as Joylene. Now she told them of her aspiration to go straight as Katharine.

'What, like Hepburn or Ross?'

'Whatever. Katharine Kane.' It would be a few months before she was accused of pirating the original name of Batwoman who had, in any case, been written out of Gotham City by editors at DC Comics.

The fags took to calling her Kate.

And so shall we.

Leonard and Javier came to LA for Thanksgiving, Javier driving their Nissan, Leonard driving Kate's used RAV (she didn't yearn for a new car).

They stayed at Huntington but came to Silver Lake on their first evening. Hugs and kisses in Patrick and Steven's living-room, a symphony in chrome, suede and bonsai. The hosts were deadpanning. Standing behind Kate, Leonard gave her a shoulder-rub. Javier held her hand. She took a deep breath.

'There's something I need to tell you guys.'

'Is there, pussycat?' said Javier, also deadpan.

'That's with a "k", by the way,' Leonard said, squeezing her shoulders. She turned so fast her neck clicked.

'You *know*?'

Deadpan expressions turned to pantomimed amazement. Lips unpursed as the four queens screeched simultaneously, porno-orgasmically. More hugs, more kisses.

'You think nobody in Tucson sees *Creamme*?' Javier laughed.

'Tell me Mom hasn't seen it. Or Ruiz.'

'Well, slimming magazines are what your mom's mostly into,' said Leonard. 'And Ruiz likes to see ovenware on the cover, not a dish like you, Ms. Kane. Of course we just beamed ourselves into Tucson to buy *Cl-ass Action 10*.'

'And *The Bigg One*,' Javier screeched. 'Ooh, that Dick Bigg! When are you going to bring to him to Seldom? Does he do gay? Would he like some tight Latino ass, d'you think?'

'Yeah,' Steven contributed: 'tight as the Lincoln Tunnel.'

Kate relaxed and glided into the general hysteria. She was home and dry. Well, not exactly home. As Leonard pointed out, how long before a regular customer from Tucson – one of the airbase guys, for instance – made the connection between Pussy-Kat Kane and Le Bayou's former foxy maître d'?

'You have to tell them, babe,' said Javier. 'Your mom and Ruiz. You need to come clean.'

'So to speak,' Steven added.

This too – at Christmas – went better than expected.

Her mother came to the door of Reception as Kate was getting out of her car in front of the Seldom Motel. Jaynette could now cross thresholds without having to turn sideways. Not exactly svelte, she weighed in at around 165 pounds, but her doughy flesh was disassembling into the constituent parts of the head-turning figure she'd once had. She wore a front-buttoning floral dress; after all the muumuus she looked homely and almost pretty again.

'Look at you,' she said as her daughter fished in the trunk for her bags, which were still from J.C. Penney. 'You didn't get those jeans at Kmart.'

'Mom, they're only Calvins. It's not like I bought them on Rodeo Drive or anything.' Some Gap outfits and one Prada dress to show off to her high-school crowd were the best things she'd brought for this trip. Her more extravagant clothes were currently hanging in the Santa Monica condo apartment into which she'd moved yesterday. Two bedrooms and a sea-view balcony; only a rental, but something else she'd have to explain to her mother.

'I thought you'd be in Versace by now,' said Jaynette.

'You think I can shop there on the money the Reverend sends us?'

'Not until they discover you for the movies, I guess.'

Was this another tease? Did her mom know? Leonard was sure she didn't, although others did: he'd run into Maria and Jimmy in the drugstore in Oracle.

'They were kinda tight-assed about your new career'. But they wouldn't have told Jaynette. Had somebody else? *Let's get this over with*, she thought.

'Actually, Mom, I have done some work in a couple of movies.'

Still in the doorway Jaynette clapped her podgy hands. 'Good for you, baby. Why didn't you tell me before?'

Kate was still standing by the rear of the Toyota. 'I thought

I'd save it up for a Christmas surprise. One of them just came out this week.'

'On TV?' Jaynette guessed. 'One of those cable channels? God knows when we'll get cable out here. I keep telling Ruiz we should move into the city —'

'Not cable, Mom. These are the kind of movies that — go straight to video.'

'Still, if it's got you started, baby. So are you, like, one of the extras?'

'No, I got a part.'

'With lines and everything? Wow!' A deep crease opened in her fleshy face as she frowned. 'Joylene, I hope you didn't have to — you know — do anything to get parts in these movies?'

Kate shook her head. 'Not exactly. But I have to do — stuff - in the movies.'

'You mean — sex scenes? What, you and some guy are making out and — the slasher attacks you, like in a *Halloween* or an *Axman*?'

Kate took a deep breath. 'No, Mom,' she said quietly. 'Like in — porno.'

'You made a porno movie?' Jaynette rocked slightly in the doorway.

'I've made four. Two of them aren't out yet.' In January they would dub the sound on *Another Bigg One*. And *Pussy Power 2* would be filmed for release in March.

Mother and daughter stared at each other. The crease reopened in Jaynette's forehead. 'Just how gross are these movies?'

'I don't do the really gross stuff. You know —' Kate blushed — 'ass stuff.' Her mother rocked again. 'They use a stand-in for those scenes – a Black girl with a lot of light on her ass to make it look like mine.'

'But you do the – regular stuff?'

Kate nodded.

'You do – like, oral-type stuff?'

Kate nodded, blushing deeper.

'The guys wear condoms, or do you wear one of those women's things?'

'The guys wear condoms. Except for the oral scenes.'

'Is that safe?'

'They reckon it is. I use an antibacterial mouthwash before and after.' Was she dreaming this conversation with her mother, in the dusty forecourt of the Seldom Motel?

'Are the boys hunky?'

'They're men, Mom. Still pretty young. And, yeah, they're hunky.'

'And hung, I guess?'

Kate smirked. 'Sure they are.'

'Are you OK with that? You know –' Jaynette's turn to blush – 'down there?'

Another smirk. 'Yeah, Mom, I take good care of myself down there.'

'Is this, like, a regular studio or some hole-in-the-corner outfit?'

'It's a regular studio. In Santa Monica. The top guy, Mr. Kazman, is the number-one man in porno. He pays taxes and everything. We all do.'

'Kazman? Sounds like a Jew. How much is he paying you?'

'Well, just for my screen-test which they edited into one of the movies he gave me seven grand.'

'Seven grand?'

'Uh-huh. Now I'm getting twenty.'

'Twenty grand?' Jaynette held onto the doorway for support.

'Uh-huh, ten up front and ten when it's released. Plus I get a percentage if the movie sells well.'

'And do they?'

'Some of them do. Duane – he's the guy who got me into this, a talent scout – says we could be talking millions in a few years' time.'

'Where did this talent scout find you? Some club on Sunset Strip?'

Kate smiled and shook her head. 'He came to Le Bayou last summer.'

'He came here?'

'Scott told him about me.'

'That nice boy from the mall you were dating? He's a – pornstar?'

'He just poses for pictures. The gays get off looking at guys like him. It's helping to put him through college.'

'And making these movies isn't interfering with college for you?'

'Mom, I quit UCLA. I had to.'

'They kicked you out?'

'No, I quit.'

'To make millions in porno.'

'If I'm lucky. Mr. Kazman's starting another company to make movies for cable TV. Adult but not so hardcore. More dialogue, more storyline. He says I can do one of those when the right story comes along. And maybe even before that someone'll want me for a proper movie.'

'After porno they'd use you in a proper movie?'

'It could happen.'

Her mother exhaled loudly; it might or might not have been a sigh. 'Well, Joylene, this ain't exactly what I was expecting after you left for UCLA, but I guess I can get used to it if it's what you want to do. I'm kinda glad your granma didn't live to see you become a blue-movie girl. She'd call you a Jezebel.'

Joylene smiled at a memory of her Granma Abigail and the 'fornicators' at the Seldom Motel. 'I like to think she'd be proud of me for making a fortune with my body.'

'I guess she might at that,' said Jaynette. 'Promise me you'll keep your father's name out of this. Bart's been good with the money for your education. It wouldn't be fair to dynamite his ministry.'

Kate nodded. 'I promise. I use a different name in my movies: Pussy-Kat Kane. I haven't been Duchat since I dropped out of college.'

'And don't take any chances with AIDS and so on.'

'Believe me, Mom, I'm not. Actually, it's no more risk than I'd be taking dating college boys in LA or even Tucson these days.'

'And I guess those boys wouldn't pay you twenty grand for a blowjob either!'

'Mom!' Laughing, Kate walked up to her mother and they hugged. Kate thought it was more agreeable – and less judgmental – to be thought of as a '*blue-movie girl*' than a pornstar.

Ruiz didn't seem too surprised by the news of his stepdaughter's new career. Next morning he and Jaynette watched *Pussy Power* (which Kate had brought as a Christmas 'extra' for the boys in the week of its release).

Kate had a reunion with Jimmy and Maria in Oracle. Her first great love and her high school best friend said they'd gotten over the shock of seeing her in porno, but Leonard was right, they were tight-assed about it. They hadn't graduated from the small-town mindset and maybe never would.

Jaynette was tight-lipped after seeing *Pussy Power*.

'I don't think I'll watch any more of your movies,' she said. 'It's not easy watching the child you gave birth to do doing that sort of stuff. Even if some of it isn't really you.'

Kate phoned Scott. He was still shooting gay stills for the talent scout who'd taken over from Duane in Arizona. He had seen her first two movies.

'I said you were gonna be big,' he told her, 'but I never expected it to happen so fast.'

'Me neither!' She told him about quitting UCLA and her change of name.

Next day she went to the mall in Tucson. He still looked cute, in his blond California way, in the security uniform. And she still had the hots for him.

She handed him a folded check. 'This is for you.' He unfolded it.

'Five grand! You don't have to give me this kind of dough, Joylene.'

'Kate,' she reminded him. 'And I do. I owe you for Duane. Like, big-time.'

'Christ, Joy-, Kate, this will see me through till I finish college.'

She laughed. 'I could get through it in an hour on Rodeo Drive.'

That evening he took her to one of the city's fanciest restaurants. Kate didn't wear the Prada dress in case the evening ended with some alfresco fucking. Which it did, even though Scott was dating a sophomore from Seattle who'd gone home for the holidays.

It was good sex, easy and familiar. The kissing was especially nice; there isn't too much kissing in porno. Yet, despite a canopy of stars in place of arcs and spotlights and the welcome absence of crew and cameras, the magic was gone. Scott wasn't screwing Kate or even Joylene Duchat, he was screwing Pussy-Kat Kane. She came, but there was no buzz.

He may have sensed this. He didn't call her over Christmas or New Year. Apart from an accidental encounter with Chris Lee in Oracle she attempted no more high school reunions. Chris told her about his activities in campus politics; yes, he'd seen *Cl-ass Action 10* – 'you were pretty hot, I guess!' – but he didn't suggest a get-together. And Maria and Jimmy didn't ask for her Santa Monica phone number when she called them on New Year's.

It was a relief to be heading west on I-10 in the Toyota on January 2. Back to her Santa Monica condo.

Back to the warehouse studio.

Back to work.

Filming on *Pussy Power 2* started in the week of her eighteenth birthday, which was also the week that *Another Bigg One* was released. What she was doing was now legitimate – legal.

8. POOR NELLIE

Reader, you must be wondering what happened to her resolve not to make more than one adult movie, just enough to get herself noticed in Hollywood – and 'nothing too gross'.

Multiples of twenty grand is what happened. Multiples which would soon become multiples of fifty and skyrocket beyond even that. Plus stills shoots. She would make the cover of *Playboy* and even *Newsweek* when it did a feature on '*The Porno Biz: illicit or legitimate?*' Interviews: all the way up to the *Catholic Herald*: '*Pussy-Kat Kane on why Porno can be healthy*'. Merchandising: '*Your own inflatable Pussy-Kat Kane – with three working orifices*' and, for those on a budget, the '*Pussy-Kat pussy*', a cushion-sized replica of her midsection – with two portals for docking.

Let's fast-forward again. To January 1999. Kate has just had her twenty-first birthday: a family dinner at Le Bayou and a party at her Silver Lake apartment where her gay friends finally got to mingle with some of their porno idols.

She moved back to Silver Lake in early '98. Santa Monica was convenient for the studio, but not every condominium welcomed a pornstar, however rich. In faintly Bohemian Silver Lake it was easier to blend in. A butch blonde wig helped the 'blending' process at local shops.

Just before Christmas she finished *Pussy Power 13*. The movies, like the guys in them, have been coming thick and fast – four per year – and the last four are on DVD as well as video. She also guested in the movies of other stars, even some for rival studios. No need to name these movies, is there, reader? Either you've seen them or porn isn't your bag.

Domestic sales have fluctuated between 50,000 (pretty good for an adult movie) to an amazing 200,000 copies. Piracy makes overseas sales difficult to quantify, but one feature writer estimated that *Pussy Power 3*, the most popular of the series, sold over three million copies worldwide, putting it up with the top titles in porno history.

At a dollar per copy, plus $50,000 up-front, the *Pussy Power* series took Pussy-Kat Kane into the stratosphere of pornstars. Even respectable newspapers and magazines referred to her as the 'Beaver Queen'; the less reputable ones called her the 'Blowjob Princess', the 'Empress of Ass Action' (a title that belonged, properly, to Brandy) or (her own title, beyond question) 'The Cunt In Front'.

She won the adult entertainment equivalent of an Oscar and other porn awards. She appeared on primetime as well as late-night talk shows. She went to film festivals in Cannes, Berlin, Tokyo and Taipei. She addressed a convention of FEM, the Female Empowerment Movement which saw her as an icon rather than as a threat, although the DAR and other conservative women's groups remained opposed to porno exploitation.

She attended mainstream movie premieres and Broadway first nights, usually with Al Kazman but sometimes escorted by a male pornstar or a Hollywood B-list actor whose publicity agent wanted to get him into the tabloids and breakfast TV.

Trying not to be photographed, a few A-listers also pursued the luscious porn-queen. One of these proved to be a major head-case with a much teensier dick than his bulging on-screen packet advertised.

There had been, as Mae West used to say, too many men in life but not enough life in her men. She hadn't found – would she ever find? – Love.

One of the men in her life died in Kate's third year in adult entertainment: 'Mr. Bigg', the 'Dick of Death', frighteningly and very publicly, from AIDS. Shacked-up with an ex-hooker who injected her drug of choice, Dick had bribed an employee of the health clinic to falsify his monthly blood tests. Gays and others were now living in uneasy harmony with HIV and AIDS, but not poor Dick: he developed a bizarre malignant form of crotch rot that unstoppably devoured his genitals. 'Dick of Death' had been a prophetic accolade.

Another health center conducted back-up tests on all employees; everyone was passed fit. Kate begged Kazman to move her into the soft-core films that his subsidiary, Namzak, was producing for cable TV, but he was reluctant; the profit from soft-core was peanuts compared to hardcore.

January 1999 was the month Brandy's rectum prolapsed.

It was also when Kate discovered that Kazman was an Arab.

There had been no second invitation to his mansion. She hadn't met them, but she knew he had a wife and five children. His kids didn't visit the studio. And he had never made a move on Kate.

He now called her Katharine. Midway through filming *Pussy Power 14* he asked her permission to bring someone to watch – 'for maybe one hour.'

'Is he in the business?' He sometimes paraded her in front of overseas distributors and rival producers.

'No, this is a personal friend. In fact, he is the son of my late nephew. He lives in Switzerland but now he is staying at the Beverly Wilshire. He has seen your movies and he wishes to meet with you. Tomorrow.'

'I'll be happy to see him, Mr. Kazman,' said Kate.

She wasn't expecting a Rudi Vallarte lookalike the next day. But neither did she expect Orson Welles. She expected to meet a Jew in his twenties or thirties, but the man who rose from a couch in Kazman's office was an immense middle-aged Arab. He wasn't wearing the headdress you often saw in the malls and nitespots, but his pristine white robe would cover a couch in Kate's apartment. It practically covered this one before he stood up. His smile revealed teeth like those of a predatory animal. Kazman had also risen to his feet.

'Katharine, this is the son of my late nephew. His Highness Prince Masood bin Khalid al-Khazi.' The name was a bigger mouthful than his teeth.

'Miss Pussy, I am joyful to meet you.' He had a sibilant fluttering voice and spoke English that sounded like out-takes from *Gandhi*.

'Mah pleasure, I'm sure,' she said, lapsing into high-school Scarlett O'Hara.

'Your films are the crown jewels of my collection.'

'You don't have, like, real crown jewels?' Kate was now dumbass pre-teen Joylene. The white robe shimmered and shook as Prince Masood tittered.

'Only these.' He held out his hands, which were unexpectedly dainty and exquisitely manicured. The third and fourth fingers of both hands sported pyramid diamond rings, all of them much bigger than the one Kazman wore.

'Like – wow,' Joylene said.

After some stilted conversation about Los Angeles and Switzerland Kate went to work. The Prince watched from behind one of the two-way mirrors. Appropriately, she was filming with Algerian super-stud Yuyu, known to his fans as 'the Arab Stallion' and 'Desert Donkey-Dick'. Kate was the housewife 'surprised' by handyman Yuyu: oral foreplay to some routine fucking made memorable by the use of an ironing board which in spite of heavy reinforcement had collapsed yesterday and narrowly missed gelding the Stallion. (Reader, don't try this at home.)

After the scene Kate showered and dressed and went back to Kazman's office. The Prince's face now had a sheen of perspiration. His lips were moist.

'Miss Pussy, you are the most magnificent woman on earth. That was the most exciting hour of my life.'

'Well, we always try to please,' she said, Scarlett O'Hara again.

'Here.' He removed a pinkie ring and handed it to her. 'A souvenir.'

'Why, thank-you, kind sir,' said Scarlett. She actually bobbed a curtsy.

'I hope to see you again.'

Kate tried for Greta Garbo, Woman of Mystery: 'Perhaps it's in our stars.'

'"*If you can look into the seeds of time*,"' Prince Masood declaimed in his reedy lisping voice, '"*And say which grain will grow and which will not.*"'

'Omar Khayyam.' If he thought she was just some trailer-trash flea-brain from Hicksville, Louisiana, Kate hoped that identifying his quote would give her a modicum of street cred on the road to Damascus. He blew her away:

'William Shakespeare. *Macbeth*. Act One.'

'Well, there you go.' Greta Garbo metamorphosed into Joylene Duchat.

Kazman phoned her at home that evening.

'Prince Masood wants – excuse me, Katharine – he wants to fuck you.'

There was silence from Kate's end of the line. 'You've never asked me to do this kind of thing before,' she said finally, choosing her words carefully.

'Other men have requested this, but I always told them no. Just because we are in adult movies does not mean we are prostitutes.' Kate admired his use of 'we'. 'This is a special favor for the son of my late nephew. And of course he will pay you for this special favor.'

So she was to be a hooker after all. OK, she fucked guys on camera for upward of fifty grand, but –

'I don't know about this, Mr. Kazman.'

'He will pay one million dollars to fuck you just one time.'

If the Prince lay on top of her she would suffocate or be crushed – a million dollars richer, but dead. Of course he didn't have to lie on top of her.

'Tell him he can kiss my ass for free every day for a month,' she said. Then she hung up and resolved to make some serious decisions about her future.

*

Broken down, the ring made earrings for herself and a brooch for her mother.

What Kate did next didn't yield a million bucks, but it saved her from being loaned to a rival studio to appear in *American Pee*. This would be only marginally less gross than the same studio's *Hot Shits!* and *Hot Shits! Part Deux*, in both of which Peaches Snatch had made colorful guest appearances.

'Mr. Kazman, guys –' (the 'guys' were Rocky and Duane, sitting with her in the producer's office to discuss the outline scenario for *Pussy Power 15*) – 'I don't wanna do this.'

'That's OK, Pussy.' said Rocky 'Let's hear how you'd like to do it.'

'I don't want to do it. I want *out*.'

'Aw, Sugar –' Duane began.

'Don't "Sugar" me. My mind's made up.'

'Maybe you need a vacation.'

'I just had a vacation.' After *Pussy Power 14* she'd taken Jaynette and Ruiz to a luxury hotel in Cancùn. Last year Kate had paid for surgery to remove the folds of skin left over after her mother's extended dieting. For a formerly obese woman approaching forty Jaynette was now fairly stunning again and even turned a few heads in a series of one-piece designer bathing costumes. Ruiz, meanwhile, was running to flab. In spite of the wealth it had brought her, some distance along the way toward the sum Duane had prophesied at Le Bayou back when she was seventeen, Kate sensed that her stepfather despised her career.

Kazman held up his hands before either of the others could speak. He had not referred again to the Prince or the million dollars Kate had turned down.

'I think we all knew this day would come. Katharine has never quite had the commitment that Peaches brought to her work.'

'I'm sorry about that, Mr. Kazman –'

He silenced her with his hands. 'Do not apologize, Katharine. Your work is electrifying. Better even than Peaches. Look at the returns. But we know you want to be a serious actress, and I think it's time to let you do this.'

'You'll let me go?'

'We cannot stop you. There is no contract between us. But no, I will not let you go. You will act for me.'

'Huh?' Kate slipped into Joylene. Movies from Namzak's Burbank studio had more plot and more dialogue than a *Pussy Power*, but their stars were neither as rich nor as well-known as she was. In the acting stakes Maria Casablanca and Helen de Jong did not exactly pose a threat to Broadway's Helen Highwater nor even to *Eldorado*'s Darla Dawson.

'You will see. Al Kazman will make Katharine Kane an actress. A star.'

Blow it out your ass, Kate felt like telling him, still in Joylene mode. But she kept her mouth wisely shut.

'This time there will be a contract. And there will be a fee of two hundred and fifty thousand dollars. Plus a percentage.'

Not such much a 'plum part' as an over-ripe fig.

Poor Nellie.

Al Kazman had spent much of the last twelve months setting up this saucy biopic of Restoration 'babe' Nell Gwynne, the Drury Lane orange-seller turned actress who becomes the mistress of (among many others) King Charles II. To be filmed on location in England with some of Britain's top comics.

A big step-up from *Pussy Power* and *X-Women*, wasn't it?

Yes and – frankly – no.

Yes, it was an incredible step-up to be working with stage and screen legends Peter O'Toole and Dame Helen Highwater. And Warren Harding and Cecil Brock (the latter aged eighty-four). And the elderly director of cherished British comedies was very patient with Kate and generous with praise for her performance.

It was a thrill to live in a Hertfordshire hotel that was practically a chateau, to shop in London's Bond Street and to spend a weekend with the Dame and her husband, who was an English lord and the most charming man Kate had ever met.

But no, it wasn't so very different from porno. Kate's costumes were more elaborate than she was used to but they came off almost as fast and at least as often. Even the script was almost as raunchy, if a shade more elliptical. A line like 'Your Majesty may berth his mighty ship within my harbor' was plainly another way of saying 'Give me that big hard cock'.

The sex was as make-believe as the dialogue. No Brandy had to take it up the ass on Kate's behalf from Richard Cromwell, Puritan turned libertine. In the celebrated nude orgy scene with four of the King's guards none of them actually screwed her. Kate only had to pretend to go down on Judge Jeffreys inside his voluminous velvet robe; the gagging noises she's making on-screen are her suppressed laughter at the series of shocked and disgusted faces Cecil Brock was pulling off-camera.

England wasn't like Hollywood. Only the Dame and Mr. O'Toole had trailers to themselves on location (a succession of palatial country houses and a time-warp village with its street markings muddied over). Kate shared her trailer, not much more than a camper-van, with a succession of comic actresses from UK TV who were unknown to her. Cecil Brock similarly had to make room in his trailer for Warren Harding and some comedians who guested, like the girls in Kate's van, for a day or two.

The one outdoor porn shoot she'd done (*XXX-Files 3*) had not required arrays of klieg lights and white screens to augment and deflect natural daylight. She'd always shopped for 'character' clothes and fixed her own hair. Now she had people to do her costumes, her makeup, her hair (mostly wigs). There were more soundmen than cameramen, plus carpenters, electricians, continuity people and others with no discernible function. The dozens of extras in crowd scenes had a large support staff and their own director who was more like a racetrack marshal.

It was a learning curve. All Kate brought to *Poor Nellie* was her work as Pussy-Kat Kane and some comedy sketches from high school. She had a voice coach for the English accent, which she modeled on Eliza Doolittle on DVD, although a Cockney soap queen would later dub some of her lines.

Her scenes with the son of Oliver Cromwell were among the first to be shot because Warren Harding was committed to rehearsing a new West End play. Kate felt clumsy and inadequate as they began shooting, but he was full of reassurance:

'Dear girl, if you've shagged on-camera, there's nothing you can't do.'

('Shag' was one of the new words she learned in England. The fans of her career as Pussy-Kat Kane were, she now discovered, a 'bunch of wankers.')

'Absolutely fabulous, darling,' Warren kept telling her.

When it came to their big sex scene in which Cromwell Junior sodomizes Nell over an apple barrel, it was Kate who had to psych Warren up:

'Some of the gross stuff I've had to do – I just close my mind off and think of fifty-dollar bills.'

He grinned. 'Well, when push comes to shoving it up your arse, I don't dare think of Her Majesty the Queen on our fifty-pound notes. It might bugger up my chances of a knighthood down the line.'

In the event, the scene was filmed with much hilarity and many blushes. It was Kate's first nude scene in the movie, shot on a closed set. Richard Cromwell, like most of the men in *Poor Nellie*, gets to keep his clothes on.

Her other co-stars were also supportive. They seemed more in awe of her than she was of them. Kate put this down to her coming from porno; in England porn actors lived outside the mainstream, ostracized, despised even. The majority of her co-stars had never seen a Pussy-Kat Kane movie.

Only an ex-soap slob playing one of the King's bodyguards tried to jump her off-camera; he did not get lucky. Katharine Kane is nude for around forty percent of *Poor Nellie*, yet she left England without getting fucked for real.

She didn't know it was her physical beauty that set her apart. The cameramen and the lighting guys took her natural beauty and made it incandescent.

'My God,' Peter O'Toole exclaimed when he saw the rushes of their first studio love scene, 'it's like watching Helen of Troy with Methusaleh!'

Historians were taking issue with the sixty-seven-year old O'Toole playing a King who'd died at the age of fifty-four.

Back in Silver Lake after four months in England she shopped, read novels, listened to music, worked out on the equipment in her apartment, ate out with friends and went to a few parties. She watched a lot of rented movies, mostly comedies and art-house productions. Kate didn't share her gay friends' (and her mother's) addiction to junk TV shows like *Eldorado* with their interchangeable studs and bimbos and über-bitches. Steven and Patrick had shown her the internet clip of Jason Howl's impromptu on-set hard-on with Tawdra Thanatos's body double – 'a Dick of Death,' they screamed. Yes, he was up there with the late Dick Bigg, but so were most of the stars of porno, gay and straight. As Steven and Patrick and millions of porn aficionados knew, the closest incarnation of a true 'Dick of Death' was Yuyu, the Arab stallion – ten-and-a-half inches. In her first scene with Yuyu four years ago Kate had thought that he might actually kill her.

Her summer sabbatical from actual – unsimulated – sex continued into fall in LA while she waited for *Poor Nellie* to be edited and scored. She didn't even use a vibrator. Was she, she wondered, all fucked out – at twenty-two? She hoped not.

Something was missing from her life, something more than sex. Love? Was it as simple as that? She'd almost loved Scott back in Tucson. Before him she'd thought she loved Ruiz, but she didn't think it now; loving one's stepfather was clearly an adolescent hang-up, a 'transference' thing. She was sure she'd loved Jimmy Hernandez.

Jimmy and Maria had died in '98. Even this didn't hurt

deeply: had time and distance softened the pain of such losses, or had porno hardened her against all pain, all loss? Kazman Productions had made her rich and *Poor Nellie* would hopefully turn her infamy to a less lurid kind of fame. But had she sold her soul to porno? Was Love missing from her life, or was it missing from *her*?

Blow it out your arsehole, she told herself in British-English when these thoughts persisted. It worked: they went away.

She was also, it seemed, on an enforced sabbatical from the cameras. When Patrick and Steven urged her to get an agent she went to see Kazman.

'Katharine, you are free to do this if you want, but you will get better deals if you wait till after our movie comes out. You owe me nothing, but –'

'I owe you everything,' she interrupted. He smiled.

'Thank you, Katharine. I am looking for another project. When I find it, if it's something you want to do I promise you that your next salary will not be less than one million. Maybe much more.'

It wasn't about the money. She already had more than the one-and-a-half-million Duane had dangled in front of her in Le Bayou. It was about having a job, a career, a life.

'Don't tell Duane I asked you about getting an agent.'

'Forget Duane. His mind – and his name – will always be in porno.'

She relayed this conversation to Patrick and Steven. 'If nothing else you could be making commercials,' Steven said.

'What would I advertise? Trojans?' They all laughed. 'Crisco?'

'Mattresses!' Patrick suggested. They broke up.

'Shampoo,' Steven quietly offered. Blank looks. "*Pussy-Kat Kane doesn't know much about* Shoulders, *but she gives great* Head!"'

Kazman Productions had a new star. Thai beauty Ivana Likyu, with her surgically enhanced mega-boobs, had debuted in *Pussy Power 13*. Ivana brought rimming back to mainstream porno, which Kate had steadfastly refused to do and which 'the wankers' had evidently missed. Ivana was hailed as 'the new Peaches'; they weren't yet calling her 'the new Pussy-Kat', but they would. Sales of her movies with Croatian super-stud Ivor Longun would eventually eclipse even those of Pussy-Kat Kane.

After nine months of celibacy Kate began to feel horny. When Jed Swann, whose movies were lifting him from B-list to A-list, obtained her phone number from a press agent and asked for a date, he got more quickly than he'd dared hope to first base with the pornstar turned not-quite-A-list actress. They spent Christmas in Mauritius. The tabloids spotted Romance in the making. More useful publicity ahead of the release of *Poor Nellie*.

The sex was only so-so, but she continued to see Jed until he went on location for his next picture. Then it was back to a gay social scene and Blockbuster rentals. Tiring of novels, she dug out her UCLA course notes and began to read history and biographies of politicians. Would they take her if she applied to resume her studies? Could Pussy-Kat Kane somehow repossess the life of Joylene Duchat? In Italy a pornstar had entered parliament. Could that happen here? Probably not in a country where the DAR and the Reverend Duchat influenced the voters.

As winter turned to spring the publicity machine for *Poor Nelllie* cranked up, Kate had fleshed out the semi-factual background she'd given herself as Pussy-Kat Kane. She was from Louisiana; her mother and stepfather now lived in Arizona where Katharine Kane had gone to high school in Tucson. Duane's role in discovering her for porno was credited but not Scott's or the 'coaching' from Mr. Dunne and some trainee pilots and truck-drivers.

Kate kept her promise to her mother to keep Bart out of the limelight. The name Duchat was, like Hoover High and Seldom, not specified. She allowed it to be inferred that she'd been born out of wedlock, father possibly unknown.

After Jaynette informed Bart that Joylene had quit college, not only the support checks had stopped coming but also those for her birthday and Christmas. Preoccupied with the Son of God, Bart chose to forget his own daughter. In Kate's view her father's brand of praise-the-Lord-and-send-a-check Christianity was what the Brits would call a 'load of old bollocks'.

The Church of Grace Here & Hereafter was riding high in the televangelical charts. Its bonfires still blazed, although perhaps a little less brightly. Pornography – 'porno-lite' at least, was part of the nation's diet. Fox News announced that DeeDee Delfein was to host a debate on her *Here's Hollywood* show at Easter: "*Is there too much sex in movies?*"

'Nowhere near enough,' Steven and Patrick chorused on seeing the announcement.

Kate groaned when she heard that Rev. Barton Duchat would be one of Dee-Dee's guests. Another was to be Benjamin Burns, Hunt Studios' senior screenwriter, who was mainly known for his scripts for the ongoing *Axman* schlock slasher series. Ms. Delfein reminded readers of her column in the *LA Times* that Ben Burns had also scripted *Claretta*, whose premiere was the first Kate had attended on the arm of Al Kazman in the year of her debut in hardcore porno, the trade she had now abandoned, though perhaps only in favor of soft-core.

Pornstars – even ex-pornstars – weren't invited to the Academy Awards at the end of March. Kate watched the show with Patrick and Steven. Helen Highwater won a Best Supporting Actress Oscar for her role in another British period comedy, one that had been financed by Hollywood's Hunt Studios; it also won screenwriting and costume awards.

The Dame and her lordly husband had sent Kate a Christmas card via the studio, a photo of them inside their stately home. Kate now sent Helen a congratulations card, a portrait of Charles II which she found in an upmarket stationer's in Venice.

Cecil Brock escorted Kate to both the London and Hollywood premieres of *Poor Nellie* – London in mid-April, LA a week later ahead of an Easter opening. They left the after-show parties early and dined in quiet restaurants Cecil knew that weren't regularly patronized by movie stars. He was an amusing and attentive companion. Why couldn't straight men be as entertaining as gays?

Should she marry a gay man, she wondered – obviously

a younger one than Cecil who was old enough to be her great-grandfather. Other actresses had done it.

'Katharine Kane's extraordinary beauty', according to the London *Times* film critic, *'carries you past any uncertainties in her performance.'*

'The porn trade's loss', said the *Sun*, *'is cinema's gain.'*

'A gold-star turn from the Blue-Movie Girl!' cried the *Star*.

In a Deconstructionist review for *The New Yorker* a leading English man of letters detected references to Wallis Simpson and more recent royal wives and mistresses.

Variety: *'Kane's performance has an edginess – a sharpness, a causticity – that calls to mind Katharine Hepburn in her early comedy roles.'*

Under the headline *A STAR IS PORN* in the *LA Times* DeeDee Delfein wrote: *'If they'd only asked Sondheim to pen some music and lyrics they could have called it* My Fair Pussy.'

Cecil reported that the 'buzz' suggested there might be BAFTA – 'and maybe even *Oscar*' – nominations next year. Kate hardly dared to dream that she might one day mount a podium to make an acceptance speech as Katharine Kane.

She was, it seemed, a star. A *legitimate* star.

Talk-show appearances and magazine interviews. Dozens of them, weeks of them. But why did interviewers invariably ask about her years in porno? And they always introduced her as the 'ex-' or 'deposed' Beaver Queen. She had to remind them that she had abdicated.

In both Europe and the US *Poor Nellie* fired a resurgence of interest in her work as Pussy-Kat Kane. Kazman re-released the early *Pussy Power* movies on VHS and DVD. Kate's 'residuals' from these re-issues would almost double her $250,000 fee for *Nellie*.

A star is Porn. It looked like it might be her epitaph.

9. REVELATION

One of the Fox News production team had called Benjamin Burns to invite him to debate '*Is there too much sex in the movies*' on DeeDee Delfein's *Here's Hollywood* TV show with the Church of Grace Here & Hereafter's Barton Duchat on the Friday after Easter.

'Is the Reverend OK with this?' Ben asked the caller, whose name was Stacey. 'Surely I'm Satan with a laptop? All that teenage schtupping I've scripted.'

'He doesn't know,' she said. 'We just told him somebody from Hunt Studios.'

Stacey was a fellow student Ben had befriended but not fucked on his BA course at UCLA. Ben, since his teens, paid for sex with increasingly upscale professionals. Stacey was plain, bookish, serious; and she'd ended up hustling for Fox News. But then Ben, in his college days, had intended to go on to write the Great American Novel, not the script for *Axman VI* or *Surfers Return*.

'I wasn't your first choice, was I?'

'Second.' He could almost hear her blushing down the line. *Fifth*, he thought; *or fifteenth*.

'You were my personal first, of course,' she added.

'Liar. Who was really first?'

'Rodney Fire.' Another UCLA alumnus, who'd also dated – and almost certainly fucked – Stacey. Rodney, like Ben, had started his career in advertising before (again like Ben) going to work for Isaac Hunt, directing schlock from scripts written by Ben Burns. Last year he'd made *Mrs. Bates* for Gorgon Pictures. A prequel to *Psycho*, *Mrs. Bates* was a box-office smash and won Oscars last month for Rodney and Zola Gorgon (and Tawdra Thanatos in her biggest role post-TV), mightily pissing off Isaac Hunt.

Lady Van-de-Meer's Wind, a British period comedy bankrolled by Hunts, had also won three Academy Awards, three lesser awards, including Best Original Screenplay – not for Benjamin Burns, but for an English novelist in his screenwriting debut. Months after the Nominations Ben still got reflux thinking about '*Windbag*', Isaac's codename for their Oscar-winning comedy.

'I immediately thought of you,' Stacey now said. She gave an awkward laugh. 'Well – almost immediately. I thought you might like the chance to defend your industry against a sanctimonious prick in a clerical collar.'

'You know, Stacey –' the realization took him by surprise – 'I think I would.'

It wouldn't be his first appearance on primetime TV. He'd been a (small) part of the razzmatazz for *Claretta*, Hunts' ill-conceived, ill-scripted (by Ben) and ill-received biopic of Mussolini's mistress. A face-off with Rev. Duchat was an opportunity to raise his profile, to be more than just a minor screenwriter at a studio that was widely expected to follow the dinosaurs (Isaac Hunt *was* a dinosaur) into extinction.

'You'll need to be well prepared. Mr. Duchat's got a pretty big burr up his ass.'

'But he's only got the one hymn on his sheet. It won't be hard to make him look like a throwback to the Salem Witch Trials.'

'Be careful, Ben. You don't want his supporters to single out Hunt movies as ones to trash.'

'We rely on the critics for that,' Ben said bitterly and trying not to face up to the fact that he had scripted the majority of Hunt Studios' recent run of all-too-trashable turkeys.

Stopping Rev. Barton Duchat in mid-flow was like sticking your finger in a dike, DeeDee Delfein would say afterward – 'Not that I've fingered too many dykes!'

There was indeed only one hymn on Bart's sheet, dearly familiar to his Baton Rouge congregation and to viewers of the Grace Here & Hereafter TV channel: the Sermon on – or rather, against – the Love-Mound. His homily on the homos and porn-peddlers degrading this Great Nation of Ours… the polluters… the corrupters… the defilers… blah-blah-blah.

Even with heavy editing before transmission DeeDee envisaged *Here's Hollywood*'s faithful flock switching channels in batches of five thousand. Normally one of TV's most loquacious hostesses, she only managed to get a word in when the minister paused to draw breath for the first time in almost five minutes.

'Thank you, Reverend. Very, um, powerful and, er, inspiring. But now I'd like to introduce my second guest who has made a major contribution to the motion picture industry. Just last year he scripted Hunt Studios' thrilling remake of *San Francisco*… Ladies and gentlemen – Mister Ben Burns.'

A burst of applause would be inserted here from the unseen – indeed, non-existent – audience, together with a few loud bars of DeeDee's theme music, lifted from Erich Korngold's classic score for the Bette Davis classic *Elizabeth and Essex*. The only ladies and gentlemen present were the cameramen and the production team. A makeup girl darted in to powder a shine on DeeDee's Roman-senator nose while Camera Two tracked Ben onto the set.

Here's Hollywood had stopped going out live after a few unfortunate incidents, beginning with the actor on parole who'd absentmindedly sniffed a few stray grains of coke off the sleeve of his sweater in front of DeeDee and a former President. Then there was the A-list actress who uttered a string of profanities when DeeDee quizzed her about the actor she'd jilted at the altar. And, notoriously, the great but ailing star (James Dean) who audibly lost control of his bowels when DeeDee fake-innocently asked why he was known, in certain circles, as 'The Human Ashtray'.

Ben's secretary had rehearsed him on a smile that looked neither apprehensive nor too cheesy. He smiled it now at Camera Two as he sank into an armchair on the opposite side of their hostess from Barton Duchat, who hovered on the edge of his seat in ecclesiastical black like a great bird of prey.

'Hello, DeeDee. Good evening, Mr. Duchat.' Ben communicated a degree of lese-majesty by omitting the normal honorific and over-emphasizing the second syllable of Bart's surname: 'Dew-*shat*'.

The Reverend forced himself to smile pleasantly at this impertinent soul (who was clearly, like their hostess, a Jew – a Christ-killer) in sore need of salvation. DeeDee revealed her own teeth that were the creation of a more upmarket practitioner than Jake Bernstein, Ben's dentist father in Culver City.

'So, Ben, how do you respond to the Rev. Duchat's accusation that you're engaged in pornography?'

'Hold on now, Ms. Delfein,' protested Bart, God's Elect in danger of being outflanked by God's Chosen People. 'I didn't accuse him of any such thing. I'm not familiar with Mr. Burns's work and –'

'Now, Reverend, you've had your turn. Let's hear what Ben has to say in defense of the industry that employs him.' She gave Ben a nudge.

'Thank-you, DeeDee. I get the feeling that Mr. Duchat won't rest until Hollywood confines itself to endless remakes of *The Ten Commandments* and *Mary Poppins*. I can't say I relish the prospect of our entertainment industry being subjected to the same kind of controls as in countries like Iran.'

He stopped and gave DeeDee a provocative smile. She arched her surgically perfected eyebrows at Bart whose color rose, patchily, through the studio makeup that had been caked onto his pallid face. The Lord's Mission did not permit time to loll around swimming-pools on mattresses, although other televangelists seemed to find some leisure to work on their tans.

'Now then, Mr. Burns, don't you go making wild comparisons just because I'm not as liberal in my tastes and tolerances as some people here in – the City of the Plain.'

'Reverend, you're in California tonight, not Kansas,' DeeDee reminded him.

'I know where I am,' Bart retorted. 'I was being allegorical. The Cities of the Plain: Sodom and Gomorrah.'

Ben intervened with a gag of his own: 'Better not look over your shoulder, DeeDee. We wouldn't want you to turn into a pillar of salt!'

A gale of laughter would be inserted here. DeeDee rewarded Ben with an Estée Lauder smirk of approval.

'I've never understood exactly what wickedness it was that the people of Gomorrah got up to,' he went on, addressing Bart, 'but your views on the Sins of Sodom are pretty well-known. What we Los Angelinos think of as "the Conservative Persuasion". Forgive me, but again what springs to mind is Iran: they hang gays from lampposts there. Is that what you'd like to see on the streets of Los Angeles – and Baton Rouge?'

'Don't make me out to be some kind of Fundamentalist Fascist,' Bart cautioned, looking hotter under the dog-collar as he struck recklessly close to the head of the nail. 'Homosexuals –' pronounced with long o's: 'hoe-moe-sexuals' – 'can repent and be saved, like other sinners.'

'But sinners is what they are, right? There isn't room for gays and lesbians in those "many mansions" Jesus Christ told us were in His Father's house?'

It couldn't be much fun to have a Hebrew quoting the New Testament back at you. Bart forced himself to maintain an appearance of calm.

'I think there may be a lot fewer mansions in God's Heavenly House than certain depraved Liberal types are hoping to find. But let's not forget the parable of the Prodigal Son. There's always room in the Lord's heart for a sincere penitent. Salvation is just a prayerful moment away.'

One of the evangelist's sound-bite Southern maxims. Ben felt ready to puke but he managed to inject another note of levity.

'Well, if you'll allow me to borrow another parable, Mr. Duchat, you're casting seeds on some mighty unfertile ground here in Sodom County!'

DeeDee's grin revealed every crown in her mouth. She had really wanted Oscar-winner Rodney Fire for this spot — she'd gotten hold of some dirt linking him to a male pornstar that she could have hinted at — but Benjamin Burns was holding up his end of the debate pretty well. Bart, an emissary of the Holy Ghost, glared at them both: blasphemers and God only knew what kind of degenerates.

'You may smile. You may mock. But beware the Wrath to Come.'

DeeDee's smile narrowed. 'Does it never occur to you, Reverend, that God just might have a sense of humor?'

'I can assure you that He does. There is laughter and joy in His Holy Court, but it is not the laughter of mockery or of smut and filth.'

Ben steered the discussion back on track.

'What you call smut and filth, Mr. Duchat, many of us consider to be just comedy and drama put out by the entertainment industry. Which enjoys the protection of the First Amendment. Or are you in favor of abrogating the Constitution?'

Bart went from red to a blotchy shade of maroon.

'Don't try and hide behind the Constitution, mah friend. I'm mighty sure that the Founding Fathers of this Great Nation under God never intended to legitimize child pornography or — what do they call them? — snuff movies.'

'Snuff movies and kiddie-porn are not legal in this country and surely never will be,' Ben pointed out patiently. 'Although the Supreme Court does sanction the sale of what is held to be acceptable hardcore porno.'

'Not the Supreme Court before which we shall all one day be judged,' said Bart at his most oratorical. 'No level of pornography is acceptable in the eyes of the Almighty.'

'Can we leave porno out of the frame,' DeeDee pleaded. 'For now,' she added tantalizingly, hoping to hang on to channel surfers.

'But all our popular teenage comedies and action movies are pornography in the eyes of Mr. Duchat,' said Ben. 'Which he wants to see censored.'

'I'm not saying they have to be censored. They just need to be – cleaned up a tad.'

'In other words – censored,' retorted Ben.

'That great American Walt Disney produced wholesome entertainment that kept successive generations spellbound. Why can't there be more of that?'

'We're back to *Mary Poppins*,' said Ben. 'That audience is still being catered for, from *Toy Story* to *Star Wars*. But there's another audience that wants to watch more challenging dramas that relate to the life going on today in our small towns and big cities. They want films like – *American Pie* and *Lethal Weapon* and *Basic Instinct*.' Ben realized he might be on shaky theological ground here. 'Are you going to deny them these films?'

'But can't you see that sex and violence on the screen is what begets the sex and violence on our streets?'

'This is the nub of the issue,' DeeDee pointed out for the benefit of dimmer viewers. 'What's your answer to that, Ben? Is Hollywood the source of all that's wrong with society?'

'DeeDee, that's bull and you know it. All that Hollywood does is to hold a camera to the world.'

'But it's people like you who choose what's put in front of the camera,' Bart countered 'You're so keen to film the harlot taken in adultery or the hand of Cain as he strikes his brother.

Why not show us the face of an innocent child or the very Hand of God in a majestic sunrise over the Rocky Mountains?'

'You can see that in an IMAX Theater every day of the week.' DeeDee tried to lighten the mood. But Bart did indeed have a burr up his ass.

'If the entertainment industry promoted more wholesome values,' he said doggedly, 'society might embrace those values. People could reach out together in a spirit of brotherly love instead of a spirit of lust and hate.'

'Mr. Duchat,' said Ben, 'you're trying to turn the clock back to an age that's long gone.'

'I am. I admit it. It's my mission from God to fashion this earth back into the Eden it was when He created it.'

DeeDee squirmed as her show turned evangelical again. Ben went into blessed peacemaker mode.

'Hollywood produces dozens of movies every year that are entirely harmless. And even where they do confront major issues of human sexuality and violent behavior, they adhere to a very old-fashioned code. Bad guys usually come to a bad end. Good triumphs over evil. Most drama is still a Morality Play, in a line that goes all the way back to – Cain and Abel.' He grinned at Bart. 'And, yes, the woman taken in adultery.'

Bart opened his mouth, but DeeDee got there first.

'It's time for a short break, gentlemen.' She turned to face Camera One. 'After the break I have another guest from the entertainment industry whose views, I'm sure, will be just as fascinating as those of Reverend Duchat and screenwriter Ben Burns. We'll be back – after these messages.'

Since the show wasn't live, the commercial break had no set length. DeeDee turned to her guests. 'Does anybody need the bathroom? A drink? No? Then I guess we'll move right on.'

'You didn't tell me there would be another guest,' Bart said. Ben intuited that they were both in for a surprise. There had been nobody else in the hospitality suite where he and the evangelist had made stilted small talk before the show.

'My producer told your secretary you'd be debating with representatives from Hollywood,' DeeDee reminded Bart. 'Mr. Burns is one. You're about to meet the other.' A technician wheeled in a fourth armchair and at a gesture from DeeDee berthed it next to Ben's. Their hostess retouched her neon lipstick and waited for a cue in her earpiece before addressing Camera One.

'Welcome back, ladies and gentlemen. I'm DeeDee Delfein and this is *Here's Hollywood*. Tonight we're discussing sex and censorship in motion pictures. My guests are televangelist the Reverend Barton Duchat from Louisiana and Hollywood screenwriter Benjamin Burns. Ben is well-known for scripting such unforgettable pictures as Dolores Delano's *Claretta* and those *Surfer* movies and the *Axman* series which have had us laughing and screaming in movie theater seats for the last six or seven years.'

Ben had expected a plug, but this was way too much. She gave him a gooey smile. 'Ben, you're as much a stalwart of the new Hollywood as Isaac Hunt is of Hollywood in its yesteryear heyday.' Ben wasn't sure Isaac would relish being relegated to the dustbin of Tinseltown's 'Golden Age', but he mustered a grateful smile.

DeeDee proceeded to blow him – and the Reverend – away:

'My next guest, ladies and gentleman – Miss Katharine Kane!'

Ben stood up as Kate entered the studio. DeeDee remained seated, as did Bart who now finally slid back in his chair as if to put an extra distance between himself and the glamorous young woman bearing down on him.

Kate wore a demure black silk dress with flimsy shoulder-straps; it revealed no cleavage and the rippling pleated skirt was knee-length. She'd bought it in London's Harvey Nichols in the week of the *Poor Nellie* premiere, thinking it would be perfect for the next formal event (or funeral) she had to attend. Her makeup was so fine as to appear almost invisible; DeeDee now resembled a drag-queen take on Norma Desmond.

Kate smiled at their hostess and gave Bart a nod that might almost have been the start of an ironic bow. She sat in the chair beside Ben who sat down too. He leaned across and whispered: 'Very foxy.'

'This dress? I'm auditioning for *Sister Act Three*!'

'Not the dress. You.'

'Have we met before?' Still whispering.

'You were with Mr. Kazman at the premiere of my Mussolini picture. We weren't introduced.' Ben wondered if he could invite her to dine with him after the recording. Would she accept – and would she fuck him? Her expression right now was enigmatic, as if she were assessing whether he was a potential asset to her career – or a pervert.

'Katharine, welcome,' DeeDee interrupted them, having allowed time for music and applause.

Kate turned on a superstar smile. 'My friends call me Kate, DeeDee.'

'Kate, we'd love to spend the next segment hearing about the fun you must have had filming your historical rom-com in England, which opened here on the weekend, but if you'll forgive me I want to bring you straight into tonight's discussion about sex in the movies. Reverend Duchat has stipulated that we show no clips of an adult nature on the show, but you've indicated that you are willing to talk about your pre-Hollywood career when you were known as Pussy-Kat Kane.'

'It was in Santa Monica, you know. Isn't that Hollywood too?' Steven and Patrick, sworn to secrecy ahead of her appearance tonight, had told her that DeeDee liked her guests to play-act and crack gags.

DeeDee flashed bridgework and gums. 'But seriously –' she prompted.

'Seriously is how I'm trying to get taken as an actress. But I don't mind talking about my earlier life in adult movies.'

Bart stared at Kate from the depths of his chair, as if trying to identify her. The Lord's Work allowed no more time to watch frivolous movies than for sunbathing, and although he had thrown many a store-bought video-cassette into one of his televised bonfires, he'd never found it necessary to remove the shrink-wrap and preview that which he was consigning to the purifying flames. Even in his criminal youth as a flasher he'd had only a passing interest in pornography, an interest which had expired long before his own purification and the era of Dick Bigg and Pussy-Kat Kane. But alarm bells were now ringing.

'You are a – blue-movie girl?' he blurted. Kate smiled at hearing the same euphemism her mother had used.

'Well, no, sir, I'm not. But, yes, I used to be in porno.'

Bart's face flashed to an incandescence beyond red; he looked like one of his bonfires. He glared at DeeDee.

'You bring me onto your show with – with – a pornstar?' he croaked.

'Reverend, she's just told you she's a serious actress, but – yes, she did use to be in adult entertainment. And before that she was Valedictorian at her high school in Arizona.' DeeDee had evidently read up on Kate's profile. 'I think her views on sex in the motion picture industry are worth hearing.'

'Ms. Delfein, I am a Man of God. I don't expect to be – contaminated by exposure to actors from the filthiest gutter of their profession.'

'In England they're already expecting Katharine to be nominated for a BAFTA next year for *Poor Nellie*, her new movie in which she plays Nell Gwynne, the ladyfriend of King Charles the Second.'

'More moral turpitude.' Thus Bart dismissed *Poor Nellie*. 'I don't know what a – BAFTA? – is.'

'The British equivalent of an Academy Award,' DeeDee told him. 'An Oscar.'

'In Moses' time a golden statue violated God's Holy Commandments.'

'Mr. Duchat,' Ben re-entered the fray, 'Do you ever watch these movies you are so quick to condemn?'

Barton Duchat frowned in Ben's direction. 'I rely on the elders in my organization to keep me informed about debasement in every medium.' He turned an unremitting expression toward Kate. 'Tell me, young woman. Does your mother know you are engaged in this vile evil trade?'

Kate stared into his eyes. 'Yes, sir, she does. I will admit that she's a lot happier since I switched to historical comedy.'

Ben spoke before the Reverend could formulate a reply. 'Mr.

Duchat, perhaps you should think of Katharine as a formerly lost soul inching her way toward redemption. Isn't the parable about the lost sheep at the very heart of your Mission?'

'I don't need lessons in Holy Scripture from –' Bart started to say 'kikes' but adroitly turned it into 'the likes of you', arguably just as offensive. He struggled to his feet and stood unsteadily in his dark suit like a well-dressed drunk. He rounded on DeeDee.

'You deceived me, Ms. Delfein. I thought I was invited onto this show for a serious debate about the dangers that our children face, not to be exposed to the mockery of – unbelievers. Beware the Day of Judgment. It is nearer than you think.'

'Oh – puh-lease,' said DeeDee with a nervous but unrepentant laugh.

'I will leave now. I do not intend to sit here and listen to an attempt to justify pornographic movies from this harlot, this – Jezebel.'

'Lighten up, Father,' said Kate. He rounded on her.

'You call me "Reverend", not "Father". I'm a pastor, not a Roman priest.'

Kate smiled sweetly at him as she shot him down onto his own pyre.

'I wasn't addressing you as a priest. I was addressing you as a parent.'

DeeDee's expression was gloating as she leaned forward. Watching the show when it aired, Isaac Hunt and Ben would agree that if Kate had not beaten her to it, DeeDee must have planned to introduce this biographical nugget which her researchers had managed to uncover. It would have been her biggest coup since James Dean's cigarette butts.

'Young lady, like any pastor I am a surrogate parent to my worldwide flock. My flock – my children – have gone their many ways into the world, as all children do. But God forbid that any of them should go into the sinkhole of depravity from which you come. My children are the Children of God: you are the very spawn of Satan!'

Kate laughed briefly. She allowed a Southern touch to creep into her voice:

'I hate to contradict you, Reverend, but I think you'll find I'm one of God's children too. When I went into adult movies I called myself Pussy-Kat Kane and now I call myself Katharine Kane.' She paused for the viewing audience to keep pace with her. 'But, as DeeDee said, I went to school in Arizona. And before that I was in Baton Rouge, Louisiana, where I was conceived and born.'

Bart reeled on his feet.

'I am not the spawn of Satan, Reverend. My real name is Joylene Duchat – *and you are my father.*'

DeeDee brought her hands briskly together but managed not to give Kate a round of applause.

Inside Bart's head something snapped with a crack that was audible only to him. He dropped to the studio floor as if poleaxed. Syndicated to the news services later tonight and then shown in context when *Here's Hollywood* aired in full tomorrow, his fall would be seen by millions of viewers in the US and around the world.

And what a fall it was. In a moment of rare irony his head thumped face down into the lap of Kate's black Knightsbridge dress. Even if you hadn't seen *Pussy Power 1-thru-14*, it looked for all the world as if – well, let's just say that 'prayerfulness' was not the word that sprang to the mind of even Bart's most ardent acolyte.

Hearing only the reverberations of that synaptic crack inside his head, Bart missed the snort of laughter from DeeDee Delfein and Ben's guffaw – two certain candidates for Purgatory. Head down and slipping toward oblivion, he also missed the look of concern on his daughter's face.

'Stretch out your hands into God's Glorious Radiance,' was what Bart said on those occasions when he attended one of his parishioners at the moment of transition from the earthly world to the celestial one. But what raced to engulf Barton Duchat at this instant was not Divine Light but a mighty red tsunami; the red of blood, of burning books and porno tapes, of everlasting Hellfire. A pungent odor clogged his nostrils: was it – *dear God!* – was it sulphur?

The wave hit, and Bart went under.

Fade to black.

10. A PHONE CALL

'Katharine.'
'Hi, Mr. Kazman. Anything new?'
'Something is new, yes. I bought another studio.'
'In Santa Monica?' His deep laughter boomed down the line.
'No, here in Hollywood. I bought Hunt Studios.'
'Wow! Does this mean you're gonna make, like, *real* straight movies?'
'Yes, it does.'
'Can I be in one?'
He laughed again. 'Yes, my Katharine. Yes, you can.'

* * * * * * * * * * * * * *

To be continued . . .

Katharine Kane and Jason Howl will meet – and make a movie together – in HOWL AND THE PUSSY-KAT, Part Three of David Godolphin's Hollywood Trilogy, coming soon to a book- or Kindle-store near you.

David Godolphin has also written as David Gee...

LILLIAN AND THE ITALIANS

David Gee

Looking for her wayward son in 1960s Venice, an English widow meets the gigolo who has shared the last four years of his life. From Carlo Lillian learns how little she knows about Andrew.

Going on to Amalfi , she meets a charismatic Sicilian prince with links to the Mafia. As they wait for news of their kidnapped sons, a bond grows between Lillian and Prince Massimo. How will it end?

LILLIAN AND THE ITALIANS is available to buy in print or Kindle editions.

Here's the opening chapter:

Part One

VENICE: August, 1966

As the train rattled onto the causeway with a klaxon roar, Lillian caught her first glimpse in thirty-one years of the spires and domes of Venice shimmering in the midsummer haze above the electric blue lagoon. Most of the buildings on the landward side were utilitarian – warehouses and multi-storey car-parks – but this was still unmistakably a city that floated on the sea, the mere notion of which was exotic to someone whose feet had always been firmly planted on the ground. Lillian felt the return of something she had forgotten from her honeymoon all those years ago: the spell that Italy could cast over a foreigner – a spell which had called like a summons to Andrew, the 'Prodigal Son' she was here to track down.

With another klaxon belch from its diesel engine the train began to slow, no longer overtaking cars and buses on the adjacent road bridge. When Lillian and George came here on their honeymoon in 1935 the train had been drawn by a steam engine which whooped and whistled. Its elegant *wagons-lits* were very nearly as romantic as the Orient Express ('We can't afford that,' said George, lumberjack turned builder). Lillian, the property developer's widow, could now afford the Orient Express but it had stopped running in 1962. Today's train had ordinary carriages and modern sleeping cars that were about as romantic as a camper van. And Lillian was alone in her stiflingly hot First-Class sleeper – a widow since last year, her children and grandchildren scattered to the winds.

Shuddering to a stop inside the terminus station, the train was greeted by a cacophony of over-amplified announcements on the public-address system and the shouts of porters and people waiting to meet the new arrivals. The last of the horde that had boarded in Milan with much noise and huge quantities of baggage now poured onto the platform. Lillian and her fellow First-Class travelers disembarked more soberly.

A porter, guessing that she was English, addressed her as 'Lady' in the voice of a taxi-driver in a New York movie. Lillian gave him the name of her hotel which she had been told was only a short walk from the station.

'Listen, lady,' the porter began in a confidential but worldly tone, leaning on his barrow, 'I make you da proposition. Porter not s'posed to go after da front of da *stazione*, but for one t'ousand lire I take you and dis cases to your 'otel. Okay?'

A currency that dealt in thousands was intimidating. Mistaking Lillian's hesitation for haggling, he gave a shrug born of long experience. 'Okay, lady. Seven 'undred fifty. Is 'alf of one pound in your money. Okay?'

'Thank you very much,' Lillian said. 'That will be fine.' She hoped there wouldn't be an embarrassing scene when they arrived at her hotel and he tripled his fee. Members of her golf club who'd travelled in Italy recently had cautioned her against the natives – rogues, they claimed, to the last man and even child.

She followed him into the main hall of the station and out to the steps leading down to the canal-side. Across the canal was a church of stained white marble with a green dome topped by a cupola with a statue above it. Fifty yards away a slim balustraded bridge, crowded with pedestrians, spanned the canal. The sunlit water was a dull shade of green, visibly dirty and more than a bit smelly. Nevertheless, with motor-launches and vaporettos and gondolas plying busily up and down, it was breathtaking. This was Venice's High Street: the Grand Canal.

The porter bumped his trolley down the steps and off to the left, into a narrow street flanked by bars and glassware shops and crammed with idling tourists. Shouting a way through the throng, the porter pushed his trolley on to the entrance to a hotel. Lillian gave him 1,000 lire out of the money Bob Sadler had provided her with and made it plain that she expected no change. The porter bowed low. 'You are a fine lady,' he said. Lillian smiled.

A hotel porter came out to fetch her bags and, once the formalities of registration were completed, escorted her to her room on the second floor. It was agreeably cool but gloomy with the shutters drawn. She'd booked a double room – single rooms tended to be tiny and cramped. The décor was Empire style: flock wallpaper, velvet curtains and bedspread, huge mahogany wardrobes and chests-of-drawers. Lillian hoped that a 500-lire tip was sufficient for this porter's labors. As soon as he left, she opened the shutters. One window gave onto a small piazza, the other directly onto the canal.

This stretch of the Grand Canal, from the railway station bridge up to the first bend, boasted no notable palaces, but Lillian was nonetheless delighted. The buildings were old and faded and in varying stages of decay; some had terraces and roof gardens; two almost directly opposite had blue-and-white mooring poles beside their landing stages; all bore marks from the ravages of water at their base. Vaporettos threshed the water as they pulled into and out of the station stop. Gondoliers exchanged shouted conversation as they passed one another.

It was noisy, it was decidedly smelly: it was *Venice*!
And her son was here. Maybe less than a mile away.
Her heart raced at the thought of seeing him. Tomorrow.

By the time she had unpacked and showered and changed into a skirt and blouse, it was early evening. Looking out of the window at intervals Lillian savored the color of deepening twilight on the faded walls of the houses and the murky waters of the canal.

Hungry from missing lunch (the dining car had been removed from the train at Brig, the last station before the Simplon tunnel), she dined on minestrone soup and a veal cutlet, served with a salad but no potatoes. Where was Andrew dining, she wondered, and who was he with? She thought of trying his telephone number again; Continental Directory Enquiries had found it for her last month; then it had taken the operator more than three hours to discover that the number was 'out of service': this, he'd informed her, could mean that the phone was unpaid or not working or even disconnected.

It would be best to just go to his address tomorrow, as planned. Back in her room she took out the piece of paper Bob Sadler had given her on the day she'd announced her decision to go to Italy and find her son. She didn't need to look at it – it was burned into her memory – but it provided a link between the day of her decision and today, the eve of its realisation.

Hastings, July

'Well, I think you'd be mad to go gallivanting off to Italy,' said Amy, never one to mince her words. Lillian had to resist the urge to throw one of the new cushions. Having said her piece Amy, who was strong on flouncing, flounced to the kitchen. Water was soon heard to flow, although Lillian had said to leave the tea things for her cleaning lady tomorrow.

Bob moved round the settee and seated himself at its other end, vigilant of the creases his wife had remorselessly pressed into his charcoal-gray suit.

'Lillian,' he began and her spirits sank at the solemnity of his tone, 'you know the disappointments Amy and I have had from our – how shall I describe them? – our *feckless* children. She wouldn't like to hear me say it, but I've come to regard them as *lost* to us.' He paused before adding bluntly, crushingly: 'Isn't Andrew lost to you?'

Lillian had spent years defending her son against criticism from his father and, latterly, his sister. She was not going to be crushed by Robert Sadler. She shook her head. 'I can't accept that,' she said. 'I know he's a – "rolling stone", he's been drifting further and further from Hastings since he left school, but I won't think of him as lost. I've lost *George*. Sylvia's as good as lost, she's so far away. Andrew's all I've got left, now.'

'Have you still got him?' Bob persisted callously. 'He's never invited you to Italy.'

Lillian twisted a white handkerchief in the lap of the black linen dress she'd worn to two other funerals since her husband's last year: an eighty-year-old woman from her bridge club and a sixty-eight-year-old former mayor whose widow took her grief on a Caribbean cruise and came back engaged to a fellow passenger. Today they had cremated the previous manager of Bob Sadler's bank.

'All the more reason for me to go and look for him,' Lillian said.

He sighed, conceding the point. 'Have you given any thought to how you'll go about it?'

'His letter last year came from Milan. There must be a British consulate, where he'd have to register as an alien. That's probably the best place to start.'

'Go to Venice,' Bob told her.

Lillian shook her head. 'I don't think he's still in Venice. That's where his first card came from, but the other cards and the letter all came from different places.'

'He's in Venice,' Bob said. He fished inside his jacket for his wallet and took out a slip of paper which he unfolded and passed to her. Squinting to decipher the three short handwritten lines without her reading glasses, Lillian read:

Andrew Rutherford Interiors
San Marco 253
Venezia

Somewhere, Lillian thought, in the loft perhaps, she might still have Robert Sadler's earnest declarations of love in that small cramped bank clerk's script which had not changed in thirty-three years. Her hand shook.

'How long have you had this?'

'Since October. American Express in Venice telexed it to us after I put your solicitor in touch with our overseas branch in London when he was probating George's will.'

'But you didn't think to give me his address before today?' She no longer wanted to throw things, she wanted to lay into him with her fists. She could not recall ever feeling so angry or so betrayed.

He met her gaze levelly. 'I discussed it with the solicitor and we both felt that it should be left to Andrew to contact you. Which he did. Lillian, if he'd wanted you to be able to stay in touch with him he'd have given you his address himself.'

Lillian felt that if she didn't move she *would* strike him. She rose and walked to the window. The garden was dry. It hadn't rained since a shower at the weekend. A clatter from the kitchen indicated that Amy was hard at work.

Lillian looked across at Bob on the sofa – thinning gray hair over a pale narrow face that always reminded her of Leslie Howard: handsome but – weak. 'I shall never forgive you for this,' she said and had the satisfaction of seeing a hurt expression on his face. She crossed to the sofa, slipped her feet back into her black court shoes and walked through the conservatory to find the watering can.

Andrew was not lost. And if he was, she would find him.

* * * * * * * * * * *